STRONG WILL

ROMANTIC SUSPENSE

PATRICIA CRUMPLER

World Castle Publishing, LLC
Pensacola, Florida
Copyright © Patricia Crumpler 2021
Paperback ISBN: 9781953271648
eBook ISBN: 9781953271655
First Edition World Castle Publishing, LLC, February 22, 2021
http://www.worldcastlepublishing.com
Licensing Notes
Cover: Karen Fuller
Editor: Maxine Bringenberg

DEDICATION

I dedicate this book to Timothy Michael Burnett, 1945-2011.
He was a fun guy and the inspiration for Charles Strong Manning.

CHAPTER ONE

The jungle noises stopped, triggering an eerie silence. Strong Manning dove to the forest floor toward the three other members of his team. Aphrodite pushed the teenager they'd been sent to rescue to the ground and hurled herself over him seconds before bullets ripped a path where they had just stood. The dictator's fourteen year old son trembled.

Lars crawled to them belly down in the leaves. "Are you okay?"

The teen moved his head, neither yes or no. He inched up on his knees and dropped his chin to see the patch of urine spreading on his linen slacks.

Jo Lynn crept next to him. "Don't worry. I've peed my pants a time or two."

The crack of bullets ceased. Strong eased up on his elbows and raised his head above the ferns. "It's now or never. Keep your heads low. I'll put down suppressing fire. Run! Go! Go!"

The others rose and fled to the Blackhawk helicopter waiting in a clearing two hundred yards behind them. Strong knew as soon as they started running, the shooting would resume.

The rotors groaned into action, and the craft lifted just above the ground. Strong held his breath as the runners bee-lined toward the hovering craft. From a kneeling position, he ripped off a full clip from his AK-47, dropped the rifle, and ran. Dodging a fresh barrage of bullets, he followed the runners. An assault of air gusted and a scuff of metal whizzed past his face. It took a second for the pain to materialize. He wiped the blood from his lip and signaled the pilot.

Aphrodite pushed the teen into the copter's open door. Jo Lynn followed close behind, nearly colliding with them as she piled in. The chopper floated nervously over the site when Lars heaved himself into the fuselage. Strong vaulted halfway in, grabbing a metal handhold. His blood-slick fingers slid as the Blackhawk started its ascent. A sturdy hand clasped his wrist and pulled him in.

"Thanks, Lars. I owe you one."

Lars chuckled. "One? Ha!"

As the craft cleared the trees, Jo Lynn moved to the trembling teen. She huddled close, her arm around his shoulders until he calmed. The youth swallowed hard, straightened his back, and touched Strong's arm. "Gracias, senor. My father, he—"

Strong held his hand up. "Don't worry. Your father knows where you are. We have your family, and you are safe."

"Senor, where are we going?"

Lars smiled wide and spoke in a cowboy accent. "Why, yer movin' ta Amurica, son."

Aphrodite wiped her finger along the edge of Strong's lip. "You wearing lipstick now?"

Strong touched his mouth. He looked at the blood and shrugged.

Lars popped open a metal first aid box and fished for the gauze packet. "Well, partner, ya been grazed. Yep, that's why they call it hazardous duty."

CHAPTER TWO

The elevator door whooshed open. Two women twisted on the floor, locked in an angry catfight. Emma Whitstone stepped back as the combatants pitched closer, threatening to roll into the elevator where she stood. The usual courthouse buzz fell silent amid the screams and curses that bounced off the marble walls.

A man, athletic-looking and tanned, hurried toward them and placed his briefcase against the nervous door. He stooped and, with both hands, pulled each young woman up, parting them. Flailing and kicking, the women tried to break his hold, but neither opponent could budge. He spoke whispered words, to which both young women nodded. He let them go — they went in opposite directions. Without a wrinkle in his suit, he picked up his case and entered the elevator.

Emma Whitstone had not been able to take her eyes off him. He turned, and their gazes touched. She'd been caught staring. His face, average at first, tipped the scales to handsome as one corner of his lip turned into a smile. He slid his slate blue eyes over her. She quickly examined the floor, but felt his focus on her.

Two floors down, Emma stepped forward, fighting the urge to take a last peek at the man who left the elevator and walked away among the crowd. She hurried to Susie Williams, who waited near the bank of elevators. Emma tugged Susie's arm. "Do you know that man, the one with the short hair in the gray suit?"

Susie's eyes narrowed. "Strong Manning."

"Nice. Is he a trial lawyer?"

"Not a trial lawyer and not nice. He consults. Brilliant, but stays in the background."

Susie, a substantial, caramel-skinned black woman, tossed her gold-striped curls. Her usual facial expression radiated, "Don't mess with me." Displeased, she could expand her light brown eyes to hurl an uncomfortable "bug eye" glare. Emma liked Susie and appreciated her ability to navigate the circuitous pathways of documents and files needed for research.

"Susie, you know everything."

"Yep. That's why your boss pays me."

"My boss? But you work here in the courthouse."

Susie halted her swift pace. "I do work here. In the months you've been in St. Louis working for Latito, haven't you noticed I drop what I'm doing to assist you?"

"Mr. Latito pays you to help me?"

"Hel-lo, Em-ma? Gianni needs information, and I help you get it. I'm gonna give you some advice. Don't ask questions about Gianni, and don't get interested in Manning."

"Too late on the second part. How is he not nice?"

Susie's expression hardened. "He's someone you don't notice but is everywhere at once. He dates women, then dumps them with no explanation. He's a cold one—a snake in the grass! Dangerous if you don't watch your step. Uh-huh, he'd chew *you* up and spit you out, Missy. Although, if I needed legal advice, he'd be the one I wanted on my side. Here's my cubicle. This is where the train stops."

Emma tapped the folder she held. "Should I say thank you for your help?"

"Forget what I said about being paid. You hear?"

Emma wasn't sure she could forget what Susie had said, but that evening when she flipped through her mail, a letter threatening a lawsuit gave her something else to think about. It also provided an opportunity to meet Strong Manning.

Three days later, she eyed the sign, "Manning and Manning," written in gold letters on the window of a one story brick building. She entered and approached the receptionist.

The receptionist nodded, rose, and knocked on one of the

closed doors. She opened it. "Mr. Manning, Miss Emma Whitstone is here for her appointment."

"Thanks, Evelyn." Strong moved a chair in front of his desk. "Come in, Miss Whitstone."

"Thanks." Emma took the seat.

"What can I do for you?"

She tried to hide her evaluative stare while handing him the letter.

Strong read the letter, steepled his fingers, and regarded her for a long moment. "I wouldn't worry, Miss Whitstone. It's possible, but not likely. Lawsuits commonly threaten everyone involved in a business, right down to the secretaries."

Emma bit her lip. "So, if Mr. Latito is sued, I don't have to get a lawyer?"

"I advise you to forget it. Probably nothing will happen, or if it comes to a lawsuit, Latito would settle. No one wants to see you in trouble." He returned the letter. "I'm curious, how did you select me?"

The question caught her off guard. She stalled her answer by returning the letter to her purse and closing it with a snap. "I saw you at the courthouse."

"Ah, yes, after the, uhm…hallway fuss. The captivating woman in the elevator."

Captivating? She struggled to keep aloof and came up with an answer. "You seemed confident. You looked…honest." His faint smile assured her he liked the answer. She let out a short breath. "I'm relieved. I have a little money saved, but I wouldn't want to have to hire legal assistance." Not sure of what else to say, she slipped her hand through her purse strap. "That's it, then; do I pay your secretary, or do you bill me?"

He left his chair and sat on the desk in front of her. "Initial consultations are free. On a condition."

"What's the condition?"

"That the consulting client has dinner with the attorney."

"You mean I take you to dinner?"

His eyes crinkled, and an amused chuckle followed. "Free

consultation, free dinner. How can you beat that?"

She nodded. "A win-win situation."

"I'd say you're definitely a winner. So, when are you available?"

She looked away for a second. "Does it sound like I don't have a social life if I say almost any time? My calendar is open tonight, the night after that, and unfortunately, every evening until next Tuesday. That's my ceramics class."

"Difficult to believe your calendar is not full, but now I get to be the winner. So, how about tonight? Seven?" He handed her a note pad. "Write your address."

"Seven is good," she said, putting pen to pad and trying to calm her fingers. A date! She could barely believe it.

For the rest of the day, the papers in her hand blurred, and her fingers slipped around the computer keyboard. Each thought about Strong Manning took her into a fog. And she thought about him a lot. What was so special about that man?

On her rushed drive home, she pictured her closet and wrestled on what to wear. In front of her mirror, she fussed with her makeup and wished she had listened to the beautician who recommended highlights to brighten her chestnut hair. A few minutes with the curling iron produced waves in the maybe too-short haircut.

Checking her watch, she took a few minutes to rummage through her jewelry box. She caressed her mother's pearls, sighing at how little she had to remind her of her folks. Was this date special enough to warrant wearing this simple but precious inheritance? She pressed the necklace to her chest and picked up a photo of her mother. Except for the light hair, she looked like her mom — oval face, full lips, dark lashes. "So Mom, what do you think about me meeting Strong? And how about his astonishing request to spend the evening with me! What makes him so attractive? The confidence he projects? His controlled vigor and the way he stopped the fight in the courthouse? Maybe. Okay, the curve of his jaw resembles Dad's...well, based on the few photos I have. Am I looking for a father figure?"

She put down the photo and silently answered herself. *Stop analyzing. What difference does it make? He's attractive, and I want to be with him. Should I question fate?*

CHAPTER THREE

On the third knock, Emma opened her front door. She liked the way Strong's eyes creased at the corners when he smiled.

"You're ready."

Emma cocked her head. "And you're on time."

He eyed her up and down and smiled his approval. "You look gorgeous."

"Thanks."

He brushed his hand outward. "Shall we?"

"Uh-huh." Her heart skipped a beat when his hand touched her waist. A warning bell chimed in her thoughts. *He's too forward.* Should she move away? She let out a sigh; that touch made him more attractive. Her hand shook as she held the key and tried not to fumble. "I wasn't sure what to wear, but I figured a girl can't go wrong with an LBD."

He pointed his key fob toward the white car in the driveway. "What's an LBD?" The car beeped.

"Little black dress."

His eyes flickered over her dress. "It's true; you didn't go wrong."

A brief wave of delight swept through her. "Nice car. What is it?"

"A Cadillac Escalade." He held the door for her. "I'm loyal to America. I buy our cars."

"Pretty paint." She touched her necklace. "It looks like my pearls."

"Oh yeah, that's masculine. I better make my next one black."

Besides oozing masculinity, he had a good sense of humor.

She slid into her seat, admiring his movement as he walked to his side and got in.

Strong started the car. "Do you like Italian?"

"Sure. Who doesn't like Italian? Pizza?"

"Catalano's is a super place. Big menu, all food names end in vowels, and delicious, whatever you select."

When they reached the entrance, the restaurant smelled of garlic and intense Italian goodness. Emma took a deep breath and let the tang of the air infuse into her.

A waiter waved and nodded his head at Strong, indicating a table in the corner.

Once again, Emma felt the wave of delight when Strong curved his hand into her waist, guiding her to the table.

The waiter greeted them with a wide smile and a bow.

"What do you suggest?" Emma asked.

Strong waved away the menus and ordered. Within minutes, he approved the wine, and the glasses were filled. Emma closed her eyes, making a wish on the clink of their toast that this would be one of many times together. Dare she dream of more?

When the food arrived, it did not include pizza. Sumptuous steaming pasta floating in pinkish, sweet-smelling sauce beckoned. It tasted better than it looked. Emma wondered if the food was actually that good, or had the company affected her senses? Halfway through the meal, she decided it was both. The man who sat across from her was the man she'd seen in her dreams. Had those dreams come true?

After the waiter refreshed their wine, a tall man came to the table holding a half-consumed glass of milk. A thick blond curl tumbled over his forehead. Appearing easy going and relaxed, his whole face smiled. "Strong, they said you were here in the dining room. Who is this lovely lady?" He spoke with a Swedish accent.

"Emma, meet Lars Johnson, an old friend. Lars, this is Emma, a new friend."

"Pleased to meet you, miss."

Strong cleared his throat. "This is a date, Lars."

"Yah, I see. Goodbye." He gave a slight bow and left.

Emma watched the man depart. "Lars Johnson? He's Swedish?"

"For tonight. Lars likes to charm ladies. He comes from Minnesota, not the 'Old Country.' He's a private detective."

"I've never met a private detective. How exciting."

Strong took a sip. "He'll be delighted to know he excited you." He tipped his wine glass toward her. "Tell me about you, Emma."

She returned the tilt and smiled into the ruby liquid, enjoying the little rift of pleasure his question produced. "Not much to say. I originally came from Maryland. My parents were killed in a car accident when I was ten, and I lived with relatives until I went to college. After graduation, my college roommate invited me here and got me the job with the Latito Development Company. How about you? I like your first name." Actually, she liked everything about him.

"My whole name is Charles Strong Manning. It's a tradition in the Manning family to name the first son Charles, with the mother's surname as the second. I dropped the Charles and just use Strong."

The waiter removed the empty bottle and eyed Strong, who shook his head.

"What's wrong with Charles? It's a good name."

Strong's face took on a hard edge. "When I was eleven, I was beaten up by a boy named Charles. I hated the name after that."

"Beaten up? Hurt?"

"Hospitalized."

"Oh, I'm sorry. Is that where the little scar at the edge of your mouth came from?"

"Uh, no." He touched his lip. "That's more recent."

"Did you ever avenge the Charles who hurt you?"

Strong took the last bit of his wine and put the glass down firmly. "He's doing twenty-five to life."

"That's a long time to be in prison. I know that has to be an interesting story."

"Let's just say I kept tabs on Charlie, and when he was implicated in an armed robbery with a homicide, I took an interest."

"Did Lars help?"

Strong gave her an evaluating stare. "As a matter of fact, yes."

"How did you meet Lars?"

"We met in the army. After that, he joined me here in St. Louis and became a cop. Later he branched out. He's the best investigator I know. Are you a spy?"

"What?"

"You have delicately probed me, and here I am, spilling my guts. I've never revealed so much before."

"On a first date?" she drank the rest of her wine.

"On any date, or series thereof. You're good. I should alert the CIA."

Was it the wine's effect or the company that thrilled her? Emma tried not to show her delight in the conversation. She felt out of her element and didn't want to appear unsophisticated. When the waiter removed the last dish, he asked if they would like to see the pastry cart.

"What would you like for dessert?" Strong asked.

You. She cleared her expression of that thought, she hoped, and shook her head. "I couldn't eat another thing. It was wonderful, but I'm stuffed."

"How about a walk to the arch?"

She dabbed the napkin at her mouth. "I'm up for a little exercise."

They walked several blocks from the restaurant to the park.

"Tell me about the army, Strong."

"After college, I wasn't sure what I wanted. A recruiter talked me into joining, and I got a commission. I met Lars in Special Operations. We've had some remarkable experiences. When we got out, I went to law school, and he went into law enforcement."

They sat on a bench with a view of the arch.

"Emma, what do you do for Mr. Latito? Do you like your job?"

"I'm an administrative assistant. I do all sorts of clerical work, and I go to the courthouse to research. I like the job; it pays well."

"Here's a piece of advice. Don't learn too much about Gianni Latito. Keep a low profile if you can."

"What are you saying?"

He leaned close. "You smell great. What is that?"

"It's called 'Joy.' Mr. Latito gave it to me for Christmas."

Strong's eyes became pieces of flint. "Does he give you expensive gifts often?"

Emma cocked her head. "He hardly notices me. He gave perfume to all of the female employees, and he's never said anything improper. What did you mean about not learning too much?"

"Emma, I think you're the type who trusts everyone. Don't trust *him*. Latito operates on the edge of legality. Stay under his radar. Ideally, get a different job."

Emma ran her finger the length of her lip to think. "Okay. I'll keep a low profile. When you say I *trust* people, are you saying I'm *stupid*?"

"Absolutely not, but trusting can have the same outcome. Look, in the few hours we've been together, I've learned that you are kind and caring; you probably assign those virtues to others. What I'm saying is to be careful. Hey, how about coffee and dessert? Think there's room now?" He put his hand on her stomach.

Her heart skipped a few beats before a heatwave flared through her body. She chided herself for liking his audacity, but she couldn't help it and mentally fanned herself to cool down. "Sounds good."

They walked to a diner with a neon pie sign flashing in the window. Emma didn't pay attention to the taste of the pie and coffee, grateful for the extra time the dessert gave them together.

An hour later, Strong waited as Emma unlocked her front door. "I'm coming in to kiss you goodnight."

She didn't protest, and he followed her in. She clapped, and a light went on.

Strong raised his brows. "Clever."

"It was here when I moved in," she said with a touch of apology. "Strong, I had a great time tonight. Thank you for the dinner and the walk. And the advice, I think."

"So, you'll go out with me again?"

Yes! She smiled and calmed herself. "Probably...."

Before she could say another word, he pulled her close and kissed her. She caught her breath. He kissed her again, longer this time, with more pressure.

After the fourth kiss, she backed away. "My knees are buckling. I have to sit."

He sat on the couch with her and massaged her neck before he resumed the kissing.

"Stop, I need to breathe." Emma moved apart for a moment to inhale and then put her head against his shoulder. "Let's just cuddle for a little while."

He kissed the top of her head. "Define cuddle."

"You're always a lawyer, aren't you?"

"Right now, I'm a cuddler."

They sat quietly for a few minutes in a soft embrace.

"Maybe you should go," she said without sincerity.

"All right." He rose and helped her up. "How about Saturday night?"

"Okay." Could he hear her thumping heartbeats? "You know, you are a very good kisser."

"And you are a good kissee." Strong put his forearm on the doorframe. "Do you really want me to go? We were having such a good time."

A volt like an electric shock shot through her at the image forming in her head—their naked torsos touching. *Stop it.* "No, I don't want you to go, but we've just met, and...."

"Yeah, yeah. Not on the first date, et cetera. I understand. Good night, Emma. It was great."

After hearing the car leave, she dropped to the couch and willed the buzzing in her loins to settle down. Within a minute, the phone rang.

"Hi, Emma. It's Strong. How many dates?"

"What?"

"How many dates until I can stay for a while?"

What should I say? "Uh, five. Yes, at least five."

"Would that be on the fifth, or would it be after the completion of the fifth — that is to say, the sixth?"

She laughed. Mimicking his words she said, "After completion of the fifth, that is to say, commencing with the sixth."

He chuckled. "Where would you like to go Saturday? I forgot to ask. I was busy."

"How about a movie, then dinner?"

"Great. Pick a movie. I'll call you Friday afternoon for details."

"You'll need my direct number at work. Can you write it down while driving?"

"I have it."

"No, I mean my unlisted, private work number."

"I know it, Emma."

"You do?"

"I have my ways, my dear. I'll call you."

Emma couldn't remember feeling happier, dismissing any wariness lurking in her thoughts. She hung up the phone and shut her eyes, picturing his light brown hair closely shorn on the sides with enough wave on the top to show the widow's peak, an arrow to his dangerous eyes. Susie said he was dangerous. The thrill-wave pulsing inside made her agree. *Dangerous to me.*

Sleep did not come easy, making it a chamomile tea night. She willed the tea to soothe her, but there would be no soothing. Susie's warning made its way back into her mind.

CHAPTER FOUR

The next few days dragged with the memory of Strong's touch stomping all over her thoughts. On Fridays, she worked at the courthouse. That Friday morning, she carefully selected her outfit for the day, choosing a royal blue pantsuit and a white blouse with a draped neckline. The blouse had just enough drop to show a hint of cleavage. She'd chosen her wardrobe thoughtfully before, but this marked a new part of her life. Her appearance had taken on new meaning—dressing to interest a certain man. Would he be at the courthouse and see her? If not, the outfit was practice for when she did see him.

On the floor where Susie worked, her desk was in the first cubicle nearest the elevator. A professionally produced sign prominently displayed said, *Pay Heed to How you Address the Mocha Amazon*. Most everyone, including Emma, paid heed.

Susie smiled when Emma stopped at the desk. "Love the suit—matches your eyes. Uh-uh, don't you clean up nice and pretty. What can I do for you today?" Emma showed Susie a folder and explained the work. Susie straightened her desk and stood. "Come on. Daylight's burning."

They entered the crowded elevator. He was there!

On his way out, Strong nodded to Susie. "Hey, Suze." He smiled, then winked at Emma.

When the door closed, Susie put her hand on her hip. "Oh, no you didn't!"

Emma opened her mouth, shut it, and then looked to the wall. They got off at the next floor. Susie shook her head in cadence with her rapid stride. Her stiletto heels hit the marble floors harder than usual. She stopped abruptly and waggled her finger at Emma. "So that's why you look like Miss America today, huh? I warned you against Strong Manning, didn't I?" Her eyes bugged. "The Man of Mystery. Put that guy *out* of your brain. No, uh-uh—not for you." She sucked her teeth. "You aren't listening, are you? Well, don't come crying when he breaks your heart, missy." The side of her lip curled up in a snarl. "From what I hear, he goes out with a woman, and then a blonde hottie shows up crooking her little finger. He shoots out of his chair all zombie-like and follows her. He just leaves—in the middle of a date. Don't get caught up with him. That's all I'm gonna say."

Emma straightened her back and engaged Susie's bug-eye. "Good."

Susie blinked, returning to her normal "don't mess" look. "Okay. Let's get to work."

Susie said no more regarding Strong that morning. Emma finished her work and returned to the office. Near five, when her phone rang, she held her breath before saying, "Hello?"

"Hey, Princess," Strong said. "What do you want to see tomorrow?"

She told him her choice.

"Spy thriller, eh? Want Greek food for after?"

"I love it."

On Saturday night, after the movie, they discussed the film on the drive to the restaurant.

"It was a good movie," Strong said. "But do you believe secret agents come away from the adventures without a scratch, or that all of the bad guys are completely evil?"

"I guess not. I never thought about it. I watch a movie and enjoy it. In Hollywood, the good guys win, and the bad guys lose; that's how the world is. It works."

"In the movies."

She adjusted her shawl. "Yes, in the movies."

Strong pulled the Escalade up to the valet at Zorba the Greek restaurant. He jumped out, helped Emma from the seat, and tossed the keys to the attendant. Sliding his hand around her waist, he guided her into the restaurant. When they stepped into the entrance, the host bent his head in a familiar way.

At the table, the server called him by name. *Does every waiter and maitre d' in St. Louis know him? Do they evaluate his dates and nod their approval?*

The dinner and wine were superb. Strong took long looks at her during the meal. She wished she could read him better. Susie was right about him being mysterious.

As they waited for the valet to bring the car, Emma pulled her black pashmina around her shoulders. "I don't know which was better, the dinner or the movie."

He kissed her cheek. "It's all great. You make me feel good just being around you. In fact, I could be in a foxhole, and if you were with me, I'd be just fine."

Okay, it was an odd thing for him to say, but she felt the same way.

On the way home, Strong played a CD of Andean music, lilting and soothing. "It's amazing the sound that comes from these primitive instruments. The pipes are made from different size reeds attached with thongs. The drum is a simple cylinder with a hide top, and usually there's a small guitar-type thing."

Emma leaned against the headrest. "Relaxing."

He pulled into her drive. "Don't get too relaxed." He unbuckled his seatbelt and leaned toward her. Her seatbelt released with a metallic ring.

Emma closed her eyes as he pressed his lips on hers. "Mmmm," she said in a whispery exhale. They kissed until the car's windows were opaque with moisture. She opened the car door. "I'd better not invite you in."

"Why not?"

"You have four more dates yet. I don't want to test my resolve."

"We wouldn't want anything to happen to your resolve." He escorted her to the door. "What shall we do next?" He leaned against the frame as she pushed in her key.

"How about bowling Sunday night?"

"You're kidding! You bowl?"

"I'd like some lessons. Can you teach me?"

He scratched his nose, thinking. "Not my first choice for a date, but let's see. I can get behind you real close and guide your arm, and…. Okay, I'll show you how to bowl. I haven't done it since high school."

The lock clicked. "Are you sure you remember how?"

"Yes. Come here."

They kissed against the door until Emma moved her head. "Goodnight, Strong. I didn't think tonight could be better than our first date. But it was. Thank you."

"You're welcome. Goodnight. Four more, don't forget."

"It will be four-most in my mind."

He shook his head at her pun. "Tomorrow night, then. Who knew I'd be taking a girl to the Pin Masters Alley?" Laughing, he said, "Who knew?"

Emma loved the Sunday night bowling instruction. Strong stood behind her, brushing against her back with his arms around her. She knew how to bowl, but his proximity affected her coordination. On her first throw, the ball waggled and threatened to gutter. Four pins were conquered.

Strong held his arms wide. "Great for your first time!"

With some guilt, she accepted his praise. Was it a lie by omission that she let him think she didn't know how? He embraced her. Okay, it was worth the bit of shame from her little sin. She took four more pins on the second throw. On his turn, he demonstrated the follow-through, but as he spoke, she slipped into her thoughts, and his words turned into a low whine. She went into deep deliberation. *Susie thinks I'm a fool.* Her shoulders sagged. She fought the sag and pulled her shoulders up. *It's not foolish. Oh, God, I've just met him, but this feeling….* She'd had crushes in high school and dated a few men in college. Those had been mild attractions at best. This feeling was new, different, exhilarating—love? Strong would not break her heart. She wouldn't let him.

Strong's face appeared in front of her. "Earth to Emma…."

"Sorry," she said. "You were saying?"

He smiled and kissed her cheek with a quick peck. "Nothing important. It's just a game, Princess. Relax and have fun." He pointed to the pins. "Pretend they're enemy soldiers, and your goal is to take down as many as you can."

Soldiers? Strong's haircut, his military comments…was he still military?

He picked up his ball, gliding on the shining alley floor like a ballet dancer, and threw it effortlessly, precisely. His muscles rippled as the black sphere left his fingers. His moves, cat-like, thrilled her. Surely he had flaws, but nothing physical she could see. Susie's words bubbled up. Emma shook them off. The clash of the pins assailed by his swift, accurate ball drove Susie's warning away.

He slid onto the seat next to her. "Your turn, Princess."

She did better the second time, extracting more praise. She had enjoyed bowling in high school, but it had never left her breathless or lightheaded.

After the games, they strolled, holding hands along the river walkway. In Emma's driveway, after the Escalade's windows were thoroughly steamed, Strong walked her to the front door, where they kissed once more. As he turned toward the car, they both said simultaneously, "Three."

Strong chose the venue for their fourth date, a dimly lit supper club where most of the music was slow and sultry. They ate a light meal and danced for hours to mellow jazz. Strong alternated the drinks, ordering club soda and ginger ale between rounds.

On the way home, Emma relaxed into the soft leather of the car seat. "Strong, tonight, the dancing—it's the best date I've ever had. Absolutely the best."

Strong's face was unaffected, but the twinkle in his eye said he agreed. "Hey, why wouldn't I enjoy rubbing against an attractive woman to good music?" He waited for her protest.

"You're so bad."

He ran his finger down her arm. "Two more dates; you'll see

how bad I am."

She put her hand over her mouth to hide her smile.

That night as she lay in her bed, she longed for his touch. A hollow formed inside her—an empty space—hungering to be filled. Emma wanted him beside her, inside her. This wasn't loneliness; this drive was new, demanding. Should she stick to her condition? Five dates. Five dates! She'd read that Bedouins could live on five dates a day. She sniffed at the irony and doubted her ability to exist while waiting for her five dates to conclude. She wanted him, required him. Sleep evaded her while she imagined the sixth date. Doubt troubled her. What was he doing on the nights they weren't together? *Don't think about it.* It was another long, chamomile tea night.

For their fifth date, Strong surprised her with tickets to *Lion King.* Before the show, they dined at a small French bistro.

"Great dress. You look good in pink," he said as they waited for their appetizers.

"A legacy from my roommate."

He pulled his head back with a questioning look. "You have a roommate?"

"Not anymore. It's her house, but she let me stay on at the shared rent price when she moved away." Emma sighed. "She got married to a wonderful guy. He has a job in Jordan for the next five years. Abbey and I are the same size, so she left me most of her things. I miss her."

Strong nodded. "Sounds like a good deal for you."

She clenched her jaw and released it. "Sure. She gets a lifetime of happiness, and I get some nice clothes."

He didn't speak but refilled her glass with White Merlot, his face unreadable.

In the car after the show, they sang a few lyrics from the musical.

"Strong," she said as they walked to the front door. "How about dinner here next time?"

"We *could* do that." He put his arm around her. "But let's go somewhere special instead." He kissed her.

"Why don't you come in? You can stay for a while."

"Next time. You'd better be vigilant; your resolve is slipping."

"I don't want to wait."

"Yes, you do. Good night, Princess."

For the sixth, their special date, Strong made reservations at the Old House Restaurant, a restored Victorian, romantic and expensive. They sat in a secluded corner where a bottle of Dom Perignon waited, chilling in its silvery holder.

"Strong, I need to talk to you about something."

"What's that?"

"Uh, I—" She was interrupted when the waiter came with the filet mignon.

Strong's cell phone rang. He regarded the number and snarled. "Shit."

"Turn it off."

"I can't."

"Don't answer it."

"I can't do that, either." He answered, and after a few contentious words, he put the slender phone in his jacket pocket.

She followed his gaze across the room and focused on a woman who walked through the entrance. The woman stopped at the host's podium and scanned the room until she locked her stare on Strong. She crossed her arms like someone who waited for a demand to be filled. Athletic with golden hair pulled back in a ponytail, her stunning looks brought stares from the surrounding tables. Strong, nostrils flared, pulled out his wallet. He handed Emma his American Express card and a hundred-dollar bill. "Emma, no questions, please. I don't want to leave you, *believe* me. But I have to go. Now."

Numb, she shrugged. "If you have to go, you have to." *Did I just say that? And who is that beautiful woman summoning him?* A lump formed in her throat. Was she losing him?

He kissed the top of her head. "Thank you. Sign my name on the charge. I'll get the card later. Take a cab home."

Something told her not to protest. "Strong, be careful."

"I'm always careful." He left, following the stunning blonde.

Always? He is always careful? Careful doing what?

CHAPTER FIVE

Emma awoke in a bad mood. "The wrong side of the bed," she remembered her mother saying.

She walked hard steps to the bathroom and took a shower, hoping the steam and the warmth of the water would shake her cross disposition. Vigorously toweling her hair helped shake off some of her funk. She flipped coat hangers back and forth in the closet to see which *haute couture* of Abbey's would brighten her horizon for the day. "Yellow. Like sunshine," she said, her jaw still tight. She liked the soft lemon color silk pantsuit, especially paired with the creamy hue of the alpaca shell blouse.

She picked up files at the office and headed to the courthouse in her tiny Fiat. She thought about the day she got her little car. That model had been the least expensive new car she could find, and it proved to be fun. The fatherly salesman at the showroom had used a parking area of a closed store adjacent to the dealership to teach her how to use the manual transmission. In less than an hour, she'd mastered the shifting and could drive like she'd done it for years. She loved the ease of parking, fitting into almost any slot, meaning she almost always found a spot, even in the courthouse lot on busy days.

By the time she reached the metal detector at the courthouse, her bad mood had passed, and she was ready for the day. At Susie's desk, she chuckled at the warning regarding the Mocha Amazon.

Susie approached from behind. "Hey, girlfriend."

"Hi, there." She held her folder high, knowing Susie understood.

"Give me a second," Susie said. "I need to finish the schedule. My boss gave me a raise, and now he's extracting payment. But it's nice that nine people report to me."

"Congratulations," Emma said, genuinely impressed.

Susie typed a few words and hit the print button. "Yep, not bad for an illegitimate girl from Mississippi. I have a white daddy out there somewhere. He didn't care enough for Mom to stick around, let alone marry her. He split as soon as she told him about being knocked up." She narrowed her eyes as if she listened to an insult. "I know, it's typical of brothers — black guys — not to marry their baby-mommas, but at least they give the kids their name and come around once in a while with diapers or money for formula."

"Oh, Susie."

"I didn't tell you all that for sympathy, you know. Just so you understand me." She locked eyes with Emma. "I've gotten ahead because I'm willing to do what it takes. You know what I mean?" She didn't give Emma time to comment. "Actually, you have kind of a long face. Everything good with you?"

Emma swallowed like she did when she needed to think before she spoke.

"Uh huh. I know I said I wasn't going to bug you about Strong Manning, but I worry about you."

"Thanks, Susie. Don't worry."

"You're still seeing him?"

What could she say? She didn't want to lie. "Kinda, yeah."

"*Kinda? Yeah?* He ditched you, didn't he? That blonde crooked her finger, and he split, right? That stupid bitch."

Emma took a long look at Susie's face. The arrogance had disappeared, replaced by pain. "You dated him!"

Susie let out a breath. "Yeah. I don't usually date white guys because of my father, but it was Strong. I couldn't resist. And you *know* how good he is in bed." Susie's eyes expanded into the bug-eye. She never missed a thing. "Ah! You haven't slept with him!"

Emma didn't answer.

"How long have you been seeing him? And you haven't

been to bed? Hard to believe. Actually, it's incredible. Strong doesn't waste time, and no woman refuses him, but...." Susie took a breath. "But truth? Oh, girlfriend! You don't know what you missed." Susie's eyes glazed over as if she watched a favorite movie playing inside her head. "Yep, that guy is special, almost worth the bad experience."

Emma pulled at her chin. "Is there any woman around the courthouse Strong Manning *hasn't* slept with?"

Susie gave a half shrug. "Married, old, or ugly. That's about it." Susie put her hand on Emma's shoulder. "I can't figure this out. You, I mean, with Strong. He's the mighty white hunter stalking big game, but you are a calico kitten."

Emma put her hand on her hip. "What does that mean?"

"It means that you are very cute, and I can see his initial attraction, but honey-chile, that boy goes for the lioness, not the kitten."

Emma pondered Susie's comment. "Well, what can I say in response, other than maybe he has tired of the lions?"

"Yeah. And maybe he's moved on and gone back to the safari. Let's get to work. No use crying over spilled milk—or Strong Manning. Hear?"

Emma nodded. She put aside her thoughts and concentrated on her work. Of course, she didn't.

When they finished for the day, they left the records room. In the elevator, Emma felt Susie's stare. "What is it, Susie?" She hoped it wouldn't be another diatribe about Strong. Although... today was Wednesday, and he'd left her at the restaurant on Friday night. She pulled out of her deep thought and listened to the conversation Susie had already started.

"I'm guessing Mr. Latito pays you pretty well. You're getting good at this stuff. I see the way you make connections from the research. Other companies are looking for people like you. You can go somewhere with your skills. In a few years, you could have a name-your-own-price career. That is, if you aren't too picky about who hires you—uhm, no questions or high morals."

"I do enjoy my work. I love the challenge, hunting and then

putting the pieces together. But I don't want to make it my whole world. I want what I didn't have growing up, a loving family."

"Well, baby, if you're looking for that with Manning, you're barking up the wrong tree."

Emma blew a short breath. *Susie just can't leave this alone.* But then, five days had gone by without a word from Strong. Had he moved on? Gone on safari?

CHAPTER SIX

On Friday afternoon, just before quitting time, her phone rang.

"Emma," the voice said. "This is Strong. I'm sorry about last week."

A whole week without a word. A burn flared in her cheeks. What should she say? Silence made the phone sound hollow.

"Emma?"

"I'm here."

The next silent gap made her wonder if the call had been disconnected.

"Em?"

Instinct told her he wasn't the kind of man who begged forgiveness, and the words "I'm sorry" rarely made an appearance. But he had just spoken those words. Dignity demanded she hang up on him. She imagined him on the other end of the phone, waiting for her response. She didn't want to hang up, but what about her self-respect? Susie had warned her.

"Em, please."

That was Strong...saying please.

"Okay. I know you couldn't help it."

She heard his breath escape over the phone. *He'd been holding it!*

"Look, our date was interrupted, but we can reschedule... right?"

She didn't want to sound too eager, but she agreed.

"I have work to catch up on, but next Monday I'm going to Nevada—on business. Take a week off and go with me."

"Las Vegas?"

"Close enough. One thing…during the day, you'll be on your own."

"It's a business convention?"

"Sort of. Come on, this will make up for the date I ruined, our *sixth*."

"I'll ask for the time."

"You'll get the time," he said in a confident tone.

Strong was right, when she asked the office manager, she got the time off. On Monday afternoon, they sat in the Elite lounge at the airport.

Emma nibbled a finger sandwich. "Do you always fly first class?"

"Or business class. I'd rather have my own plane."

"You have a pilot's license?"

"Yes."

"I didn't know that."

He took a sip of his drink. "There are a few things you don't know, I'm afraid."

Emma ran her finger around the rim of her wine glass. "There's something I need to tell you about me."

"Okay. What is it?"

"I haven't had sex before."

His face remained unchanged, but surprise echoed in his voice. "How *old* are you?"

"I'm twenty-six. I know, it's difficult to believe. I just never met anyone I cared enough to be with in that way."

"Not even in college?"

"I worked when I wasn't studying or in class. I've had dates, but—"

"Don't explain. So, now you've met someone you care enough for in *that way*?"

She looked down at her hands. "Yes," she said softly.

"It will be a new experience for both of us." He reached for her hand and played with her fingertips. "This little piggy went to market; this little piggy stayed home. These little piggies went to Vegas, and cried wee-wee-wee and got boned!"

Emma blushed. Then she laughed. That charming crinkle formed on the side of his eyes. She relaxed and finished her wine. In a few minutes, she left for the ladies' room and refreshed her makeup. As she returned to the booth, she halted and watched. Strong pitched nuts in the air and caught them in his mouth. He caught them every time. She stayed in place, observing his movements. When she returned to the table, a few nuts remained in the plastic cup.

She shook the cup toward the snack area. "Want some more?"

"Saw that, huh?"

Should she comment? It seemed so out of character for him.

He raised his eyebrows as if he read her thoughts on how low-class catching nuts looked. "Eye-hand coordination exercises. I do them every day." He took a coin from his pocket, flipped it mid-air, and caught it on his knuckle. Tossing it again, he demonstrated his routine. He caught the coin on each hand, then his palms, his forehead, cheeks, and then his nose. "I don't usually do the coin thing in public, but I wanted to impress you."

"Uh, yeah, impressive."

He held up a cashew. "Want to try catching? Improves your reflexes, and good for relieving stress."

She tossed the nut but missed it by a wide margin. He effortlessly snatched it in its path toward the floor. She waved her hand away from a second chance. There would be a lot to learn about Strong Manning. She willed herself to relax, enjoy, and learn.

In the airplane, the plush seats of first class and the multiple champagnes relaxed her further.

"How ya doing, Princess?"

She rested her head against the soft leather cushion. "I could so-oo get used to this luxury."

He put her palm to his lips. "I hope you do. I'll make every effort to convert you to royalty, my princess."

His princess? If only. She studied his face. His expression remained aloof, but his eyes twinkled. She thought that would be the way she could read him — by his eyes.

At the baggage pick-up, Strong put a twenty in her hand and said she should take advantage of the airport slot machines while he waited for their luggage. After figuring out how to insert the bill and select the bets, within a few minutes, the top light on the slot flashed. The attendant reached her before Strong returned, and when he brought the bags, Emma waved a handful of cash at him.

He whispered, "Getting lucky early?"

"Looks like it," she whispered back as a shiver tingled her spine. *Gonna get lucky.*

When the doors of the terminal parted, she wasn't ready for the blast of hot, dry air.

"Even in spring," Strong said. "It's always an oven. Sometimes a hot one, and sometimes on low. But," he waved his arm toward the strip, "it's Vegas."

Emma stared at the distant array of flashy hotels. "So what happens in Vegas stays here?"

He paused, looking intently at her. "Maybe not."

She wasn't sure what he meant, but the words and the tone made her feel…what? Secure? Something good, she knew. Was this a time to be wary? Even if it was, she wouldn't ruin anything by wondering or giving in to suspicions.

Emma scanned their room at the Hilton, starting with lush ivory carpeting around to the silk drapes cascading like silver waterfalls framing tall windows that let in soft light. She went to one of the windows and looked down at the hotel's entrance. Beyond the entrance, she could see the side of the convention center. *Good, the center is close by — more time to spend with him.* She assumed he would be there during the day, not too far away.

As soon as the bellman left, Strong joined her at the window and put his arms around her. He tucked her chin up. "I like this view better."

She slipped her arms around his neck and kissed him. He unbuttoned her blouse. She caught her breath with a whispery sound and immediately assisted with his buttons. As he walked her backward, she played her fingers through his flaxen chest hair.

Their clothes lay in small piles in a path to the bed. He gently pushed her down onto the silky sheets. She quivered as he placed kisses around her chest and belly.

He pulled back from her and stared, smiling. "God, you're beautiful. And perfect." He cocked his head. "What? You don't want me to tell you that?"

"I like it. It's just that no one has ever said that before."

"Really?" He gathered her in his arms and held her snugly against his body. "You should be told that, and often, because it's true."

He released his embrace and brushed his lips over her shoulder, running kisses across her neck and down to her breasts. Jolts of electric joy soared through her body. She moaned breathlessly. He moved his kisses to her hips and around her navel.

"What are you doing?" she asked as he continued lower.

"You'll like it, trust me, and...relax." He placed her hand on his groin and whispered, "Touch me."

As she slid her fingers along the warm, hard flesh, the empty feeling she'd experienced returned with a vengeance. The hollow formed, this time deeper and keener. The demand to be filled raged inside. He gently parted her legs, and his tongue explored her. Showers of delight cascaded like a surfer's dream wave. The hollow need increased but alternated with the intense pleasure his tongue delivered. She had imagined what this would feel like, but her imagination hadn't come close to the real thing. Within minutes, a massive tsunami of ecstasy exploded inside. She writhed; the intensity of her orgasm made her cry out as if she were in pain, the line between pleasure and pain creating a knife-edge. Strong gently held his hand against her lips to stifle the sounds.

"That was fast," he said, moving his lips close to her ear. "Oh, Princess."

When she could speak, she pressed her cheek against his.

"Strong...."

"What, honey?"

"Make love to me now!"

"No, we're going to take our time and do it right. You're not ready."

She clenched her teeth. "I am. I'm ready."

"We'll know when you're ready."

He covered her body with kisses and suckled gently at her breasts. She endured this sweet torture until she called out, "Strong!"

"Here." He took a condom from the nightstand. "Put it on me."

This was new. Not that she didn't know what to do, but... *just do it.* She carefully slid the latex, wet with lubricant, down his warm erection. His soft noises encouraged her.

He snapped the light off. The hairs on her neck tingled as he ran kisses up, down, and around.

She wanted to beg, say please, anything to quench the demand raging within. Each kiss, caress, nibble, pushed her closer to the edge. Her heart raced; her head pounded; a fire burned. Burning desire? She now knew what that meant. And he alone could conquer the blaze that consumed her.

"Strong!"

In his soft baritone, he said, "Okay. Now." He rolled lightly on top of her, still kissing, running his lips over her cheeks, chin, and neck. With a gentle nudge from his knee, he parted her legs. Emma thought her heart would pound its way out of her chest. She could feel him pressing against her. She'd not experienced anything like it. *In, in, in!*

He took hold of her hips. She couldn't move and didn't want to. He pushed a little way inside her. What had felt incredibly right began to feel wrong. Smoothly and gently, he pushed further.

It hurts! She clenched her teeth and pressed her lips together. She wouldn't make a sound. She didn't want to move, but instinctively she tried to push him off. He held her tight; she couldn't budge. He thrust slowly inside her. This wasn't what she expected. Would this never be over? He pulled out and pushed in again. *Oh, make this fast.* Tears formed, and she was glad it was dark. It wasn't what she expected at all. But it was what she wanted—no, demanded. He pushed, one long hard thrust. Somehow she knew this would be the last. He shuddered and, putting his lips against her cheek, made a guttural sound of unmistakable pleasure. He lifted from her, supported his weight on his knees, and rolled over next to her. She quickly wiped the tears away so he wouldn't know. He held her close in the silent darkness.

In a few minutes, Strong went into the bathroom. He came back and turned on the lights.

"Here." He gently touched a warm washcloth to her. "Oh, Ems." He pulled back the cloth spotted with blood. "Are you okay?"

"I'll live," she said, forcing a smile.

Strong fluffed up the pillows and put his back against them. He pulled her to him and wrapped his legs around her hips. Silently he kissed her neck and shoulders. Caressing her arms, he worked his way up, pressing and kneading until he reached her hair. His fingers spread wide and massaged through her hair and down to her back.

She relaxed. "What did I do to rate a back rub?"

"Everything." He intensified the massage. "I'm sorry I hurt you."

"It wasn't too bad," she lied. "About what I expected." She wriggled free and stood next to the bed.

"Come back," he insisted.

"In a minute," she said, and headed for the bathroom. The sting waned but remained to remind her of what had just happened. Strong had made love to her. She closed her eyes, thinking about it, reliving the moments. The small hurt was replaced by another emotion, satisfaction. She returned to the bed. A new feeling, pleasure, joined her satisfaction because she realized she could read his eyes, and they told her he cared, maybe more than cared.

"How about a nice warm shower?"

"I think I'll just rest for a moment."

He kissed her shoulder and left her resting against the pillows. The sound of the water soothed her further. Did she want to be soothed? She hopped out of bed and went into the bathroom. The translucent glass from the shower door cast odd lighting on his body, emphasizing his contours. She went in. Strong leaned against the marble tiles. His muscles, outlined with soapy foam, caught her attention — and her breath.

He lathered her with soap. It felt wonderful. He handed her the bar. She started with his back and lathered him from neck to ankles. Tan lines indicated he went out in the sun shirtless. In front, she soaped his chest, making patterns in the golden curls.

He put her hand on his groin. "I'm really dirty down there. See that you pay close attention to the grime."

She laughed. A shower had never been this much fun. She paid close attention to the grime, with satisfactory results. She dropped the soap and stroked his erection.

"I think we should wait, Princess. At least for a few hours."

Maybe he's right.

The toweling dry was almost as much fun as the shower. He followed her into the bedroom, keeping pace while he dried the last of her back.

"Now that we're so clean, what should we do?"

He tossed the towel into the bathroom and pulled her close. "You smell good," he whispered.

"Fragrant soap."

"Not the soap, Princess. You."

Strong let go of her, flipped open the suitcase, and took out clothing. "Hungry? I feel like a thick, juicy piece of meat."

"That is exactly how you felt," she said, picking up her case.

"Good one. Shall we eat out or in?"

"Out, if you mean we are going to a restaurant."

He chuckled. "We'll find a steak house for food and eat in later."

She kept her back to him as she dressed because she couldn't stop grinning, and she didn't want to look like a kid in a candy shop. She chose Abbey's matched set of dark green pants and short jacket and a burgundy Hermes scarf with green in the print.

While she put on her makeup, Strong rummaged through a folder of paperwork. She finished her face and stood by the desk. When he looked up, he said, "Fabulous," pronounced like a verdict.

After dinner, they walked along the strip, dodging throngs of people who snail-strolled and caused jam-ups on the sidewalks. Strong pulled Emma by the hand to circle around clots of folks who gaped at the Bellagio fountain shows, and later the cannon fight at Treasure Island.

Emma hardly noticed the close-packed swarms that impeded their progress. Walking with Strong obliterated the notion that they were surrounded. She linked her arm through his. "Just think, Strong. If it hadn't been for that letter about Mr. Latito getting sued, we wouldn't be here together."

He stopped his movement to look at her. "Maybe."

She unlinked her contact. "What do you mean?"

"Well," he said, drawing out his words, "if you hadn't come to me, I would have found a way to meet you — officially."

"I still don't —"

"I saw you one day checking in at the metal detector by the courthouse entrance. You caught my eye, and I wanted to know who you were. So...Chauncey Metcalf, the guard at the detector, owed me a favor, and...."

"What favor? And what did Chauncey do to return it?"

"I got his brother off from a DUI. I asked Chauncey who you were. He looked on his list and gave me your name."

"You asked about me?"

He pulled at his chin. "Uh, yeah. I also...uh, had Lars check you out."

Emma had to force her mouth closed from its open position. "You investigated me?"

"Nothing deep. You know, age, address, record —"

"So when you had me write my address, you already knew

it?"

He squinched his face. "Yeah."

"And when you asked me how old I was at the airport, you knew that, too?"

"Uh huh."

"You checked my record?"

"A minor check — tickets, convictions — "

She spoke with clenched teeth. "Personal history?"

"Nothing personal." He smiled and tried to kiss her cheek as she pulled away. "I mean, I didn't know you were a virgin."

In the midst of her annoyance, she realized she'd checked him out, too. Before she made the appointment, she Googled the local Mannings, adding attorney to the search. Four names came up — Charles Rockford Manning, age sixty-two, Charles Strong Manning, thirty-four, Joseph Peter Manning, thirty-two, and Sarah Deseree Manning, twenty-nine. On the office door, the gold letters Manning and Manning suggested Strong shared the business with a relative. His father? Brother? Sarah Manning was young — probably not old enough to be a full partner, so that let her out.

"Earth to Emma," Strong said. "Man, you can really tune out."

She shrugged. "Not tuning out, pondering."

He pulled her slowly into a stroll. "Pondering? Something so important you fold inward?"

"Not really."

Strong took her hand and turned from the street toward the huge building looking like a Roman Palace. "Let's ponder Caesar's Palace."

They walked through the huge casino and into the forum.

Emma's head turned up. "The ceiling looks like the sky. It really does. And the lights — just like daylight."

"Smoke and mirrors, Princess. This is a good example of not believing what you see."

"How about what I hear? Can I believe words?"

"You can from me."

She turned her head slowly to grab his attention. "Uh huh. A lawyer who never lies."

"Hey, that's a slur upon my chosen profession. But...."

"But what? You always tell the truth?"

"How about you?"

She rolled her lip for a few seconds. "I'm not going to say I've never lied, but I *try* to tell the truth. My mother said honesty is the best policy because it's hard to keep track of lies. You don't have to think about what's true. It's there in your head."

"Your mother sounds like a wise soul."

Emma sighed. "I miss her so much. She's been gone over fifteen years. I don't remember a lot."

"Tell me about your mom."

"She and my dad ran a school for hearing impaired children, teaching sign language, lip reading, communication skills. They were kind, decent people. I would like to follow in their footsteps and work with children—not necessarily disabled, but I wouldn't mind doing that. The opportunities for teaching double or triple for teachers with special skills."

"Your degree? Communications, right?"

"Double major. Communication and education. I started a Ph.D. but ran out of funds. That's why I moved here and took the job with Mr. Latito. I'm saving up to finish the postgraduate degree."

"Not that I'm sorry you came here, but couldn't you have applied for grants and loans?"

"I had some grants, but I can't bear the thought of those loans hanging over my head."

"How about your relatives? The ones who raised you after your parents died?"

"Them?" She spit the word as if it burned her lip. "They took the money meant for our education."

"*Our* education? Who's our? Do you have siblings?"

"Yes. A brother."

"In that case," he said, with a grin, "I have to talk with Lars. He's slipping. That bit of information wasn't in the background check he did on you. Your aunt and uncle? They cheated you?"

"It's complicated," Emma said, her tone wistful.

"They took money meant for you and your brother?"

"My parents had large insurance policies. I think it totaled around a million dollars, but my Aunt Hester and Uncle Gene 'invested' the funds. The investments tanked…to nothing, they claimed."

"How did that happen? Weren't the funds allocated in the will?"

"Yes, but my relatives, our guardians, used our money."

Strong's eyes went flinty. "Right. They lose the money from one place, and it shows up in another account. Helped, no doubt, by crooked lawyers who took a percentage. They're the ones that give us a bad name." He squeezed her hand. "We can get what's left, you know."

"What about the statute of limitations?"

"There are ways, Princess. Say the word."

"No. I don't want to drum up all those unpleasant memories and bad feelings that have taken me years to overcome. My aunt and uncle…didn't treat us very well. I had to clean the house, babysit their little kids after school, and have dinner waiting. Joey—"

"Your brother?"

Emma nodded. "He had to keep the lawn perfect, clean the garage, and do whatever dirty work Uncle Gene wouldn't do. And Uncle Gene kept control with his belt."

"Corporal punishment for discipline is a gray area, but child abuse—"

"It was abuse." As her stomach twitched, she shut her eyes. "Poor Joey." She swallowed hard to prevent choking on her words. "He ran away when he was sixteen. I haven't seen or heard from him."

Strong slid his arm around her waist. "Oh, Princess." His fingers caressed her back. "I can have Lars find him for you."

"I don't know." She let out a long breath. "If he wanted to find me, he would have. He contacted my mother's best friend,

Lilac Simmonds, where we lived in Maryland when I went away to college. She gave him my address. I never heard from him. After Joey left, the old lady, Ada, who lived next door to Aunt Hester, was nice to me. She contacted Lilac to see if we could get some of our family mementos. We found out that Lilac had sent a box of my mother's things and photos. Aunt Hester threw them away because she said it would have made me too sad. Ada got Lilac to make copies of what photos were left, and that's how I got the few I have now. Mother had put her pearls into the jewelers to be reknotted right before the accident. I'm so lucky because Lilac knew about it and paid the jeweler to get them out. She hadn't sent them in the box with the other stuff because I was so young. When I was fourteen, Ada got them from Lilac. I kept the necklace under my mattress."

"Hester never found them, eh?"

"She was allergic to mites, so I did all of the dusty work. She never knew about the pearls." Emma sighed a long breath. "If that kind of deception counts as a lie, then I guess I do lie."

Strong kissed her cheek. "It doesn't count, Princess. But I'd like a few minutes alone with your aunt and uncle."

Emma skated on a fine edge between tears and anger. She gritted her teeth and sought a distraction. "Oh! Look! Godiva chocolates." She increased her pace. "I'll let my nose show the way."

A five-minute wait in the aroma-filled shop gave Emma ample time to decide what she wanted. She gave the clerk exact instructions. "I only want dark chocolate—nuts, especially. And, oh, there! I love chocolate-covered cherries. Do you have coconut? No creams. Uhm, toffee, yes!"

With the gold foil box tucked under her arm, Emma, recovered from her unpleasant memories, smiled at the Roman centurion who smartly brought his arm over his chest in a salute. She giggled, but the centurion nodded seriously.

As they walked away, she whispered, "Where do they find all of those huge men?"

Strong shrugged as if everyone should know that answer.

"Talent agencies. Same place they hire the fake slave girls. Smoke and mirrors, Princess. Smoke and mirrors."

They ate at a small café in the forum. Outside of Caesar's, they rejoined the mobs on the strip. Each time Emma saw an advertisement, she asked to go there.

"We're only here six days, Princess. Prioritize."

"Well, my first priority is to stay in bed with you."

"That's my girl!"

Am I his girl? The one? If only that could be true. She sighed. "Cirque de Soliel, that's second, and I'll figure what comes after that."

"Some of those things you can see during the day while I'm gone," Strong said as they hailed a cab to the Hilton.

"I don't want to go without you."

"We'll come back when we have more time together."

Was that a hint to the future? A promise?

In the room, Strong stripped down to his briefs. "It's late. We should get some sleep. I have to get up early tomorrow."

Emma fell asleep in his arms, feeling safe, protected, and cared for.

She sat up when the cell phone alarm played. Strong, still dripping, ran in from the bathroom and turned it off. "Crap, I didn't want that to wake you."

She stretched and smiled. "I'm glad."

A quiet knock on the door sent her padding into the bathroom.

Strong wrapped a towel around his waist, answered, and admitted a room service attendant, who rolled a linen-draped table into the suite. When the attendant left, she came from the bathroom and sat near the table. Strong stacked the silver warming domes away from the plates. Smoked salmon, bagels and cream cheese, coffee, and juice.

"I've got to hurry, Emma. I'll be late. There'll be a car for me in thirty minutes." Strong ate and dressed. "Here," he said.

"What's that for?" Emma picked up five one hundred dollar bills he spread on the bed.

"Use it for gambling, or shopping, or whatever you want."

"I can't take that kind of money from you."

"It's not from me. It's expense money. I won't need it today." He tapped it. "And there's more for tomorrow. Take it."

"I'd rather have you."

He pulled her close and kissed her.

"Are you sure you can't be late?" she asked.

He pulled his shirt from his pants. "Yeah, the car can wait a little while."

She hopped into bed and pushed the sheets away. *Will it hurt?* The foreplay felt wonderful. He stoked her fire with nips and nibbles, then bid her to mount him. After slipping the condom on his erection, she nervously balanced on her knees and situated her position over him. Easing down painlessly, his hands on her hips, she felt filled, but the fire wasn't out. He flipped her over on the bed and moved rhythmically until she hummed inside. The hum gave way to a spasm of electric joy. She barely noticed his moan as she let out a cry, a pleasure wail.

When they stopped breathing hard, Emma sat up. "Oh, Strong. I never imagined it would feel so good. Look at all the time I wasted! It's wonderful, *indescribable!*"

"It's not always like *that.*" He headed for the bathroom. "Oh, it's always good, but it's extra good with you. Like you say, indescribable. We've got some chemistry going, Princess. Pure chemistry. And God, talk about a hair trigger. You are something." He put on his pants and looked at his watch. "Shit, I'm going to hear about this."

"Will there be a problem?"

"Yeah, but it was worth it." He put his wallet in his pocket. "See you here around seven tonight. I don't dare kiss you goodbye, or I'd never leave. Have a good day." He opened the door. "Spend that money!" Then he said almost inaudibly, "Your tax dollars at work."

At half past six that evening, Strong returned. He sat on the bed. "How was your day?"

"I hit the jackpot at the Wheel of Fortune slot machine. I won all of the money back plus three hundred more. That was fun.

You look tired; do you need to rest?"

"A short nap. No." He held up his hand. "Don't touch me—I need a siesta."

"Okay, hands off. For now. Sleep. Hmm," she said, examining his face. "Did you have part of your meeting around the pool? You have a little sunburn. I can see the outline of sunglasses."

"Uh huh, something like a pool," he said, pulling back the bedspread. "Give me an hour. Go commune with the Wheel of Fortune."

Within an hour, she had doubled the hundred dollar bill she shoved into the slot machine, the one with the mermaids that swam around the screen and sang when the right symbols lined up. Returning to the room with her booty, she marveled at how the brief nap had done its restorative job. They enjoyed dinner and saw the Cirque de Soliel. Returning around midnight, they made love. Emma slept in Strong's arms, the peaceful, safe sleep she had come to adore.

Before sunrise, the phone rang. Strong shook his head. "Shit. That can't be good."

"Why?"

"Only one person knows where I am. Only one reason to call." He snapped on the light and put the phone to his ear, saying nothing. He argued a few times and hung up. "Emma, I'm sorry."

His face, the usual calm and unreadable visage, warred with eyes that spoke many words—regret, concern, anger, and affection. The expression on his face delivered bad news.

"You have to go? Oh, Strong."

"Emma, look at me. I have to, or I wouldn't. I'm not abandoning you. Please understand."

"I know you're not dumping me, Strong. If you didn't want to be with me, you would say something like, 'It's not working out, but it was fun.'"

He nodded his head and picked up his watch from the side table. "Ten minutes." He dressed, bent over her forehead, and kissed her. "There's money in the drawer. Charge everything you need to the room. It'll be paid for. Leave all of my stuff. Someone will get it for me. You'll have to fly home by yourself. I won't be back by then. Take care of yourself." Then he left.

It happened so fast. He had been asleep at her side, and now she was alone. She pulled her legs to her chest and circled them with her arms. A few minutes trying to sort her feelings didn't help. On an impulse, she sprang from the bed and looked out the window. From their fourth story room, she could see the well-lighted porte-cochere of the hotel. A dark sedan pulled up. Strong approached it. The blonde, the one from the restaurant, got out of the front seat. A tall light-haired man, looking like the man named Lars, got out, too. The three conferred for a few seconds. Strong got into the front, the blonde in the back with Lars. Emma could barely see, but the car had two in the front and three heads in the back seat.

The blonde again. Emma sat hard on the bed. The lump that formed in her throat expanded and became tears. *It has been so good.* She reviewed his words and believed that he didn't want to go, that he wasn't abandoning her. He'd left before, didn't he? And when he returned, the relationship turned up a notch. She'd have to trust him. But it didn't mean she liked the fact he left with that woman…the blonde hottie.

The clock on the nightstand said five. Sleeping now was out of the question. She dressed and went to the twenty-four hour café and ordered breakfast. The half-full casino beckoned. People ate and gambled at all hours of the day and night. But here she was now one of them. She played the slots for a few hours, winning.

Having more luck at the slots than she wanted, she returned to her room and packed her things. The concierge arranged for her flight and called a taxi. She waited in the elite lounge, the finger sandwiches and champagne no longer a delight. Her emotions mixed into a toxic brew. Anger faced off disappointment, and worry wrangled with fear. By the time she boarded the plane, she had put all of the feelings on hold. She fell asleep watching a movie that played on a screen embedded in the back of the seat in front of her.

CHAPTER SEVEN

From the hotel, the team drove to a small airport outside of Las Vegas, where a Gulfstream Five waited. They wasted no time in the take-off.

Assistant Secretary Roland Spencer put his pen down as Strong took his seat. The plane's engines roused and increased their roar.

Officially named by the government, the Theta Mu Team was a finely tuned and well-oiled machine. They were the best in the country, maybe in the world. They knew they were good because they always came back from their missions — came back when other teams didn't.

Spence, the administrative arm of the group, had said they needed to be crafty, silent, like mice. Strong used the initials of their name and suggested they call themselves "Tricky Mice." Each time they received their mission information, they rededicated themselves to each other, and they had all saved each other many times over.

Lars, glass of milk in hand, took a seat next to Strong. He lowered his voice. "Hey, what's with the face?"

"What?" Strong relaxed his jaw.

"That grim look. What are you worried about?"

"I left Emma at the hotel. This is the second time I've had to ditch her, but St. Louis is a thousand miles away from Vegas."

Lars rolled the rim of his glass against his cheek. "Emma…. You mean Emma Whitstone? The one I researched?" He sipped the milk. "Hmmm. The Sunday school teacher. So? She's a big girl and can get back on her own. You never worried before about leaving a woman."

"True. But it's bothering me now. Emma's...different."

Lars stretched his neck from side to side. "That's an understatement."

"What do you mean by that?"

"Nothing; she's just not like the usual chicks you dig. Since I've known you, your women have been in-your-face aggressive or knock-out gorgeous. This one's exceedingly cute, but frankly, I don't understand the attraction."

Strong didn't answer.

"I thought she was a client."

"She was. Now she's an...interest."

"An interest? That goody two-shoes? So squeaky she's never had a moving violation? Why did you bring a woman on a training session?"

Strong looked away, hoping Lars would understand the gesture.

Lars took a sip from his glass and wiped his white mustache with his hand. "But really. Come on, she's not your type, buddy."

Obviously, Lars didn't understand. Strong rubbed his neck muscles. "My *type*?"

"Too nice."

Strong clenched his teeth. "Haven't you ever liked a nice girl?"

Wrinkles gathered horizontally on Lars's forehead. He put his glass down hard on the small table between them. "Yeah. I *loved* a nice girl until her brother threatened to cut my balls off."

Strong folded his arms on his chest. "She was too young."

"She was in college. Your mom didn't have a problem with me."

"My mother didn't know what you were doing."

"Right. It's okay for you to shtoop *my* sister, but I wasn't allowed to—"

Spence came to them and cleared his throat. "If you two ladies are through with your afternoon tea party, maybe we can have our briefing?"

In the field, Strong was in charge, and no one questioned him. He didn't like Spence's tone, but Spence took his job seriously, and even the leader of the team needed to listen to the briefing. Lamb-like, Strong followed Spence with Lars behind. Jo Lynn and Aphrodite sat at a small rectangular conference table, manila envelopes waiting in the middle. Spence took two of the envelopes and slapped them on the table in front of Strong and Lars.

"Open," Spence said. The team complied. "Page one. This is a bad one. Clear your minds. Everybody, blank page. Ready? We have a comptroller for a drug cartel who has a lot of information and is ready to spill. He has a family in Medellin. No problem. We have the Zetas on them. But the cartel is suspicious, and they have embedded our man at their main lab. We have to get him out. Take note, Manning. This has the Black Rose's marks all over it."

Strong looked up from the paperwork. "Black Rose? In South America?"

"Why not?" Spence thumped the folder. "They've expanded — weapons to the terrorists, hash from the Middle East, and now cocaine from Colombia. You took out five men last year, all relatives of the Black Rose. You're on the top of their hit list, and need I say how bad that could get?" No one spoke. "Okay, let's go over your parts." He cleared his throat. "We're flying to Colombia, so we have a few hours to discuss the mission." He looked at Strong. "Manning! Focus."

Strong flinched. "I'm listening. Colombia."

"Okay, hand over your wallets, cell phones, and jewelry. You know the drill." Spence held a leather briefcase open to accommodate the items. He handed passports with photos to Strong and Jo Lynn. "You two are tourists. Samuel and Hazel Goodwin of Philadelphia. And you two," he addressed Lars and Aphrodite. "You are the Rosses, Robert and Jill, missionaries from California."

Spencer waited until they fixed their attention on him. "We are relocating Raphael Valencia, the accountant, and his family.

Raphael is a VIP to our government. It will be touchy, but I know this team can handle it." Spencer removed a file from his briefcase. He took out a photo and tapped it. "This is Raul Martin, our contact in Colombia."

Lars took the file and examined the photo. "Is he one hundred percent?"

Spencer shook his head. "Eighty percent. He has a family in Cartagena. It's almost impossible to be one hundred percent when there's a family. It makes an agent vulnerable. He's okay, but it never hurts to be on your toes." Spencer continued. "You have luggage with everything you need. Aphrodite, don't cut your hair so short again."

Lars swished his fingers through Aphrodite's spiky hairstyle.

She took a swing at his hands. "Don't touch. You know that."

Spencer pointed at Lars's head. "Your lovely girlie curls have to go, Lars. Jo Lynn, there is a kit with barber tools. Do a 'missionary' cut on our golden boy here."

Jo Lynn snorted. "Hey, I know some missionary stuff, but it doesn't include haircuts."

Strong did not participate in the banter. "What's the time-frame?" He flipped through the file and read.

"However long it takes to get Valencia and his family out of Medellin. The cartel has a tight watch on Valencia. You four will have to finesse our 'senor' away from the compound under the Cartel's nose. But that *is* what you do." Spence passed wallets around already supplied with new driver's licenses, American money, pesos, working credit cards, and pictures of unknown families with their faces photoshopped into the group.

"Hey Spence, my wedding set has a diamond solitaire. You guys went all out this time," Jo Lynn said.

Spencer tapped his third finger in response. "Give the big one to Strong, Mrs. Goodwin. We think of everything."

Aphrodite opened her make-up case to find the little plastic jewelry bag. "We just have plain bands. I want a diamond, too."

"You are missionaries—they don't splurge on frivolities. Trust us."

Lars searched his toiletry kit. "There aren't any condoms in my case."

"Are you going to have sex with Jill Ross?" Spencer said in his business tone.

"No," Aphrodite said emphatically. "Not Aphrodite or Jill Ross. No one touches me. You all know that."

Spencer pointed to Lars. "That is why you two get to be the missionaries."

Strong showed the open case to Lars. "I have a dozen. Hey," he addressed Spencer. "You must think we'll be there for a long time."

"Hopefully, no longer than twelve screws for the Goodwins."

Jo Lynn held up a number of shiny foil discs. "I have some extras in my kit. Are the Goodwins newlyweds?"

"Why not?" Spencer said. "If it works as a cover."

For the next two hours, Roland Spencer went over the mission. The team had worked together since they met in the army. They were a machine in perfect working order, and as Spencer laid out the overview, the team inserted the details. When the plans were set, the players reclined the seats and rested.

"Twenty minutes until touch-down," Spencer said loudly.

CHAPTER EIGHT

After two weeks with no word, Emma debated calling Strong's office. His cell went directly to voicemail, and she had already left an earlier message. The opportunity to check his building came via a roadwork detour that rerouted her past Strong's office. His parking slot was empty. Week after week, his car didn't show up in his parking space. Four weeks—a long time, but nothing. She remembered his expression when he told her he didn't want to leave her, and she believed him. He hadn't said how long he would be.

Six weeks passed as she flip-flopped anger with concern. She couldn't stand it and called his office. Evelyn said she'd take a message and give it to him as soon as she could. At least that lined up with the empty parking space.

After eight weeks and another call to Evelyn, Emma tried not to think about him at all. The roadwork had concluded, and she took her old route to work. The days at the courthouse had been especially difficult. She stayed on edge, hoping Susie wouldn't bring Strong up. It had to happen sometime. And it did.

"Hey, Susie. How are you?"

"Fine. You haven't mentioned your attorney boyfriend lately, and you're acting all heart-wornish. Did he dump you?"

Emma didn't reply. She flipped the page of the oversized book and ran her finger down the column.

Susie stepped closer. "When did you see him last? If you don't mind my asking."

Of course, Emma minded, but she didn't want to get into the "I told you so's." Her finger paused over the name she wanted.

"More than two months. But he's not in town. I've called, and his secretary said he hasn't returned. He didn't dump me. He's away on business."

"Uh-huh. And the moon is made of cheese. Look, sweetie, I'm familiar with Strong. He knows how to please a woman, and as he breaks off the relationship, he makes you feel like you are doing the dumping. I have first-hand knowledge." Susie rolled her eyes and sung a few bars of "Smooth Operator."

"Here." Emma ignored the commentary and put a slip of paper into Susie's hand with a little more force than necessary. "Can you look up liens for this person?" It was a direction rather than a question.

"Sure," Susie said. "I'll call you if I find anything."

"Good." Emma forced her focus on the work, hoping she didn't seem aware Susie had left.

On the Monday of the ninth week, even though the construction had completed, Emma took the route that passed by Strong's office. The Escalade! It was there. Her heart did a double-beat. As she slowed to get a good look, the car door opened. A man wearing a hat got out. He leaned in and brought out...a cane. She stalled the Fiat. Cars honked. Flustered, she turned the key, but she hadn't engaged the clutch. The little car lurched. More horns. She couldn't take her eyes off the man as he limped into the law office of Manning and Manning. The horns blared in steady blasts. Forcing her attention on restarting the car, it turned over, and she shifted back to first. Stepping faster than her usual pace, she made it to her desk in record time. Without putting her purse away, she called Strong's office.

Evelyn answered. "Law office."

"Evelyn, this is Emma Whitstone. Is Mr. Manning in?"

"Yes, he's back from his trip, but he isn't taking calls. He's sequestered in his office to catch up on work. I'll tell him you called when he asks for his phone messages."

Strong was back. But the man coming out of his car didn't look like him. What exactly had she seen? The back of a man wearing a coat and a hat. But a cane? Limping?

Emma broke early for lunch and told the office manager she wasn't returning for the day. Her mother's words bubbled in her mind. "Cookies." When she had been small, she recalled her mother bringing cookies to people who were ill. Emma stopped at the store on her way home and bought the ingredients for assorted cookies—peanut butter, sugar, and chocolate chip. It had been years since she made them. Maybe she'd never made them by herself. The cookies she usually made were what Abbey called "pancooks," store-bought dough cut into slices and cooked in a frying pan the way pancakes are made.

Making something from scratch was a challenge. But it would give her a reason to come by the office. Did she need a reason? Should she go there? He hadn't called her. Nine weeks. She'd make those damn cookies, and if he didn't have a good excuse, she'd throw them at him. Would she do that? Maybe.

At three, she arrived at Strong's office with a warm plate enclosed in cellophane, tied with a bow. "Evelyn, I know he's busy, but I brought him a welcome home present."

"He doesn't wish to be disturbed, Miss Whitstone."

That's too bad. I will disturb him. She firmed her voice, not enough to annoy Evelyn, but enough to let her know it was important. "Would you take these to him, and please keep the door open so he can see me."

"Okay," Evelyn said with trepidation. "He's been in there nonstop since this morning. I brought him a sandwich, but I don't know if he ate it. I think he could use a break. Give it to me." She sniffed the plate. "Mmmm, chocolate chip cookies?" Evelyn rapped on the door, paused, and opened it. "A welcome home present, Mr. Manning."

Strong's desk was loaded with stacks of papers and files. The wastebasket overflowed. "Find a place to put it."

Peeking in, Emma smiled when the smell caught Strong's attention. She concentrated her stare, hoping to make him look at her. He looked.

"Emma!" Strong grabbed the plate. "Come in."

Trying to stay collected and nonchalant, she made her steps

smooth, she hoped, and elegant. She flinched when she saw him close up. His hair had been cut short, almost shaved. Over his ear, fine bristles surrounded bare skin on either side, showing the scars of an inch-long row of stitches. He looked thinner, paler, and had a steely edge to his face.

"Mr. Manning," Evelyn stammered. "I'm sorry. You said not to be disturbed, but —"

He smiled. "It's good, Evelyn. Shut the door behind you." Evelyn left, and the door made a soft click. He shifted his smile wider, producing crinkles around his eyes. "Princess...."

Emma lifted the plate from his grasp. Her anger built as she waited to hear why he hadn't contacted her for so long. "I saw your car in the parking lot." She tapped the plate. "Welcome back."

He took hold of the desk's corner, seized the cane leaning against the wall, and stood. A slight wobble nudged his usual nimble gait. His eyes followed her gaze, moving from the cane to the stitches over his ear.

"You've lost weight. Were you sick? Are you all right?"

He chuckled. "Almost as good as new." He held his arms out in invitation. "It's so good to see you."

Concern equaled the anger she felt at not hearing from him, but she couldn't keep the question bottled up. "Why didn't you call me?"

"I wasn't able to contact you before."

"I was worried. In nine weeks, you couldn't call me once?"

As if lights had turned on, his gray eyes leveled a serious look. "No. I couldn't. You *need* to believe that."

Although his moderated voice delivered the words without emotion, she received them like ice water had been hurled in her face. She'd never been good at picking up innuendo, but she read Strong clearly. What he meant was she needed to believe him if the relationship could progress, and she exceedingly wanted it to progress. She swallowed hard.

His eyes softened. "I got home late last night. I left you a message on your cell this morning."

"You did?" Still shaken by the invisible ice bath, she fumbled the cell out of her purse. There it was! The phone icon indicated she'd missed his call. She checked the ring indicator. It said "off." Sometimes when she picked up the phone, she touched the volume unknowingly.

"No problem," he said, and reached outward, inviting her into his caress.

Clearing a spot on his desk, she put the plate down and stepped into his embrace. He squeezed her gently and kissed the top of her head, his cheek lingering on her hair. "I'm okay. God, it's good to feel you. I couldn't stop thinking about you."

She pulled away from him and took a long look. "What happened?"

"I met with an unfortunate accident." The muscles in his cheek tightened, telling her not to ask further. "Look...." He took ungraceful steps and embraced her again. "I really want to see you." He held up three fingers. "Scout's honor. But I want to give you my full attention." Sweeping his hand over the piles of papers on his desk, he sighed. "Sarah handled most of the work while I was away, but—"

"Sarah?"

"My partner. Didn't you notice the sign outside? Manning and Manning."

"I thought the other Manning was your father."

A flash of contempt took over his face. Hatred? She'd not seen that before. Could Susie have been right about his dark side? She had nailed it when she referred to him as a man of mystery, a deep persona, one you couldn't fathom.

He wiped the look from his face and regarded the plate. "So, you brought me a present?" He pulled the bow on the cellophane. "These smell good. Did you make them yourself?"

"Yes. I learned how to bake cookies."

"Great! I haven't had lunch."

"Strong...." She took his arm and helped him back to his chair. "Are you going to be okay?"

He nodded stiffly. "On Wednesday morning, I have to get

this redone." He tapped his leg. "I lost a piece of femur, but the medics messed something up." He didn't elaborate further and stepped around his words like someone avoiding cracks in the sidewalk.

She sensed not to ask questions.

He leaned the cane against his desk. "Will you take me to the clinic early Wednesday morning?"

The request surprised her. "Of course, if I can get the day off."

His face became serious. "You'll get the day off, honey." He scanned the paperwork. "Let me get back to this stuff." He slid a cookie from under the plastic wrap. "I'm really glad to see you. And lunch, too!" He took a bite. "Mmm. I pretty much need to rest tomorrow."

She leaned over the desk toward him. "Can I help you?"

He laughed. "No, Princess. If I let you help me, I wouldn't get *any* rest. Pick me up at my place at six-thirtyish Wednesday." From a slim drawer underneath his desktop, he fished for a card.

She read it. "Your home address?"

"It is. Thanks for being willing to take me." Limping, he walked her to the door. Annoyance crept into her thoughts as she realized she'd just been dismissed. She stopped in front of the handle so he couldn't open it. But he *had* asked her to take him for the "fix," and she understood that was some kind of special request since most people had their loved ones do that.

His hand snaked around her to the handle.

Her annoyance notched up. But he had called her—her mistake for not seeing it—and she had come uninvited. She did want him to get his work done. A soft sigh preceded a slight nod, but before she left, she took a quick scan of his face. Maybe the shaved head made him look thinner, but overall he looked like he had gone through something awful.

Emma left Strong's office deep in thought. Was that how their relationship would be? How many times would Strong leave abruptly and not tell her why? And she needed to believe whatever small bit of explanation he offered? Could she do that?

On her way to the car, she wondered what had happened to him. Would he tell her?

CHAPTER NINE

Strong was right. Mr. Latito's office manager gave her the day off, no questions. She checked the address on the card for directions so she'd be ready.

On Wednesday morning, as she drove closer, the neighborhoods got nicer, more elegant. Strong's home was perched on the brow of a low hill overlooking woods below. She pulled the Fiat into the semi-circular driveway. Leaning on his cane, he waited for her at the end of the porch walk, looking much better than she'd seen him on Monday. The sparkle in his eye had not dimmed.

"Hey, Princess. You've made my morning." He handed her the key fob for the Cadillac. "Take my car, okay?" She helped him into the passenger side. Other than directions, he didn't speak for the short ride to the clinic.

The place wasn't a public hospital, and she wouldn't have recognized it as a medical center if he hadn't told her to park there. It was an unassuming three-story unmarked building faced with dark stone. Glass doors parted as they entered. A woman in business attire seated at a single desk greeted them with only a hint of warmth. She used her phone to summon an escort. Emma sensed the need for quiet and held her questions and comments. Within a minute, a white-uniformed man brought a wheelchair. Strong sat in it and gave the guy his cane. Emma followed the quick pace through the corridors until they reached wide closed double doors. The orderly keyed in a code, and the doors swung open inward. Curtained cubicles lined the walls. In one cubicle, Lars waited on a seat by a bed.

He smiled at Emma. "Okay. That explains it all." He winked at her. "I usually bring him to get repaired."

She stiffened. "Usually?" *How often does Strong need repairing?*

Strong shouldered off the orderly's help and got into bed. He reached for Emma's hand. "I want your face to be the first thing I see when I wake up."

Emma stifled her worries and took the chair Lars pulled up next to the bed. She watched the orderly start the IV. Within minutes, Strong closed his eyes. Emma swallowed hard. What was she supposed to say? Do?

The orderly pushed the bed out of the cubicle without comment.

Lars moved his chair closer to her and extended his hand. "Don't worry. He'll be okay," he said without a trace of an accent.

She wanted to ask about the medical center that had few patients and no outward signs of a clinic. The memory of Strong's words to her in the airport regarding things about him she didn't know increased her worries. He wanted her to accept him without questions. If it was important to him, should she hold her peace? Maybe. For now. But it didn't mean she wouldn't speculate.

Lars's stare brought her out of her thoughts. "How ya doing?"

"I'm okay. I'm surprised that the, uhm...." She looked around at the empty cubicles. "Hospital would let me be there when he wakes up."

Lars raised his eyebrows. "If you stay around long enough, you'll find that Strong pretty much gets his way, in all things."

She wasn't sure if this was an observation, a warning, or an insult. But she wouldn't react to it. She slid an e-reader out of her bag and began reading. It was difficult to concentrate. Even though she would not look up, she knew Lars appraised her.

Two long hours later, a nurse and an orderly wheeled Strong back trailed by various beeping machines graphing his vital signs. The nurse pulled a chair next to the bed. Using a stylus, she wrote on a hand device. She didn't speak. Emma didn't ask questions.

After a half hour, Strong opened his eyes. He ignored the nurse and smiled at Emma, and then at Lars. "Nice to see you."

He spoke in thick words. "My best friend and—"

Emma tensed. What would he say?

The nurse cut him off. "Pain, Mr. Manning?"

He closed his eyes halfway. Shifting his position, he said, "Oh, yeah."

The nurse tapped a button on one of the machines. In seconds, Strong relaxed. His eyes fluttered. "And," he said, pointing to Emma. "My girl." He fell asleep.

His girl. Was it true? The man who could have almost any woman he chose wanted *her*?

The nurse said she'd be back and left. Emma felt Lars's glare. They had a minute-long staring contest. He blinked first.

"I already know you've checked me out," Emma said, starting the conversation.

"Uh...uhm...you do?"

"Strong told me. I checked him out, too."

Lars laughed. "Bet you didn't find out much."

She had to laugh, too. "Enough."

She hoped their short banter had broken the ice enough to quell the tension that had been there since she arrived. The stiffness edged down a notch. Lars's tanned face had fine features and strength. He was definitely handsome. Based on current standards of beauty, Lars scored high. Higher than Strong? She couldn't compare; she loved Strong. *Loved? Yes. No question.* She smiled.

"What?" Lars asked.

She tried to think fast. Looking at Strong, she said. "He seems so innocent when he's asleep."

Lars looked at her askance. "Yeah, he kind of does. Don't let that fool you."

Without speaking, she bent over Strong and brushed his cheek with her fingers.

A man in scrubs parted the curtains. "Hi. I'm Doctor Childs. The surgery went well. I'm turning this case over to Doctor Herman, the clinic resident. I'm heading back to Philly in an hour or so. I don't expect he...," pointing to Strong, "will have any problems." He produced a business card and looked back and forth between Lars and Emma.

Lars took the card.

Dr. Childs regarded the beeping machines for a few seconds. "If something happens that needs my attention, don't hesitate to call." He nodded and left.

In the quiet of the curtained area, Lars doubled his stare at Emma. Her first impulse was to shrink. Why should she? Strong had asked for her. She sat up in the chair, straightened her shoulders, and with steel, she hoped, showing in her expression, she went back to her e-book.

"Hey," Strong said weakly.

Emma turned off the e-book, and Lars put down his magazine.

Strong fumbled for the bed control and raised the head. "Anyone hungry?"

Lars nodded. "Starved."

Emma scooted her chair close to the bed. "I'm hungry, too." She checked her watch. "It's almost two. I could go out and get something."

"Or," Strong pressed a button on the control, "something could come to us."

The nurse came in. "Mr. Manning?"

"Lunch. Something nice."

"Right," the nurse said, and disappeared.

Emma fluffed his pillow behind his head. "I wonder if you should eat so soon."

Lars clucked. "He always wakes up with an appetite."

Always? How often does this happen? Lawyers don't get hurt that often. He's into something dangerous. I need to know. Is Lars trying to tell me something?

Lars kept his gaze on her. Emma let the comment slide. "Well, the nurse will bring what they think is best."

Strong extended the non-IV hand. Emma took it and kissed his palm. Lars rolled his eyes and went back to the magazine, *Sports Illustrated.*

"Did the surgeon come in?" Strong asked.

Emma told him what Dr. Childs had said. As she finished, Dr. Herman stopped by.

"Childs is the best. You had some nasty stuff going on in your leg. He cleaned it out. It'll hurt for a while, but it looked good when he closed."

"When can I get out of here?"

"Tomorrow, if you stay in bed all day and tonight. No activity for a few days when you get home. Bed rest." He smiled at Emma. "Real rest. No distractions, okay?"

Strong nodded. "I guess you go home alone tonight, Princess."

"I'll come and get you tomorrow," Emma said.

"Lars will take me home and look after me. I'm afraid you'd pose too much of a distraction."

Dr. Herman left, and soon after, an orderly came in with a rolling tray, linen-draped like fancy room service. Large metal domes covered the plates.

"No candles?" Strong asked.

"Soup for you," the orderly said. "Philly steak sandwiches for your guests. The chef made these in honor of Dr. Childs."

Chef? What is this place?

The orderly pulled the dome off the soup. "Consommé for the gentleman," he said like a waiter. "If you tolerate it, you can eat real food tonight."

When the orderly left, Strong winked at Emma. "Can I have a bite? I love Philly steak."

Lars cut a third of his sandwich apart and gave it to Strong. As he bit into it, Strong said, "Ahhh. Now throw that flavored water away."

Lars tossed the broth down the sink.

Emma stayed until after dinner, chicken cordon bleu—three servings brought on the elegant cart. After dinner, Emma left at the same time as Lars.

While she was at work the next morning, Strong called and thanked her for being at the clinic. He promised to call her with updates on his healing and to take her out when he was able to walk.

By the next week, he called and said he was back in shape and caught up with his work. He invited her to dinner at a quiet country French restaurant.

After dinner on Tuesday, they went back to his house to see a movie. They nestled in each other's arms, kissing, and after fifteen minutes, he clicked the controller off. They had not seen one bit of it.

"Strong," Emma said, "Lars mentioned something like you always wake up hungry after getting repaired. And—"

Strong kissed her, stopping her question. He put the remote on top of the long cabinet that held the television. Nodding his head toward the hallway, he held his hand out. She took his and allowed him to escort her to his room. An odd feeling surfaced as they headed down the hall to a large room, but maybe this wasn't the right time to probe. She admired the lights of the city from the bedroom's expansive picture window. *Such a lovely nighttime cityscape. I'll bet all of his dates like that view.* She tried to shake that thought. The strange feeling she had added to the memory of Susie's comment about Strong dating all the women from the courthouse who weren't married, old, or ugly. The concept stuck its sharp point into her.

Strong chose a CD from a collection in a drawer. "Do you like classical music?"

Emma shook herself out of the jealous path her thoughts had wandered to. "What? Oh, classical music. Yes. Some. The church I attended in college started their services with Bach's *Jesu, Joy of Man's Desiring*. That might be my favorite."

"I know that piece. It's mesmerizing. I've chosen one for us tonight. You'll love it. This one is perfect; I think it's my favorite Vivaldi piece."

As they made love to the music, she agreed with his promise—the music heightened the love-making. His foreplay matched the changes and beat of the instruments and melody. As the music settled into a regular beat, Strong's plunges became rhythmic, and her body anticipated the passes until she felt the hum that heralded the crashing tsunami of sensory overload. She missed the end of the concerto when her orgasm drowned out any sounds.

Even in the dark, his voice conveyed his smile. "By the decibel level of your squeal, I know you enjoyed that. I think you enjoy sex bet—"

She shot up rocket-style and flipped the light on the nightstand. "Better than other women you know? You're comparing me?"

"Hey, wait a minute. I'm not comparing you to any other woman."

"Have you made a study of the multitude of females you've enjoyed Vivaldi with and came up with an average?"

"Where is this coming from, Emma? I thought you'd enjoy making love in a way you've never done before."

Before? I've never done this before in any way until I slept with you. "You can safely say I have not enjoyed this particular fashion of screwing."

"Screwing?" He sat up and pulled her to him. "That's an odd word coming from you."

"It's the word I'm using now that I'm being introduced to your 'style' and choice of sexual activities."

"What are you talking about?"

"Using classical music for your...." What word did she want to use here? What would properly fit? "For your *bootie calls.*"

He put his head back and laughed. "Bootie calls? That's not Emma talking. That's Susie. Let's not insult Antonio Vivaldi."

She pulled away from his arms. "Ah, so that Vivaldi tune is one you save for special encounters? You know what? I want to go home."

"Fine. Get your clothes on." He kicked away the sheets and left the room. The water in the guest bathroom echoed from the hallway.

She cleaned in the master bath and dressed quickly. In a few minutes they sat in the car. The ride was silent until they were a few blocks from her house.

"I don't know what set you off."

She didn't look at him. "I don't want to be another pea in the pod."

"What? That sounds like one of Susie's clichés."

"So what tune did you use when you screwed Susie?"

The car came to an abrupt stop at her driveway. He hopped out and opened her door. She hadn't seen that expression before. Grim? Angry? Defensive?

He leaned his face close to hers. "Why don't you ask Susie?"

Emma used all of her will not to run to the front door. She didn't look back but knew Strong hadn't left where he stood when she got out. Her fingers located the door key in her purse, and with a fluid movement, she opened the door and shut it fast behind her. Clapping the lights on, she froze to her spot.

What had she done? Did she make a mistake about wanting to be his only partner? No. Her mother's words charged through her mind. *If it feels wrong, then it's wrong. Don't fool yourself.* Being in Strong's bed where he had been with how many women—the unmarried, young, and pretty ones of the courthouse? His ritual of making love to his favorite music made her feel cheap, common. She wouldn't have that kind of relationship; she wouldn't be the next pea in the pod.

Had she lost him? The sound of the car's tires crunching on the gravel announced he'd left. What did she expect? That he'd pound on the door and apologize? Apologize for what? That he could have almost any woman he wanted, and in any way? Did the others care about being one in a string of hot lovers? She definitely did. But it was Strong—the man she loved.

Emma ran to the window in time to see the Escalade's taillights turn the corner. Had it just driven out of her life? Tears streamed down her cheeks. Sleep would elude her for sure.

CHAPTER TEN

The next morning, Wednesday, added to her misery, for she did most of her courthouse research on that day and Friday. She selected a navy suit with a pink silk blouse. Abbey's taste in clothing was flawless. Emma doubted she would have chosen such beautiful clothes even if she'd had the budget. This blouse had chevron pleats meeting below the neckline to the tapered waist. It screamed expensive. She hadn't worn it before, but now she wanted to look professional. Dating Strong had elevated her concern for appearance. She could take that from the relationship at least. Instead of low heels, today she'd wear Abbey's Ferragamo navy sling-backs. And nylons. Although most women didn't wear them anymore, she couldn't wear a business suit without them. She chose sheer navy hose, enough to be serious but accentuating her legs. She locked her front door behind her and closed her eyes. She didn't want to face Strong and hoped he wouldn't be at the courthouse. Most of her work would be on the bottom floor. Maybe she could talk Susie into using the stairs.

Her trip to the courthouse was uneventful, and she hoped to keep it that way. But then, when she entered the courthouse, she saw Chauncey Metcalf. Right. Perfect, the guard whose brother Strong had helped to beat a DUI. She unclenched her teeth and signed the log.

"Good morning, miss," Chauncey said.

She eyed him with all the malice she'd stored since the previous night.

His forehead crinkled. "Miss?"

"Emma Whitstone, but you already know my name." She

stomped past him, her fabulous shoes clacking on the granite floor. She couldn't ignore the stares from a few eyes in the line, and she sped up her pace, using the stairs to reach Susie's floor.

Her shoes echoed smartly as she approached Susie's desk.

Susie's eyes appraised her. "Why, ain't you just like five pounds in a one-pound bag. You pretending to be a lawyer?"

"No. I'm trying to change my…whatever. Is there something wrong with trying to look good?"

Susie pulled her head back, the motion that usually preceded the bug-eye. She smiled instead. "Nothing wrong at-tall, girlfriend, not with trying to look good. I suspect there's something more, but you can tell me at your convenience."

Emma stiffened. Susie didn't miss much. "Do you mind if we take the stairs down?"

Susie's grin transformed into a benevolent smile. "Don't want to encounter the boyfriend, eh? Good. Glad to see you're taking my advice."

Emma looked down at the Ferragamos, trying to take some pleasure at their beauty.

"Uh huh," Susie said, standing up from her desk. "Want to talk about it?"

Holding up the folder, Emma said, "I just want to do my work and get back to the office."

"Whoa." Susie shook her head, sympathy radiating from her eyes. "Worse than I thought." She grabbed Emma by the arm. "We're taking the elevator, and if you see that bastard, look him in the eye and say good morning. That's what he'd do, and you're better than he is."

There was no use in trying to change what Susie had decreed. Maybe she was right. Maybe dignity called for a high head and no regrets.

Luckily, Strong made no elevator appearance. The two women made their way to the records floor without incident. As they began their work, Emma suspected there would be questions because Susie wasn't the type to leave things alone.

After Emma found a few of the documents she needed, Susie

started her inquiry. "He dump you?"

"No. I need some time away, that's all."

"You dump him, then?"

"Susie. No one dumped anybody."

"No, uh-uh. That's not how it works with Manning. I hope it was you that called it quits."

Emma looked away. What *had* happened? She asked to go home—and he took her there. Had she called it "quits" by doing that?

"Look," Susie said, peeking around to meet Emma's eye. "You can't put turds in the oven and expect to pull out biscuits."

"What?"

"Bacon always curls upwards."

"What are you talking about, Susie?"

"Nature. Manning ain't going to change his ways. He's a selfish, cold womanizer…at best."

"Wait. What do you mean at best? What is at worst?"

No bug eyes, but they narrowed, and Susie's face darkened. "Not sure, but I'll find out. There's more to that guy than what shows. I'm a first-rate researcher. I'll get to the bottom—"

Emma touched Susie's arm. "Don't, please. It's none of our business." Oh, how she wanted to say it was none of *Susie's* business.

"Normally, I wouldn't care who does what to anybody else, but I like you, Emma, and I think you are…uhm…vulnerable. You're so pretty; there are lots of guys who'd go for you. If you're into black guys, and there are a lot of reasons why you should be, I can introduce you to some friends. I know a few basketball guys—money—who can show you a good time. Wait a second… you like lawyer-boys. I could fix you up with Antwan Givens, an assistant district attorney, handsome and smart. He's the next Johnny Cochrane, really going places." She laughed. "You know the amazon sign at my desk? From him. He'd give that Manning a run for his money. I'm seeing an architect now. We can double."

"No thanks. Not because they're black, I just don't want to date anyone right now."

The bug-eyes popped. "You mean anyone *else* right now because you're still stuck on Manning. You'd better get over him."

Before Emma could protest the last comment, Susie's pocket made a cricket sound. She reached into her pocket and glanced at the phone. "Oooh. Sorry, honey. I've got to go."

"No problem. I'll finish this on my own."

Susie cocked her head. "I doubt that. You're good, but you need me."

Emma had enough. She put her hands on her hips. "No, I don't need your help — not in this or in my relationships."

"You think?" The bug-eyes got a little larger. "Okay. See ya." She stomped away, in even strides on stiletto heels.

Emma pulled a chair over to the huge drawer she'd been working on. She slumped over the hundreds of files that had yet to be computerized. *Terrific. I've lost Strong and now my friend at the courthouse. Even though she's compensated to help me, she cares about me. Am I right? I thought Strong cared.*

Allowing herself a few minutes of pity, she dug into the work, sorting through thousands of Jones families to find the information Mr. Latito required.

Not wanting to encounter Strong on any floors or in the courthouse lunchroom, she skipped lunch and stayed at the records department until almost five. She would have to come again tomorrow. In the morning, she would definitely stop at Susie's desk and make amends. Susie was right about the work, even if she was wrong about meddling in relationships.

At home, she undressed, first kicking off the lovely shoes, surprised that her feet didn't hurt. She had barely thought about them, meaning they had been comfortable to wear — one more point for Abbey's taste in apparel. Emma toyed with ideas of what to have for dinner, although she felt no hunger. As she sunk into the softness of the couch, the doorbell rang.

Hardly anyone ever came to her door. Maybe it was Strong! She rushed to the peephole. A man in a dark uniform with packages stood outside. Not thinking about Strong's warning regarding people at the front door, she answered.

"Ma'am," the man said. "Emma Whitstone?"

"Yes."

"I have these for you." He had a long box tucked under his arm and a small box in his left hand. "May I come in and set them up?"

"Set them up?"

"Yes, ma'am. Can I come in?"

She swung the door wide, and the man entered. He opened the long box, and before he separated the mass of green tissue, the powerful and sweet smell of roses wafted out, filling the room with their vivid scent. When he parted the wrapping, he pulled out an arrangement filled with long stemmed red roses — way more than a dozen. The flowers had been placed in a cut glass vase.

"You'll need to put water in them, Ms. Whitstone. See these little jelly things around the stems? They provide the moisture for shipping, but you need to hydrate them right away to make the flowers last."

The roses had captivated her so much she couldn't take her eyes from them.

"Ms. Whitstone? There's another package."

"Oh." She looked at the box he'd put on the table.

He brought out a box opener, carefully cut the cardboard, and removed the black tissue. The object turned out to be a metallic box, heavily carved, probably silver. It showed wear in some of the corners, suggesting its age. The man wound a bottom key and opened the lid. A tune played, and inside the mirrored chamber was a note that said two words, "Emma--------ning."

"Thank you, ma'am," the man said, backing away.

Her thoughts cleared for a second. "Wait. I need to give you a tip."

He put up both hands. "No, ma'am. I've already been handsomely tipped. Have a good night."

She saw him to the door and returned to the mysterious music box. She reread the puzzling note. What did it mean? The familiar tune made her sway. Wait! She hummed along. This was the tune that preceded the services at the Methodist church, the place that paid her to teach hearing impaired children for Sunday School. Warmth radiated inside as she unraveled the mystery. She, *Emma*, was the Joy of Man*ning*'s Desiring!

Before the thrill of the gifts really sank in, the doorbell rang again. *Let it be him.* But the peephole revealed a short woman holding a box and a letter.

"Miss Whitstone?" the lady asked.

Emma nodded.

"For you. I'm told not to accept a tip because I got a really big one from the sender."

Even though the messenger was abrupt, Emma thanked her warmly before shutting the door. She hurried to see what Strong had sent. It had to be from him.

The package opened easily and contained a large gold-foiled box. The smell of chocolates announced the contents. The top flipped up, and a note from the candy company sat on the first tray. It was dated that day. "Thank you for allowing us to please you with our craft. These chocolates are made fresh daily in our small Belgium factory to your specifications. All of the ingredients are the finest in the world. If you are not one-hundred percent thrilled with each confection, please let us know. We feel confident that you will love each bite designed especially for you. M. Schmidt, Antwerp."

Fresh? Daily? Antwerp? Belgium? She examined the confection placement map included with the letter and, her appetite restored, located a chocolate-covered cherry, looking like a dark sculpture. It nestled in a tiny lace doily on the top row of a velvet tray that looked like it would accommodate earrings. Of course! It was a jewelry box when emptied. She admired its form before she took a bite. The taste trickled on her tongue and never had one tasted so good. It made the inexpensive Christmas cherries pale in comparison. No, there could be no comparison.

Wait. The messenger left a letter, too. She popped the rest of the piece in her mouth and opened the letter. In his masculine and firm handwriting, it said, "Emma. Can we talk? Lunch? Tomorrow? Noon? I'll call you at your office around 11:30. Strong."

Emma shut her eyes hard and whispered a prayer. "Thank you, Lord. And Herr Bach."

CHAPTER ELEVEN

"Good morning, Susie," Emma said. "You were correct; I did need your help yesterday. Here." She handed Susie a plastic baggie with six chocolates. "A peace offering?"

Susie took the bag and turned it around, admiration in her expression as she viewed the little doilies holding the confections. "What are these?"

Emma rolled her lip. "Turds from a biscuit."

"What?"

"From Strong."

Susie rolled her eyes. "Sure they're not poisoned?"

Emma reached for the bag, but Susie, with a move like lightning, pulled it away. "I'll take a chance."

"Try the round one. It's a cherry."

Susie took her time opening the bag. She sniffed the chocolates a few times before selecting the fat round sculpted cherry. After the first nibble, she bit it in half. Emma recognized the dreamy effect forming on the face of her friend, the Mocha Amazon. These bits of delight involved more sensory stimulation than just taste. The sound of biting through the thick chocolate shell echoed in the mouth, the feel as the outer covering melted on the tongue, the smell, and the rich red liquid that oozed from the bite produced a phenomenon more than a luscious sensation.

"An example of the whole being more than the sum of the parts, right?" Emma said when Susie opened her eyes.

For the first time, Susie had no words. Emma smiled, recognizing the breathing out and in again to capture the remnants of the perfect taste. She pulled a chair up to Susie's desk, understanding that those chocolates needed leisure to work their magic.

After the second selection, Susie closed the bag and shoved it in her drawer. "Maybe I should lock it." She did. "Okay, Missy, let's finish what I'm sure you didn't get to yesterday."

"Thanks, Susie," Emma said, handing the file across the desk.

Susie looked at it and nodded. "We'll be done by noon."

Emma bit her lip. "By eleven? Please?"

Susie stood and deckled the papers in the file. "Uh huh, noon date. I guess if Manning sent *me* candies like that, I'd meet him for lunch, too. Come on, girlfriend. We won't talk about what a jerk you're going to dine with, okay?"

"Okay—I think," Emma said, and followed Susie down the hall to the elevator.

As they waited for the elevator, Susie shook her head and sighed. "I'd sure like to introduce you to Antwan, though. Think about it."

Susie took a wad of papers from Emma's file and moved like Wonder Woman. At eleven, Emma said so long at the Mocha Amazon's desk, where Susie unlocked her drawer and took out the bag of chocolate delights.

At eleven-fifteen, Emma slid into her chair that swiveled in front of her desk. *No messages, good*—she hadn't missed anything. She worked on the information she'd gathered at the courthouse but had to force herself to keep her eyes on her keyboard as she entered the data.

At eleven-forty-five, her desk phone rang.

"Hi."

"Hey," she said, not knowing what else to say and not wanting to sound too excited.

"Can you meet me at Ralph's?" Before she had time to decline, Strong shifted his tone into the done-deal sound. "It's a place about a mile south of the courthouse—"

"I know where it is."

"Good." He'd dropped the sure sound, and she detected a bit of relief. "I only have the time the judge allows for lunch recess, so do you mind driving there?"

"I don't mind." Why did she say that? But then, the roses, the candy, and the music box.... No problem. She'd drive. Miles, if he asked.

"I'll see you at noon. Tell the host at the entrance you're meeting me. Bye."

The conversation was the usual clipped communication she'd come to expect. He rarely wasted time with excess words.

At twelve sharp, she stepped into Ralph's, where the mixed smells, particularly the smoky aroma of barbecue, assaulted her senses. A young woman dressed in a green T-shirt sporting "Ralph's" and black pants greeted her.

"Welcome to Ralph's. I'm Nelda. Table for one?"

"I'm meeting Strong Manning here."

The young woman's eyebrows ascended. "Okay. Follow me."

They passed the dining room and headed in the direction of an alcove, where the woman opened a door that said "private" on it.

"I'll be back," Nelda promised. Then she was gone, leaving Emma in a small private dining area. She pulled out one of the six chairs and sat at the oval table. Old-fashioned wood paneling hung with old English dog-and-horse hunt paintings contrasted with the barbecue smell emanating from the swing door located in the back of the room near a serving buffet.

She checked her watch. Seven minutes after twelve. A bowl on the table had small packaged hand wipes. She opened one and unfolded the lemon-scented sheet. After swabbing her hands and cramming the wad into the old wrapper, she checked her watch again, finding two more minutes had elapsed.

The rear door swung open. As it slowly closed, sounds and movements from Ralph's kitchen caught Emma's attention. Another young woman brought a tray laden with a water pitcher, two glasses, the usual cutlery items, a small bowl, and a platter with steaming pasta.

The woman, whose nametag said Krista, smiled and filled

the water glasses. "Lemon slices? Mr. Manning doesn't take them in his water, but would you like some?"

Emma hadn't noticed Strong didn't take lemon in his water, and it annoyed her that a serving girl knew. How often did he come here?

"No thanks." She did want lemon, so why did she say that? What was wrong with her?

"I'll come back later and take your order," Krista said.

"What are these?"

"Oh, appetizers. Mr. Manning likes them. I'll be back."

Emma's watch indicated twelve minutes after twelve. Time felt so messed up. She'd swear she'd left the office an hour ago, but it had been twenty minutes. The smell of the appetizer offered a diversion. The pastas…brown puffy pillows, but crispy. Two long-tined forks flanked a bowl of red sauce. She stabbed a pillow and took a bite. Fried ravioli! She kept her mouth open to allow the air to cool the small bit that burned her tongue. The bowl didn't steam, so maybe dipping that would help cool the morsel. She dipped and blew before the next bite. She finished the pillow and put the fork down to wait for Strong. Twelve seventeen.

At twelve twenty, he came through the door. "I got waylayed as I left the courthouse." He scanned the table. "Tried the raviolis, eh? Aren't they great?"

She toyed with a comment regarding the waitress's knowledge of his preferences while he took a chair next to her. He stabbed a steaming pillow and dipped it in the sauce. A drop of red fell from the pasta, and he caught it with a napkin before it made contact with his silk suit jacket. She'd never seen anyone so coordinated. The peanut training!

Krista came through the swinging door. "Hello, Mr. Manning. What can I get you?"

"I need to eat light today. How about a salad? Gorgonzola?"

She turned to Emma. "What would you like?"

"I'll have the same," Emma said, unimpressed with the waitress asking for Strong's order first. He must be a good customer. Krista left.

Strong bit the next pasta in half and leaned toward Emma. "I'm glad you came."

Emma stared at her empty fork. Confusion always killed her appetite, even if these puffy little marvels tasted delicious.

Strong's fingers drummed on the table. "You said you didn't want to be a pea in a pod. Does that mean you don't want to be in my house because I've invited other guests there?"

"Invited other guests? Other women."

"I understand."

"You do?"

"I think so."

They sat quietly. Strong bit a pasta cushion in half and put the fork next to her lips. "Have a bite. Keep up your nourishment."

He could be charming. She bit the other half. "Thank you for the flowers. They're beautiful."

"Glad you like them. By the way, in my whole life, I've only sent flowers to two other women besides you."

Two other women?

He stabbed a puff and smiled. "My mother and my sister." He dipped it, blew on it, and offered it to her.

She held the fork and turned it around to keep the sauce from falling. "Those chocolates were unbelievable. Belgium?"

He nodded. "And the box?"

Emma drew out the answer by slowly nibbling the ravioli, touching her tongue to the sauce. "I am the joy of Manning's desiring?"

He slapped the table with the palm of his hand. "I knew you'd get it!" He took the fork from her and put it on the platter. "It's true, you know. From the first time I saw you across the lobby in the courthouse, I knew you'd be the joy of my desire."

She allowed the shivering wave of satisfaction to warm her and searched for the appropriate words. She couldn't match the lyrical beauty of what he had just said. She wouldn't even try. Was it predatory bullshit? No. Not when he went to this much trouble. And he wasn't the type to chase a woman just for great hook-ups. There had to be more than that. "The music box looks like an antique. Where did you get it?"

"I have my ways, Princess. Let's just say a few people lost some sleep finding it."

"I don't know what to say other than thank you. I don't mean to be difficult, but—"

"I can deal with difficult. But *bootie call?* Susie seems to be rubbing off on you. If I had to describe our relationship in two words, bootie calls wouldn't be the ones I'd choose."

"What two words would you choose?"

"Something special."

She laughed. "You think fast on your feet. It must be the lawyer training."

His tone headed toward anger. "I do think fast on my feet. But that isn't what guided me to those words. You *are* special to me. What do I need to do to convince you?"

"Strong, I feel, uh…."

He held up his hand. "Don't explain. Look, I want to make you happy. So tell me, Emma, what do you want?"

Dare she say it? "Monogamy."

"Okay."

Don't say really! "Really?"

"Yes, and you say where we can be together. My house is out, obviously. We can go to your place or a nice hotel. Or…I can get a new place."

"A new place? A house?"

"Why not? You can help design it. We'll have a bedroom with sixteen mattresses so you won't feel the pea, my princess."

"Don't be silly."

"Actually, it's not so silly. The bonus of the acquittal on this trial will give me enough for a nice place."

"You're going to win? For sure?"

"Well, it's never for sure, but we have definitely established reasonable doubt, and that's what we need to acquit."

"I didn't think you took trial cases."

"I don't care for courtroom theatrics, but I consult, and we're getting near the end, so I'm second chair. Robin Andrews, who hired me, is intimidated by the ADA, Givens. He's really something."

"Antwan Givens?"

Strong pulled back from her and took a long look. "You know him?"

She speared a ravioli and answered with a two-syllable, song-like, "Hmmmm."

"Uh huh." He stared at her for a moment, not a muscle changing on his face. "The monogamy runs both ways, you know."

"I know."

"I don't mind going nose to nose with Givens in court. But I'd have to get nasty if he went after you." Keeping his eyes focused on her, he expertly impaled a fried pillow and lowered it to his plate. "And Susie," still not looking, he squished the fat pasta until the filling oozed from its sides, "should mind her own business."

Emma stared at the squishy appetizer. Part of her felt smug at his jealousy. Another part felt uncomfortable.

The waitress came with their salads. "I brought some extra gorgonzola for your salad, Mr. Manning. I know you like a lot."

"Thanks, Krista. That's all for now unless the lady wants something."

"I'm good," Emma said.

When Krista left, Emma said, "They really know you here."

He nodded. "I own twenty-five percent. This room is mine or is used with my permission. Lars checks it out every so often."

"Checks it out?"

"For bugs—uh, listening devices. I have meetings here. I keep them private."

The urge to ask for more information overcame her. "You invest in restaurants?"

"Not really. I invest in people's lives by getting them acquitted. Those who can afford it happily pay big. In this case, Ralph was in a pickle, and he offered me the percentage to clear him. I accepted and got him acquitted. I don't take the percentage of profit. I have him use it to fix up the place and keep this room for me. My left-over profits go to the Public Defense Fund to help defray expenses. Win, win, win. You know?"

They ate quietly for a few minutes.

Strong checked his watch and put his hand over Emma's. "I have to go. This judge is very strict on time, and he is extra hard on me."

"He doesn't like you?"

"Worse. He's a friend of the family." He drew on her hand with his finger, seeming reluctant to leave. "We're good, right?"

"We're good. I don't know why I'm so surly about...things."

"Not surly—refined, particular, and you know what you want. That's part of the reason I'm so attracted to you." He dabbed the napkin to his mouth. "Tonight, I'll be working late with the law team to get ready for summation. We have a lot to do, and I won't be available until we finish. Okay? After that, you and I will get together."

"All right. I understand."

"And...about the music in bed? I play classical to help me think. I'd been listening to it while considering the details of this case. I thought about you and how nice it might be to make love to the music. I chose a Vivaldi I thought would work. It did, too, as I recall."

"So, you never —"

"Made love to any other woman with classical, or any other kind, of music? Just you."

Regret flooded her mind. His disclosure didn't require a comment. She didn't say anything.

He stood and pulled out her chair. They walked to their cars conveniently parked next to each other. Emma laughed. It looked like a mamma car, the Escalade, had a baby, the little white Fiat.

Strong held her door. "Ever think about getting a bigger car?"

"No. I like Esmeralda."

"Big name for such a little thing."

"Haven't you ever heard that good things come in small packages?"

He smiled. "Yes, I have." He kissed her cheek. "Yes, I have."

CHAPTER TWELVE

Five days later, Strong called, asking Emma to take Friday and Monday off so they could go to Mexico. That afternoon he took her to a passport agency. She had the passport in time for the trip. Mr. Latito never gave her a hard time about days off.

They flew to San Jose Del Cabo and rented a car. Less than an hour's drive brought them to Cabo San Lucas, where a mountain perched over the beach had been turned into a resort. As soon as the bellman left them in their room with its view of the ocean and an occasional breeching whale, they raced for the bed, shedding clothes in seconds. Emma made up for what she considered lost time by requesting doubles.

Strong had no problems complying with her requests, and after a "double," Strong fluffed the pillows against his back and pulled her arm, gently helping her lift. "Here, sit up — I want to admire your tits. I only get to see them while you're on your back."

"Strong...."

He cupped her breasts with his hands. "Beautiful."

Emma shook her head. "Small."

"It's the shape that counts, perfect cones." He pushed his face in between her breasts and kissed both sides. "You know, sometimes I watch you walk. You have just the right amount of bounce — a sexy little jiggle."

"Me? Sexy?"

"Absolutely."

Her nostrils flared, and she let out a quick breath. "I know I'm plain."

"Plain? You are the most gorgeous woman I've ever met." He kissed her cheek. "It's true. Ems, you are beautiful inside and out."

She rested her head on his shoulder. "Oh, Strong, you can't imagine how I feel."

He raised her palm to his lips. "Yes," he kissed the inside of her hand, "I can."

The next morning they sailed to the Sea of Cortez on a chartered fishing trip. Emma hooked a shark, but it fought so hard she couldn't reel it in. Strong took over, and the crew helped land the fish. After a photo, Emma insisted the boat captain release it. The captain wanted it to hang next to his boat for advertisement. Emma insisted, and Strong talked to them in Spanish. Reluctantly they released it. Strong caught a huge striped marlin. They had the same argument, and this time it took the promise of a large tip to release the animal.

From the day out on the ocean, Emma needed a bath. Their bathroom overlooked the ocean from a large corner glass window, a view from two sides. The showerhead became a waterfall flowing over tile shelves with a flick of a lever. Emma washed her hair, turned the shower into the cascade, and slipped into the water of the tub.

Strong, nude, came in. "May I join you?"

She sat up to make room. "Of course."

In two seconds, from the time she assented to when he stepped over the tub's wall, his erection formed.

She pointed. "Impressive. Like the speed of light."

"I'm glad you're impressed." He slid in next to her and kissed her. "You're on birth control, right?" He continued. "Moments like these…. Well, once in a while spontaneous sex is —"

She rolled her lip and looked away. "No," she said to the wall.

"No, what? No spontaneous sex or no birth control?"

"I'm not on anything. We can't do it here."

"Emma?"

He normally didn't want explanations about her decisions,

but his saying her name with the rise at the end clearly demanded she give him one.

Her lip made a thin line before she spoke. "I brought condoms with me for our 'sixth date' in case you didn't have any, and it turns out we didn't have that date. I didn't know if I would see you again."

"But —"

"When you invited me to Las Vegas, I didn't have time to see a doctor…plus you left me again. Remember?"

"I remember." His voice had a controlled, displeased sound. "But now we're seeing each other regularly…and having regular sex."

"And I have an appointment in two weeks."

"Two weeks?"

"Appointments are hard to get with gynecologists. Plus, he was out of town for a few weeks, so he's backed up."

"I can fix you up with my brother-in-law, a gynecologist." He sponged her back. "Let me dry you."

"Thanks," she said with relief. "Can you do it fast?" She cast her gaze to the flagpole sticking its head above the water.

"We don't have to hurry. He'll be here for a long time."

They laughed, towel-dried each other, and made love *a la condome.*

As she lay in his arms, she pressed her face into his neck, breathing in his clean man smell. This was what she wanted — to be next to him, forever. His hand ran up her back, ending in a soft neck massage. She turned her face to him. Before she was able to stifle the words, they poured from her. "I love you so much."

For a second, the look on his face made him almost unrecognizable. What was that look? Fear? Pity? Despair?

He pulled her close in a grip of steel. "That's unfortunate," he said in a whisper.

Her heart sunk. "You mean for me?"

"For us. Oh, Ems, I don't —"

She cut him off and finished the sentence. "You don't love *me.*"

He put his lips to her ear. "I didn't say that, Em. I didn't say *that*. It's unfortunate for both of us. Remember at the airport when I said there are things you don't know? Please understand. I'm not husband material."

Husband? He's thinking on those terms? She snuggled into the crook of his neck. "You'd be good at anything you wanted, Strong."

He kissed the top of her head. "Who knows?" He didn't say anything for a few moments. "How about dinner? Lobster? I haven't had seafood for a while."

She moved from his embrace and headed for the bathroom. By the time she opened the door, he had left the bed and put on clothes. After a long stare at the dresses she'd brought hanging in the closet, she selected a sage-green silk sheath. The princess seams defined her figure, and the plain lines would look good with her pearls. The bolero jacket with its small turned collar made her neckline the focus. The outfit was a designer work, and she had always liked it. After putting a few touches to her makeup, she peeked from the bathroom into the suite's sitting area. Strong and his dime dance partner did their routine. He caught the coin over and over—on his finely sculpted cheeks, his forehead, and nose, doubling then tripling the nose landing. Was he honing his muscle skills or dispelling stress? It had to be stress, the pressure she'd caused by her love confession. Regretting her words, although true, she'd not say them again. The last thing she wanted was to drive him away with her feelings.

She forced a smile and stepped into the room. He played with the coin in a new way, holding his fist out as the dime rolled across the hills and valleys of his knuckles with no perceivable hand movement.

When he saw her, he flipped the dime in the air and caught it in his palm. The coin disappeared into his pants pocket. "You look wonderful—as always. That dress is great. I haven't seen it before."

She sighed slightly. "Abbey had what appears to be an unlimited clothing budget."

"Yeah, but you make the dress look good, Princess."

"I'll tell her how appreciative we both are for her good taste in my next email."

CHAPTER THIRTEEN

After the Cabo trip, Emma didn't hear from Strong, other than a message left on her phone that said he'd be gone for a while.

For a while? What does that mean?

She worked at the courthouse with Susie the following Friday. Susie had backed off somewhat on her anti-Strong comments. On this day, she hadn't said a word about him. Emma walked with Susie back to the cubicle.

As they parted, Susie called to her. "Busy tomorrow night?"

Emma returned to Susie. "I don't think so."

"Want to have some fun? Go with me to a club."

She had gone out with Susie to a few social events and had a good time. Who knew how long Strong would be gone this time? "Okay."

Susie smiled. "I'll swing by your place around eight."

On Saturday evening, Susie tooted the horn of her sleek BMW convertible — black with white interior. Emma wore gray slacks with a silver lame top. She wouldn't have chosen lame for herself, but Abbey always looked great in this set. It surprised Emma how good she looked in the outfit. The blouse had a dropped square neckline and showed plenty of cleavage. A quick glance in the mirror on the way out created an impulse to hike up the top to minimize the décolletage. The lame didn't move easily. The boob slot would have to stay.

The club's music was so loud they had to shout to talk. Several drinks appeared on their table, compliments of unknown admirers. Emma refused invitations to dance until Susie pressured her.

"Dance with the next man who asks you," Susie said.

Emma couldn't think of a reason not to dance. She agreed. The next man who came to their table was a tall, handsome black man who had a warm smile and a self-assured attitude. After the dance, the band took a short break. Susie introduced the man as Antwan Givens.

"The ADA?" Emma asked.

"Guilty," he said.

Susie's eyes sparkled, and she excused herself to the ladies' room. Emma knew the meeting had been planned and suspected Susie's trip to the bathroom meant she had departed for the night.

"I can't stand the loud music," Emma complained.

"I don't like it either," Antwan said. "Let's get out of here. How about some coffee?" He cocked his head. "Don't forget, there's always decaf."

She laughed. The music blared again. "All right," she shouted.

Antwan held the door on his red Jaguar. It purred out of the parking lot. They drove for a few minutes into a less-nice part of town.

"Don't be nervous," Antwan said. "I'm taking you to my auntie's restaurant. It's safe. Everyone knows me."

In the parking lot of an older building, a teenager approached them. "Watch your car for you, Antwan?"

"It's Mr. Givens. And, yes." He pulled out a ten. "Keep good watch."

"Yes, sir." The kid took the bill.

Auntie's Restaurant was buffet style, with food steaming in a row of trays, like soldiers at attention. Formica and steel tube tables with vinyl covered chairs, clean but worn, said the restaurant had seen a few years.

A large black woman with gray streaks in her hair hugged Antwan. "It's good to see you, boy."

"Aunt Gladys, I'm not a boy."

"Yes, you are and will always be. Our bright and wonderful boy." She winked at Emma. "We're proud of Antwan. Can you tell?"

Emma laughed. "Not really!"

"I like her, boy. Dinner for two? Tell me what you want. I'll bring it to you."

"Brisket?" Antwan asked.

"Of course. And greens, and sweet potatoes, and…you let me pick." She turned heel and headed for the serving line.

Antwan shrugged. "She'd pick for us anyway. Don't worry. It'll be fantastic."

Aunt Gladys brought a large tray to their table laden with over-flowing plates. The food was delicious, flawlessly seasoned, along with the perfect textures. Emma chatted with Antwan and learned how he made his way through school with scholarships and hard work. He was a polite and interesting person, and she enjoyed her "date" with him. After dinner, he drove her home and saw her to the door. He kissed her cheek goodnight. Susie's sly plan had provided a good time on what would have been a lonely Saturday night, and no harm done.

Luckily, Strong's message "gone for a while" meant a week. On Monday afternoon, Strong called her at work. He had just returned. Could they go out? She invited him to her place, where she wanted to make dinner.

"Dinner at your place? Okay. Pot roast, maybe? I loved it when I came home from school and smelled the pot roast my mom cooked."

"Your dad's favorite meal?"

The way Strong paused gave her a shudder. "*My* favorite meal. But whatever you want to cook is great, Princess."

"Pot roast sounds fine," she promised, hoping Google would help her. "Come tonight after six."

She took off work early and bought what she needed.

At six, Emma lifted the lid to the pot roast and stirred. It was almost done, but the potatoes were a little firm. It needed a few more minutes. She heard the doorbell and wiped her hands on the apron. She hurried to answer it.

"Good evening," Strong said with both arms behind his back.

She clasped his neck and kissed him. "Come in."

He withdrew his arms and gave her a vase of roses with one hand and a bottle of wine with the other.

"Flowers! Thank you." She rubbed her nose against his cheek. He sat the vase on the dining room table already set for dinner.

He followed her into the kitchen and sat at the little table.

"Would you like a drink, Strong? I have Wild Turkey."

"When did you start hitting the sauce? Not good, Princess."

"I remembered you ordered that when we were in Las Vegas. I bought it...quite some time ago." There was a hint of annoyance with the time reference, but her delight in his presence allowed a widening smile to take over. "I am so glad to see you."

"I'll take a little Wild Turkey."

She brought him a glass and the bottle. The lid on the pot rattled, reminding her that it still simmered. She gave the contents a stir, and as she worked, she felt him come behind her. He kissed her neck and slid his hands around her waist before he turned her around and kissed her, long and drawn out. Emma wrenched free long enough to turn the stove off and untie her apron. She hated her body's furious demand for his attentions. She could barely control herself, and she needed control to keep from feeling...what? Cheap? Easy? It wasn't how she was raised. How was she raised? Her mother had given her values. What did she get from Aunt Hester? Hard work and tongue lashings?

Was it just the sex she craved from Strong? Sleeping with him was the best part of her life, ever. Not just the incredible feeling of his body in and on her, but the safe, protected sleep. It had taken her years to fall asleep easily, to not cringe at noises, wondering if Aunt Hester would stomp into her room and rip her out of bed to redo a task not done to satisfaction. Aunt Hester didn't use a belt, but she could wield her hand or a flyswatter effectively.

"Honey?" Strong asked.

"Sorry," she breathed out.

"What's wrong?"

"I don't want to talk about it now."

"Okay, then. Put everything out of your head. Just enjoy."

Strong picked her up and brought her into the hall. "Which one is your bedroom?"

She pointed, the thrills shooting around her body preventing speech.

He placed her on her bed and kicked off his loafers. They unbuttoned and unzipped as fast as they could. She pushed the bedspread off with her foot.

He sat up on his knees, his erection rubbing against her thigh. "Did you get the pills or something?"

"Not yet. You'll have to use a condom."

He sat back, squatting on the bed. "Shit. I was in such a hurry to get here I forgot about them."

"Oh, Strong. No," she moaned.

His head fell on his chest. "Christ."

She ran her hand over his erection and moaned her disappointment. "Strong!" He slid over her, kissed her neck, and licked at her breast.

"No. Stop." She wriggled out from under him. "I can't take the chance. I might get pregnant."

He faced her and put his hands on her shoulders. "We'll get married."

She pushed him away. "What kind of high school crap is that?"

He rolled off the bed, grabbed his clothes, and slipped his legs into underwear. He struggled to enclose his thickened shaft in the fabric. His pants strained at the zipper.

What had she done? "Strong?"

He didn't speak as he continued to dress.

"Strong, I...I—"

He held up his hand to stop her words.

She slumped back against the pillows. She'd done it this time. Why couldn't she hold her tongue? She could have just ignored his statement. Could she let him leave? What could she say? That she was sorry?

"Strong, listen—"

"No. You listen."

Is he leaving me?

He took her hand. "I've been doing this all wrong. What I meant to say is, marry me."

No words came to her. Her breath came fast.

"Okay. How's this?" He went down on one knee. "Emma Whitstone. I love you. Will you marry me?"

Speak. Before he changes his mind. Little sounds preceded the meek, "Yes."

She threw her arms around him, pulling him back toward the bed.

"Uh, uh," he said. "Just in case you think I'm trying to," he chuckled, "fool you into giving out favors, we'll wait. When do you want to tie the knot?"

"Tomorrow. So you don't have a chance to change your mind."

He shook his head. "I won't change my mind. That's not my style, Princess."

That, she believed.

"Tomorrow, huh?" He fished his wallet from his pocket and handed her his American Express card. "Obviously, you'll take tomorrow off. As soon as the most expensive store in town opens, buy a dress. I want you to wear something that isn't Abbey's for your wedding."

She pushed the card back. "I'll get something, but from my own money."

He rolled his eyes and put the card back. "Getting independent already? Good. Look, I'll try to schedule a ceremony for early afternoon."

"You can do that?"

"Yeah. I have friends in low places."

"What?"

"I know a judge who will marry us." He drew out his cell phone. "Hold on. I just thought of something." He spoke into the phone for a few minutes and hung up. "Get dressed and come with me."

"No dinner?"

"You're hungry?"

She shook her head vigorously. "No!"

They drove to a jewelry store. The jeweler brought out a tray of rings, but Strong said to show them better ones.

"I don't need anything big or fancy," Emma said as the jeweler went back for a third tray.

"He owes me money. Pick something opulent."

Strong selected a diamond Emma said was gaudy but quickly stuck out her finger to accept it. He selected a diamond band, too.

He picked up her hand to admire the shine. "'Oh, pig, are you willing to sell for one shilling, your ring? Said the piggy, I will. So he took her away, and were married next day by a turkey who lived on the hill.'"

"*The Owl and the Pussycat!*" said Emma.

Strong nodded to the jeweler and asked for a tray of earrings. He picked oval diamond studs. "Engagement present," he said.

She put in the earrings, and Strong escorted her out the door.

He grinned. "Let's see, what is the next line of that poem? Oh, yes. What a beautiful pussy you are, you are. What a beautiful pussy you are."

"You are full of surprises," Emma said, sliding into the seat of the Escalade.

"Oh, yeah."

"Had you been thinking about proposing?"

"No."

"When did you know you loved me?"

"Probably in Las Vegas, but tonight I couldn't deny it. Plus, yesterday, I heard Antwan Givens broke up with his girlfriend and is free to date. I can't take any chances."

She flushed and hoped he didn't see it in the dark of the car. Did he know she'd gone to dinner with Antwan? How could he?

"Strong…how…?" She took a breath. "You could have any woman you want. All those smart, pretty, powerful women. How am I so lucky?"

He put her hand to his lips. "You're right. I can have any woman I want. And I have her. I've known a number of ladies, smart and pretty. Emma, *you* are smart and pretty, plus a whole lot of other qualities. On our first date when we kissed on your couch? I knew you were worked up. But you made me leave. I've never experienced that before."

"That was good?"

"Oh yeah. I couldn't stop thinking about you."

"I should warn you about my knee-jerk reactions."

He laughed. "Oh, baby, I'm very much aware of your reactions."

She shook her head. "I thought I'd lost you when I threw that fit about all of the other women you…bedded in your house."

"Lost me? No. That was the clincher, Princess."

"My fit?"

"Uh huh. You thought you were part of a routine, and you weren't having it. Your gut told you it was beneath you. Actually, I thought I'd lost *you*."

"Really?"

"I didn't know what to do. I almost swung the car around and banged on your door. But I thought it would turn you off."

Oh, how wrong you were.

"I spent the whole night arranging for those gifts, hoping you would come around."

"Come around? I was overwhelmed."

"Whatever. I felt relieved that it worked. Ems, you are the kind of woman I'd introduce to my mother. The kind of woman I want to raise my children."

Children.

He held her hand as they walked to the car. Their conversation left them both quiet. He drove her back to her place and lingered at the door.

She examined her diamond in the porch light. "Are you coming in to kiss me goodnight? Like our first date?"

He shook his head. "I don't want any temptations to keep me from my resolve."

"What resolve?"

"No sex until marriage."

Emma laughed. "Really?"

"What did I say about not changing my mind?"

She sighed and unlocked the door. "Until tomorrow then?"

"Come to the office around noon. I'll call you if it's to be later."

Emma stepped inside the door and poked her head out. "I love you."

"And I love you, too."

She headed to the kitchen to clean up from the unclaimed dinner. "You, pot roast? How useless." *Useless? It got him here and into my bed. And...!*

She whirled around the small kitchen. That hollow-in-the-loins feeling plagued her, but she reviewed his words over and over. Her dreams had come true. Almost.

Chapter Fourteen

Emma arrived at the office at noon.

Evelyn looked up from her computer screen. "Hello, Miss Whitstone. Why, don't you look pretty today. Love the suit."

Emma loved it too. She'd seen it from across the store at Saks. Square shoulders with short sleeves, the jacket had ombre coloring by connecting strips of heavy silk starting with white and getting grayer at the bottom until the hemline was dark slate. She added a charcoal cashmere sweater shell underneath. The V-neck of the jacket allowed just a peek of her pearl necklace.

"Mr. Manning. Miss Whitstone is here. You said to let you know as soon as she came in. And Ms. Manning said she'd be here at twelve-thirty."

"Ms. Manning?" Emma asked.

Evelyn cast her gaze to the closed office door across the room. "Sarah Manning. Mr. Manning's partner."

"Oh, right," Emma said. She still had a lot to know about Strong. Was she making a mistake? Should she wait and learn more about him? *Hell, no, you idiot.* She smiled at her own admonition. She wasn't making a mistake. This is what she wanted. She turned so Evelyn couldn't see the huge smile forming.

Strong came from his office. "Hi. You look...," he turned his head right and left, "Fabulous. Ready?"

She squelched the smile and nodded.

"Sure?"

She nodded again, afraid she'd break out in joyous laughter if she spoke.

"Evelyn, hold down the fort. I'll be back sometime this

afternoon."

Evelyn reminded him about the work piled up from his recent absence. He thanked her for the observation and told her to take messages while he was gone.

In the car, Emma found her voice. "You didn't tell anyone?"

"No one's business. But to tell the truth, I thought Evelyn would see your ring and ask some questions. She usually notices things like that. It's one of the reasons I keep her at such a high salary. That, and she doesn't ask about me leaving so suddenly. And, of course, she's a good assistant.

"What about Sarah?"

"My cousin? Oh, you'll have to meet Sarah." He said it in an odd way. "Thank God for her. She sees to most of my cases when I'm gone. She has one of the finest legal minds I've ever met."

"I thought you were the fair-haired boy."

"She's five times as smart as I am. She has a fine sense about what leads to follow and picks up on the smallest detail. It's amazing."

"Is she a trial lawyer?"

Strong took his eyes off the road and looked at Emma with a strange expression. "Uhm, noo." His lips formed the word "noo" in a rounded circle. He pulled the Cadillac around the block from the courthouse to a parking garage. At the ticket kiosk, he keyed in a code. The barrier lifted, but instead of turning left to find the elevated floor parking, he drove to what looked like a dead end. Two doors swung open, and he drove down a ramp to a valet-attended underground lot. The valet opened Emma's door. Strong tossed him the keys.

Emma gazed around the parking area. "I didn't know this was here."

He pulled at his chin. "Yeah…well, you're not supposed to. By invitation only."

She put her hands on her hips. "And you have an invitation?"

He shrugged. "Friends in low places, Princess. Ready to change your name? Wait, you are taking my name, right?"

"What if I don't? What if I keep Whitstone?"

He made a thinking face. "It might mess up our first son's name. You know, Charles Whitstone Manning. We might have to name him Charles Whitstone Whitstone, or he'll have one of those awful hyphenated names...you know...."

"I'm taking Manning," she said. "I worked hard enough for it."

He laughed. "So you did, baby. Come on." He took her hand. "The judge said twelve-thirty sharp. We have twenty minutes to do the paperwork."

The next stop was the license bureau. He had called ahead, and with his connections, there was no waiting; the paperwork was ready. Their third stop was to Judge Tullis, an old family friend.

"Are you sure you want to do this, young lady?" Judge Tullis asked. "This fellow is pretty ornery."

"I'm sure. Maybe I can help him be less ornery."

"A worthy goal, indeed. Let the proceedings begin," the judge said, and married them.

After the kiss, the judge threw a handful of shredded paper at them. Strong shook the judge's hand, and the judge hugged Emma. The older man moved his head from side to side. "Well, if I hadn't seen it for myself, I wouldn't believe it. Behave yourself, Charles."

On the way out, Strong said, "He still calls me Charles. He was at my christening and can't change gears."

In the valet parking lot, he didn't need to give them a receipt; the valet knew to get the car as soon as they got off the elevator. The car burped to a stop in front of them.

"There you go, Mr. Manning." The attendant rushed out of the seat and opened the door for Emma.

"Thanks," Strong said, and put the car in gear.

"Aren't you going to tip him?"

"I give them a big tip once a year. And extras when I get trial bonuses. They always know when the verdict comes in favorably."

"Really?"

"And I never have a scratch on old Nelly Bell here."

It reminded her of Antwan giving the young man a ten-dollar bill to watch his car.

"What are you thinking about? I've never known anyone to focus inward like you."

She wasn't about to tell him her thoughts included Antwan Givens—or why she could focus inward. She'd learned that skill when Aunt Hester flailed the dreaded fly swatter.

"Hey, Mrs. Manning!"

"Sorry. What?" She smiled. "Mrs. Manning! How wonderful."

"Where do you want to go to lunch?"

"I'm not hungry. Not now."

"Me neither. Do you mind if I go back to work? That way I can close the office this evening. I have some important work that has to be completed today. Besides, sometime this afternoon, you'll have to go back to your place and make room in your closet and whatever else you need to do for another person."

That took her by surprise. She hadn't given a single thought to where they would live. Of course, the fuss she'd made about all the women who'd been to his place meant he wouldn't expect her to live there, even if it made more sense.

"Right. I'll make room, but now that I know about this private parking lot, can I get invited?"

"Maybe you should ask Susie. She parks her car here."

"How do you know that?"

"We had a bit of a fender-bender. That's how we met."

"How did she get invited to park here?"

Strong's eyebrows rose. "I can't tell you that because I don't know, but I can tell you one thing...this property belongs to Latito." Strong drove to the office and parked in his space. "Come in for a little while. Maybe you can meet Sarah."

They had been gone for a little more than an hour. Evelyn looked at the clock on her desk. "Short lunch, Mr. Manning."

"Uhm, we didn't get lunch, Evelyn."

"Would you like me to order something?" She smiled at Emma. "Will you be staying, Miss Whitstone? I can order something for you, too."

"Order in. Good idea. We might be hungry in a little while. Thanks, Evelyn. Let's see. How about Forbidden City? I'll have orange chicken. How about you, Mrs. Manning?"

Evelyn did a double take and scanned Emma up and down, stopping at her hand. She popped out of her seat. "Oh! Strong! And Miss—"

Emma said, "You can call me by my first name." She winked. "When there aren't any clients around."

Evelyn had the "snagged" look and laughed. She hugged them each singly and then together. "So, what would Mrs. Manning like for lunch?"

"Orange chicken sounds good."

Strong put his hand on Emma's shoulder and turned her toward his office. He called over his shoulder to Evelyn. "Don't disturb us for a while, okay?"

"Right, boss," Evelyn said in a relaxed manner, a change from what Emma had seen before.

Strong let Emma pass into the room and closed the door. He took her purse. "See that wall?" He pointed to the west wall, decorated with a solitary painting.

"Yes."

Strong removed the painting and leaned it against his desk. "That's not a wall. It's a honeymoon suite at the Ritz."

He gently pushed her against the wall and slid his hand up her skirt.

"What are you doing?"

"Removing your pantyhose. This is the honeymoon suite, remember?"

He unbuckled his belt and let his trousers fold to the floor. Emma pressed against the wallpaper and smiled as her skirt bunched upward over her hips. Strong removed her lovely jacket before running his hands into the cashmere and back against her bra closure. Movements swift and deft left her without the support of the lacy undergarment.

"I haven't been to the doctor yet."

"I'll take a chance if you will," he whispered.

She didn't answer but pressed her lips against his. In her mind, she wished she could control her lust, but the war between mind and body proved momentary. She, like her new husband, could be ready in an instant, even a nano-instant. Emma's panties acted as if they had been greased the way they slid down her legs, assisted by Strong's supple sock-clothed toe.

Did she just tell him to hurry? In case she didn't, she whispered, "Hurry."

The wall-turned-honeymoon suite thudded slightly from their activity.

Laughing, Strong put his hand over her mouth when she emitted the high-pitched wail, providing a reliable sign of her orgasm. His laugh turned into the low moan with which he announced his. They slipped down the wall onto the carpet into each other's arms.

"I hope that's a bathroom," she whispered, pointing to the door on the far wall.

"Yep," he said, almost out of breath.

Neither one moved for a few minutes.

Strong kissed Emma's cheek, stood, and looked around for his trousers. He extended his hand and helped her up. She snagged her panties with her foot and tossed them into the air. Strong caught them effortlessly.

"Like catching nuts, eh?"

He smiled. "Maybe I can practice by juggling panties, bras, and—let's see. Oh yeah, pantyhose."

She took her lacy low-riders and smoothed down her skirt. "I hope I don't look like I just—"

"Just had a honeymoon?" He escorted her to the bathroom door. "I'm sure Evelyn won't notice a thing."

When they'd freshened up, Strong opened the door. "Hey! Sarah! Come meet someone special."

Emma peeked over Strong's shoulder. A woman, a dwarf, walked in a stiff gait toward him, her dark curls jiggling.

"Sarah, this is my wife, Emma."

"Wife?" She spoke with a high-pitched nasal sound. Emma waited for the next words to see if Sarah had been joking with her voice. "I can't believe it. Strong! Married."

Sarah had not been having fun. Her grating voice sounded like nails on a chalkboard. Strong's comment about Sarah not being a trial lawyer became clear. It didn't matter the level of her legal brilliance. Unfair and sad, people, being the way they were, would never take Sarah seriously either as a defender or a prosecutor. The poor woman didn't have a chance in front of a jury.

"I'm pleased to meet you," Emma managed to muster. "Strong says you are a great help to him. Thank you."

Sarah thumbed at Emma and spoke to Strong. "I like her. You better treat her right, cousin." Then she peered at Emma with a piercing stare. "Right now, you're wondering about the chance of having dwarf babies. Put your mind at ease, Emma. I was adopted. No blood relation to your honey-boy."

Emma's mouth worked without sounds. It was the exact thought that had popped into her mind. Like Strong said, Sarah had a brilliant mind and caught on to the smallest nuance of behavior. "Wow," was the word Emma managed to say.

Sarah picked up her phone messages from Evelyn and headed for her office. She stopped at the threshold and smiled to Emma. "Welcome to the family."

"Thanks," Emma called out as Sarah disappeared past the door.

Strong shrugged. "Next, you get to meet the rest of the Mannings."

Emma nodded. "The rest of the family? I can't wait."

After they finished lunch, Strong surveyed his desk. "I have work to do, Princess. And so do you."

"Right. I have to make my house our home. When should I expect you?"

"I have to go to my place and pick up some things, so I'd say around eight."

She bent close and whispered in his ear, hopefully, low

enough to evade Evelyn's detection. "Can you bring your CD player and Antonio Vivaldi?"

Strong bit his lip. "I can, and I will."

In her car, Emma stared at the steering wheel. She'd been married for three hours. Shouldn't she feel something exhilarating? She held the key near the ignition slot, frozen in her seat. The wedding...could she call it a wedding? They were wed, so it met the qualification. Qualification? Nothing else about the nuptials had met her dreams. No blame on Strong—he would have done anything she wanted regarding a ceremony. With a deriding chuckle, she inserted the key and turned on the engine. Who would she have invited? Abbey lived out of the country. Susie most likely would have refused, and she had no idea where her brother Joey lived. With her hand on the gear shift, she reviewed her present life. She'd been in St. Louis for less than a year. Friends were on a short list and no family. Family? Would Strong's family let her join their ranks? Would she *want* to be part of them? Other than that, she loved him intensely. What did she know about him? As she pulled out of her husband's office parking lot, she resolved to find out more about him and more about whatever took him away. And that blonde hottie who crooked her finger to summon him, her husband.

***

At eight thirty, Emma jumped from her seat on the couch at the sound of tires crunching on the drive. She ran to the car and helped Strong with the boxes in the trunk.

They stowed the boxes in Abbey's old bedroom, and removed items Strong would need in the next few days. Two of his suits took their place next to the clothes Emma chose to leave in the closet.

"What's for supper, woman?"

Her new title as "woman" became the icing on the cupcake of her new status—Mrs. Manning. She'd spent several hours daydreaming blissfully about the years ahead. "Leftover pot roast or Chef Boyardee Spaghetti-O's."

"Hard choice. I have fond memories of Spaghetti-O's too.

Okay, the chef wins."

When the microwave dinged, dinner was served.

Strong lifted his loaded fork. "Long live canned Italian. I shall love you, Emma, better than these tender little circles, and that's saying something, indeed."

"I love you better than anything," Emma said in a whisper. "And that's saying everything."

"My princess." Stone clinked his glass of ginger ale with hers.

"My chieftain," Emma responded.

"Chieftain? By God, you've read Burroughs?"

"Every one of his books. The John Carter series was my favorite."

With almost blurring speed, Strong scooted back the chair and pulled Emma up into his arms. "When it's right, it's right. Right, Princess?" He kicked her chair out of his way and carried her to the bedroom.

She laid her head on his shoulder. "You know, my doctor's appointment is tomorrow afternoon."

He placed her on the mattress. "And?"

"I've been thinking about Charles Whitstone Manning. What I mean is…."

"You would like to meet him?"

"How about you?"

"Whatever you want, Princess. In for a penny, in for a pound. And I'm way in."

"So you are, my chieftain."

"Antonio Vivaldi is ready for us. Are we ready for him?"

"Yes," she said breathlessly.

"This piece is better than the last selection."

"How can that possibly be?"

"You'll see." He popped the disc into the CD player. "Listen to the first part."

They sat together on the bed.

"Can you hear the beat? There's an understatement, lusty and forceful. But sweet and spirited."

"I hear it. But why are we sitting here? Did you lose your lust for me?"

"Ah. Softly, slowly, catchee monkey."

"This monkey needs catching now."

"What a woman." He chuckled. "Oh, yeah. Uh huh. Harpsichords? Mandolins. Do you hear the organ's beat, like thrusting? Perfect timing."

"Thrusting, yes. Strong…thrusting…."

"Hold on. You need to hear this. Crescendo! The climax! And if everything follows the music, that's when the orgasm happens. I said it was the climax."

"Is this formula sex? Structured lovemaking?"

"No, it's making love to the sound of beautiful, moving music."

"This is a new facet of you, Strong."

"Yeah." He pushed her down on the bed. "The softer side of Strong."

"But, I want—"

"Yeah, yeah, you'll get—"

"The harder side of Strong."

CHAPTER FIFTEEN

In the morning, they went their separate ways. Emma had a thick folder on her desk waiting for her trip to the courthouse. Two things bothered her. One, that Mr. Latito owned that special parking lot and hadn't invited her to use it. How did Susie rate? Two, what barrage of insults would she endure when Susie saw the ring and learned about the marriage? She wouldn't let Susie say anything negative. She'd stop it before Susie could start.

Susie's desk looked unattended. The clerk in the neighboring cubicle said Susie had called in sick to spend time at the hospital because one of her friends had been severely injured.

In the elevator, Emma learned Antwan Givens had been brutally beaten and might not survive. Poor Antwan. She made calls until she found out what hospital Antwan was in, but his critical condition meant no visitors except family. Emma couldn't concentrate on her research. Even though it was early, she packed it in for the day, and for the first time, didn't worry about unfinished work. She hadn't told anyone at the office about getting married. Except for the payroll clerk who needed the name change, no one would care. Certainly not Gianni Latito. She already had the afternoon off for that gynecology appointment.

She saw the gynecologist, but after thinking about having a baby, refused the birth control. After asking his opinion, the doctor proclaimed her fit and healthy and wished her luck on getting pregnant.

On her way home, she alternated images between Antwan in the ICU and holding a baby, Charles Whitstone Manning, in her arms. She couldn't wait until Strong got home. The clock struck the hours, five, six, and seven. She reminded herself that Strong didn't work a nine-to-five, but by the time Abbey's old clock chimed seven-thirty, Emma's mood had dampened. A half-hour later, Strong's key clicked in the lock. Emma's mood soared.

They ate a simple meal, the left-over pot roast and Chianti. After the clean up, Strong pointed to a box he'd brought in. "Where can I put these? They're just jeans and T-shirts, my rough clothes."

"We can use Abbey's dresser," Emma said.

Strong brought the box into Abbey's old bedroom across the hall from Emma's, which he asked to be his office. Emma tugged on the bottom drawer of the dresser.

"Here," he chuckled. "Let a man do the hard work." He tugged and then tugged harder. Applying more strength, the drawer gave way. From the back of the cabinet, a wiry object took flight. Strong retrieved it mid-air and held it upright.

Emma paled. She grabbed her throat and backed up in extended steps.

"Emma? What's wrong?"

She trembled, unable to speak.

"Honey, it's just a flyswatter. See?" He waved it at imaginary insects.

Emma backed out of the doorway.

Strong took a long look at the object in his hand. His jaw muscles flinched. He threw the horrid thing into the open closet and, with bare movements of his lips, said, "Hester and Gene Ludwig are going to pay." He rushed to Emma's side. "Are you all right?"

"Yes," she croaked between swallows.

He embraced her and kissed her cheek. "Nothing will hurt you, ever. I promise."

"I know," she said.

CHAPTER SIXTEEN

At breakfast on Saturday, Strong finished his coffee. "Princess, it's time to meet the family. I've asked my sister and mother to join us for dinner tonight at the Hastings Inn. Ever been there?"

"No. Way too expensive for my budget."

"Not anymore. It's a nice place. Fine food and quiet atmosphere. It's the restaurant the Mannings use for special occasions. It will be a surprise for them."

"Should I be nervous?"

"Absolutely not. You'll love my mother. And my sister, although wacky, is adorable. You'll see."

Strong and Emma got there first. Stringed instruments played by a quartet sent soft notes of classical music into the background at a tasteful volume. A hostess dressed in a long black dress showed them to a brocaded booth. Another hostess brought them four leather-bound menus. A server brought water in stemmed glasses. The faint sounds of tinkling dinnerware and the low lighting presented elegance. Tucked away in a corner booth, they kept watch for the guests.

"There's my sister," Strong said, waving his arm. Seconds later, he touched Emma's shoulder and pointed to another woman entering. "My mother." He stood while the ladies scooted over the plush cushions. "Mom, Lizzie, this is Emma. Emma Manning."

Strong's mother, with dark indigo eyes and deep auburn hair, looked like Maureen O'Hara. Although still striking, she must have been a stunner thirty years prior. Lizzie, attractive in a cute way, looked like her mother. Strong, ashen hair and light eyes, must have resembled his father.

"Emma, this is my mother, Katherine Manning, and my sister, Dr. Elizabeth Manning-Chu. She's a pediatrician."

"It's just Lizzie," the younger woman said.

"Hello, Lizzie and Mrs. Manning."

Katherine smiled. "You can call me Kate. Oh! You have the same last name. Are your people from Ohio?"

"She's Emma Whitstone Manning, Mom. She's my wife."

Kate and Lizzie looked at each other and then stared at Strong.

Lizzie shook her head. "I didn't think it was possible. What do you think, Mom?"

"I don't know what to say." She addressed Emma. "When did this happen?"

"He asked me three days ago, and I didn't want to give him time to change his mind. We were married the next day."

"Well, congratulations," Kate said. "Strong and Emma. I would be upset that you didn't tell me beforehand, Strong, but I'm so happy that I can't get angry with you. Son and daughter-in-law, gee."

"Gee," echoed Lizzie. "Wow. So how did you meet, Emma?"

Emma took a sip of water. "I saw him when I went to the courthouse. He caught my eye." She winked at Strong. "I asked a friend, Susie Williams, about him. She said he was brilliant."

Strong gave Emma a sideways glance. "Susie can't stand me. What was the rest of the description?"

Emma rolled her lip to stifle her laugh. "She said you were cold and not very nice. An operator. A snake in the grass!"

Lizzie's eyebrows went up. "Someone who knows you."

"But it isn't true," Emma said. "He's warm, gentle, kind, and thoughtful. That's the Strong I know."

Lizzie pointed her finger at Strong. "Gentle? Warm? All right, Buster, who are you and what have you done with my brother?"

Their humor was interrupted when the waiter asked if they were ready. They all looked at the menus and ordered.

When the waiter left, Lizzie said, "What about your family, Emma?"

"I don't have one to speak of. I want to start our relationship off with honesty, so I will tell you that after my parents died in an auto accident, my brother and I lived with my father's youngest sister and husband. They took us in because they got most of our inheritance, not because they loved us. We were treated like interlopers," she cast her gaze to the table, "and worse." She brought her head up. "My brother left when he was sixteen. I haven't heard from him again. I often wonder what happened to Joey. He was always good to me."

"Joey," Lizzie said. "Isn't that a coincidence? Joe is our brother's name, too."

Emma turned to Strong. "You have a brother?"

"Two brothers," Lizzie answered. "Strong is the oldest, then Joe, then me, and the youngest is Perry."

"You never mentioned brothers."

"Bad blood," Lizzie said. "He doesn't speak to Joe and only tolerates Perry. I am the family moderator, so to speak."

Strong glowered at Lizzie. "Hey."

"Family honesty, like Emma said. It's a good policy."

Emma looked at her hands. "Oh." She grappled for a word to distract the growing discord. "Uhm, what about Mr. Manning? What happened to your father?"

Strong's face became more intense. "We don't talk about that drunken loser."

A moment of awkward silence preceded Emma's words. "You shouldn't say that about your father. It hurts your mother's feelings."

His lip went up in a half sneer. "No, it doesn't. She hates him."

Emma's voice lowered. "That's not true, Strong. Maybe *you* hate him, but she still cares."

"You don't know anything about this family, Emma."

"I know from the look on your mother's face. A person can be angry with someone, but still be in love."

Kate dabbed the table napkin to her eyes.

Strong pointed. "Look, you made her cry."

Kate sniffed. "No, she didn't. I've had this little cry in me for a while now. It's good to get it out."

Strong pursed his lips. "Damn it, Emma."

Lizzie slapped Strong's shoulder. "Don't talk to Emma that way. She's right. Mom does still care for Daddy. You and Joe are the biggest obstacles keeping them apart."

Strong put his hand firmly on the table. "This conversation is closed."

The waiter brought bread in a silver basket covered with linen. Another waiter brought tall, graceful wine glasses and made a show of the bottle. He poured a small amount into Strong's glass for approval. After Strong's nod, the server poured the wine for them.

Lizzie wrinkled her nose at Strong. Then she looked at Emma. "Too bad Dave, my husband, can't be here. He's on call and had a delivery tonight. This is his first week with a new gynecology practice. He loves it." Lizzie took a few bites of a breadstick. "Hey, how're the garlic rolls, Mom?"

Kate nodded, recovered from her cry. "Very good." She took Emma's hand. "We are so happy to meet you, honey. In the midst of surprise at the news, I neglected to say welcome to our family."

"Thank you. I will try my best to make a good home for Strong. And our children."

"Are you pregnant?" Lizzie asked.

"No. But I wouldn't mind. I want children."

"Well, you have come to the right place. Pun intended!" Lizzie laughed at her naughty joke.

"Lizzie," admonished Kate.

"Okay, sorry. I don't care who you are, though, that was funny! But, seriously, Dave can see to you during pregnancy, and I can be your baby doctor. Mom, can you picture Strong as a daddy?"

"No." Kate took a big sip of wine. "I'm still working on imagining him as a husband!"

Strong put his hand on the table again. "This conversation is closed, as well."

Lizzie pointed at Strong and laughed. "Uhm, brother, look around you. Three women and one man—one newly henpecked married man. You're not the king. We'll talk about whatever we want, right ladies?"

Emma laughed, knowing she wanted Lizzie as her friend. Their food came, and the conversation lulled.

Halfway through her lasagna, Lizzie elbowed Kate. "Mom, wow, I can barely comprehend that Strong is married." She cocked her head. "So, how did that happen?"

"I fell in love," Strong said.

Both Lizzie and Kate stared at him.

Lizzie shook her head. "I never thought I'd hear him say something like that. In public, yet. Incredible."

Kate's expression emanated pride, hope, and relief. "Almost unbelievable. It was wonderful to see him smile when he introduced Emma."

Strong patted his chest. "I'm sitting right here, guys. Besides, I smile."

Lizzie sent a puzzled look to Kate. Kate shook her head. "I can't remember a time, say, in the last fifteen years that I saw him happy." She patted Emma's hand. "Oh, my dear. I hope you're sturdy enough to deal with him."

"Hey," Strong protested. "I am sitting *right here.*"

Lizzie swished her hand mid-air in front of Strong's face, dismissing him. "Listen, Emma. We love him so we can tell the truth. Strong can be harsh; he needs a soft pillow. I think you're sturdy but soft, perfect for Strong. You didn't flinch when he got grumpy. But don't tolerate too much of his grumpiness."

Emma shook her finger at Strong in mock reprimand. "Five minutes of grumpiness a day only."

Lizzie nodded. "Uh huh. Strong chose well; maybe he knows what he needs."

Kate studied her wine glass. "I hope you're right, Lizzie."

"Hey!" Strong used his thumbs to point at himself. "Right here, you know!"

The women laughed. Strong's expression, usually stoic,

glowered again. He placed his napkin on the table and excused himself to the men's room.

"Why don't you have lunch with me Saturday?" Lizzie asked.

"Good," Kate said. "You girls get to know each other."

Lizzie leaned from her chair, eyeing Strong as he departed the dining area. "Mom, will you please talk to Daddy? He phoned me today and said he's tried to call you, but you hang up. He loves you, and he's sorry for what he did. These years have been so hard on him. The years without you. He said it was his mid-life crisis; she didn't mean anything to him. Please?"

Kate's eyebrows came together. She bit her lip. "Not now. Maybe later."

Lizzie spread her hands wide. "Well! That's a step in the right direction. At least it's a maybe."

Emma sat quietly, believing she had witnessed a critical family moment.

When Strong returned, they finished the meal, with small talk as the focus of conversation.

That night after Emma prepared for sleep, she found Strong in his recliner reading.

"Strong, why don't you come to bed?"

He didn't look up from the papers. "Go to bed without me."

Emma pushed his legs over and sat on the edge of the recliner. "Are you angry with me?"

He didn't answer.

"Strong!"

"You three talked about my father when I was away, didn't you? I could tell by the look on Mom's face. My father is not part of my world, which makes him not a part of yours. Remember that."

"You should remember what I said in the restaurant about being angry but still being in love. Those feelings can coexist. I love you."

He looked up from his work. "I love you, too."

Within twenty minutes, he joined her in bed. They made love.

CHAPTER SEVENTEEN

The next morning, when Strong stepped into the kitchen, Emma pulled two cups from the cupboard and poured coffee, determined to take her place as "wife" in their new marriage. She handed him his cup. He sat at the table and sipped.

She kissed his forehead. "Toast?"

He nodded and stared at his cup for a few seconds. "Emma, I want you to change jobs. Latito's office is not a healthy place to work. Why don't you just quit? You don't have to work."

"You don't want me to contribute?"

"I make enough money. And we'll get you a decent car, too. Put in your notice."

"I love my little car. And if I resign, what will I do all day?"

"Take a painting class, read romance books, eat bon-bons. Whatever you want."

She became aware of the line forming between her brows. "I don't know. I'll think about it. Can we get a dog?"

"That's not a bad idea. Uhm, I want to meet with Lars tonight. Catalano's for dinner?"

"Okay." The quiet of the room made the scratches of butter-on-toast sound abrasive. First, she'd met his family, now the friends—all of the important people in his life.

She needed to leave first because her drive to work was longer.

"Catalano's? Six-thirty?" he said, after their goodbye kiss.

She held out her cheek for a second kiss. "Sounds good."

At work, she took a long look around her office. She hadn't made any close friends. Susie at the courthouse was the nearest thing to that. Could she live without this job? Maybe she could go back to school, finish her post grad? Have a baby? What was the hurry? She'd have to think about it.

Six-thirty came fast. When Emma pulled into the restaurant's parking lot, Strong sat waiting in his car. They walked in together. A few minutes after they were seated, Lars approached the table.

"Hey, Dude. Hey, uhm....." The Swedish accent no longer apparent, he talked like a surfer.

"Emma."

"Yeah, Emma. Hey, there." He pulled out a chair and sat backwards. He relaxed his chin on the chair top and engaged Strong's attention. "What's new?"

"Emma and I are married."

"Uh-huh. Nah." He squinched his face. "It's not like you to play jokes."

The muscle in Strong's jaw twitched. "You're right. No joke. We were married three days ago."

Lars sat up straight, and the languid surfer look disappeared. His voice changed to serious. "Do you have any idea—?"

Strong put his hand up, palm towards Lars. "Of course I do."

They sat in silence, staring at each other.

In the quiet, Emma spoke. "Are you not happy for your friend, Lars?"

Lars shifted his eyes to look at her. "There will be a few people who won't be happy." He shook his head and glared at Strong with silent accusation.

Strong stood. "Let's take this outside." He turned to Emma. "We'll just be a minute."

They exited the restaurant in stiff, hard steps. From the window at the table, she had a clear view of them as they strode through the well-lighted parking lot. They stopped at a dark-colored Jeep. Lars gestured as Strong stood with his arms crossed against his chest in a defiant stance.

Emma's parents had taught their children American Sign Language, and lip reading was second nature. Lars had his back to her so she couldn't see his mouth, but she read Strong's words.

"It won't affect the team. Screw Spencer and screw you. Screw you all. Deal with it."

After a few minutes, Strong put his hands up and formed a T, like a football referee calling time out, and walked away. Lars leaned back on the hood and looked to the night sky. After a few seconds, he left his position on the hood and headed for the restaurant. When Strong stepped into the entrance, Lars caught up. They returned to the table a few steps apart. This time Lars sat in the chair the normal way. The feeling in the air was heavy and uneasy.

Emma folded her hands on the table. "I feel like I did something wrong."

"You didn't do anything wrong." Strong reached his arm around her shoulders. "And neither did I."

Emma waited for Lars to speak, but he looked away. She didn't need this. "Strong, I'm not hungry. Can we go home?"

"We can." He pulled the chair for her. "Lars, this is FYI only. I'll deal with what I have to."

They drove through Burger King's take-out for their dinner. There was little conversation in the car as Emma clung to their bag of fast food. At home, as Emma distributed the burgers, Strong came behind her and kissed her neck. "Here's something I've learned. That is, don't agonize over things you can't change. It only makes you feel worse."

She fished the napkins from the bag. "I'll try. Lars is your close friend. He wasn't happy. Is that something I can change?"

"It'll work out." Strong opened the catsup package and squirted red over the fries. He pointed to the sandwich with the potato strip and did an imitation of the cartoon character, Homer Simpson. "Mmmmm, burgers!"

Knowing it was an attempt to make her smile, she forced one. After the meal, he made another trip to his house for clothes and paperwork. Emma stored his clothes while Strong worked in the office until bedtime.

The next morning they ate breakfast in the small kitchen. Before he finished, he brought up the meeting with Lars.

"I'm going to speak with Lars again this evening. You need to be there."

"Maybe he won't want to see you. Especially with me there."

Strong swallowed the remainder of his coffee. "He'll be all right. He's had time to think about it. He understands the concept of not worrying about things he can't change."

"I'd feel uncomfortable to be with him."

"Don't. Don't allow people to influence you. Lars and I are involved with each other in business and friendship. He'll flex. You need to adjust as well."

"Why don't you ask him to dinner here tonight?"

Strong's lips turned up just a bit. "On your turf, eh? Good thinking. I'll call him."

Later that morning, in her office, Emma answered the private phone. Lars had accepted the invitation to dinner.

That evening Emma peeked from the kitchen as Lars handed Strong a bottle of wine. Strong backed from the door to allow Lars to enter. "Come in. Would you like a drink?"

Lars nodded. "Got milk?"

Lars followed Strong into the kitchen, where two glasses sat next to the Wild Turkey.

"Hello, Lars," Emma said.

"Hey, Emma."

Strong poured generous servings of the bourbon. He brought a carton of milk from the fridge and put the container next to the bottle.

Lars poured the milk into the liquor and started to make a toasting gesture, but checked his action. "Have you told her yet?"

Emma turned about. "Told me what?"

"Regarding his part-time job."

"Strong?"

Strong used his foot to push out a third chair at the small table. "I couldn't tell you anything before we were married. But now I will. Sit."

She sat.

He took a drink and put down his glass with a small thud.

"Okay. Don't ask questions, just listen."

"But—"

Strong put his finger to his lips. Lars pointed to her and put his hands around his ears. Emma, recognizing the primitive sign language, nodded. She pointed to herself and cupped her hands around her own ears.

Strong's jaw muscle flexed. "I am part of a four-person extraction team, and we work for a little known agency of the government."

Emma's eyes widened. "Extraction? You kill people?"

"No questions!" He lowered his voice. "No, not usually. We rescue people."

"Not usually." She felt the flush burning her face. "Is it dangerous?" She'd ask questions, all right.

"If it wasn't dangerous, they wouldn't call us," Lars said.

"Emma." Strong leaned in toward her. "The bottom line is, every so often I get called, and I go. I don't know when I will return, and I won't be able to contact you while I'm gone."

She put up her hand. "Don't tell me not to ask questions."

"All right, you can ask, but I might not answer."

"Who's on the team?"

"Me, Lars, and two women named Jo Lynn and Aphrodite. We formed a team in the army and have worked together since. Besides the team, sometimes I do hostage negotiation, mediation, and legal consultation, in Latin America. That's it, Emma, that's what I can tell you."

"Except," Lars added, "if he dies, you'll get a wad from Uncle Sam."

Emma put her hand to her mouth. "Oh, Strong!"

Strong glared at his friend. "Lars, you're an idiot."

"I know," Lars said, and poured more milk into the Wild Turkey.

Strong put his arm around her waist. "Hey, try not to worry. We've been doing this for a while. And I'll tell you as much as I can, okay?"

The smell of the baked chicken from the oven didn't have

the same appeal as it had earlier, but it would burn if left in any longer. She went into robot-mode, serving dinner quietly, much like she had when she slaved for Aunt Hester and Uncle Gene. She refused help for the clean-up, needing some thinking-time.

After Lars left, Strong came behind her and wrapped his arms tightly around her as she stood at the sink. "I know it's a shock. I wanted to tell you in stages."

"Maybe it's better this way," she said quietly.

He put his lips to her ear. "Maybe," he whispered. "I don't want you to worry."

She turned to face him. "I'll worry."

He took a towel and dried the dishes. Neither spoke, allowing silence to help settle the tension.

With the work done, Strong took her by the hand and led her into the bedroom. They showered and made love. That protected, secure feeling she'd developed from sleeping with Strong felt shattered. His job was dangerous? On call at all times?

CHAPTER EIGHTEEN

In the morning, Strong kissed her at the front door.

"Since it's Saturday," Emma said, "and you have to go to your office," she handed him lunch in a paper bag, "I'm having lunch with Lizzie."

"Oh, great. There won't be a single family secret left by the time you finish the appetizers."

"I plan," she said as she straightened his tie, "to be very quiet, hoping to hear all the dirt before we butter the rolls."

Strong shook his head and smiled. "*Bon appétit.*"

Emma found Lizzie at a back table, pulling green olives off a long toothpick with three wide-flared glasses lined up like soldiers. "Theeth are the beth part," she said, chewing the olive. "I askth for extra olifs."

"Hi," Emma said. She slid into the booth.

Lizzie swallowed and eyed the loaded skewers marinating in the glasses. "How's married life treating you? God, that was lame. I can come up with a better opener than that, like welcome, new sister-in-law."

"Thanks. I feel welcomed." Emma pointed at the drink. "Is that a martini? I've never had one."

"Perfect time to try something new."

"Okay," Emma said.

Lizzie waved to the waiter and held up her glass. She touched Emma's ring. "I didn't notice it the other night, but nice rock. My brother went all out, I see."

"It's showy, but I'll admit I love it. I hope we really can afford it."

Lizzie took another olive from the pick. "He can afford it. He doesn't talk about it, but he's worth some bucks. Ask him. And here's some advice. You'd figure it out for yourself, but I'll save you some time. When you ask him questions, be specific and don't let him flim-flam you. He has a way of telling the truth in an untruthful way. So, is Strong showing you around? Are you meeting people?" She popped the olive in her mouth.

"So far, I've met you, Kate, and Lars."

Lizzie's eyebrows lifted. "Ah, Lars!"

"You know him?"

"Mmm." Lizzie sighed with exaggerated shoulder movement. "Lars broke my heart. Among other things!"

"Oh," said Emma, accepting her olive-heavy martini from the waiter.

"I dated Lars when I was home from college. He's one of the good guys. You would think someone that handsome would be arrogant or shitty, but he is as nice a person as I have ever met. Lars is the best. And, uh…gifted, you might say."

"Were you in love with him?"

"At the time, but dear brother had issues with it. Oh, it was okay for Strong to boink Lar's sister, Inga, but when Lars started poking me, Strong got irate. That's the Strong double-standard in action."

Emma pulled a skewer from its gin and vodka bath. "Boink and poke. Clearly medical terms you've learned from your gynecologist husband." She bit the olive with a grin.

"Clearly," said Lizzie. "You know, people wonder if a gynecologist loses the mystery aspect of lovemaking because of what he does all day."

"Yeah," said Emma. "That's a good point. And, mmm, this *is* good."

Lizzie removed the last olive by grabbing it with her teeth and pulling away the pick.

"Well, the mystery is still there, even at the end of the day. My Dave is as randy as any other young male." She chewed. "He says he can be compared to a race car enthusiast. When the hood is up, the engine is the concern, like sparkplugs, battery, carburetor, etc. The parts need to be in good order so the car can function at top performance." She swallowed. "But when the racer is behind the wheel, the only thing he cares about is stepping on the gas and making it go, and he doesn't think about his previous work under the hood. The only thing that matters is the sweet adrenaline from the movement of the machine."

"Wow," said Emma. "Good analogy. You met him in medical school?"

"Right. Breaking off from Lars was probably the worst time in my life, but then I met Dave. Oh, I don't want to sound pompous, but he is one of the finest doctors around. And nice, too. I didn't think anyone could be as nice as Lars, but then I met Dave."

Emma drew a circle on her napkin with her finger. "Lars hasn't been all that nice to me."

"Nuh-uh! Lars? I can't imagine that."

"Well, imagine it."

Lizzie pushed the untouched drinks away.

"You're not going to drink them?"

"Nah. I never drink the martinis. I just like the marinated olives. Enough to get a tiny buzz, but not too much, see?"

"Okay. Want some of my olives? I like them, but there's a whole bunch on this other pick."

"Yeah, they know to uber-olive me and my friends here. Thanks." She took the pick. "You know…Lars…I can't understand him being uncool to you. Maybe it has something to do with that…uhm… secret thing that Strong and Lars do." She examined an olive. "You know about that, don't you?"

"Just that it's secret, and I'm not supposed to ask questions or talk about it."

"Yeah, what a pain. Strong comes back from his trips with bandages or a limp. Mom pulls him aside, wondering if he's okay. But he's always okay. He pussyfoots around but doesn't give her details."

Emma let out a long sigh. "I doubt I'm going to get much more from him, either." She waited until Lizzie looked square at her. "And since he doesn't want me to talk about it...I'm not going to."

Lizzie smiled. "Gotcha." An absent little smile formed. "So, what *do* you want to talk about?" Her eyebrows shot up in a double raise. "Family secrets?"

Emma took an olive from the loaded skewer, and not making eye contact with her new sister-in-law, said, "I thought you'd never get around to it!"

"Where do you want me to start?"

Emma's thoughts refused to shape themselves into words. "Uhm?"

"Let's see. You know what? You remind me of Becky, Joe's wife. She's a sweet person. A little shy, but perfect for Joe. Yep, opposites attract. Joe is like Strong in many ways, except maybe not as stubborn. It's why they couldn't work together."

"They worked together?"

"Strong, Daddy, and Joe shared a law practice. Daddy had an affair with one of the secretaries. When they found out about it, Joe and Strong threw him out of the building—bodily, into the parking lot. It was horrible."

"So then Strong and Joe kept the practice?"

"For a while, but Strong is difficult to work with. He's smart and sees what Daddy calls the big picture. He thinks about a problem, identifies the solution, and then doesn't understand why people won't accept his advice, which, by the way, is usually right. His calm, brusque manner gets to people."

"What happened? You know, when he worked with his brother."

"About a year later, he and Joe came to blows. Fistfight. I know, unbelievable, but true. Strong bought Joe out, kept Lars and the building. He and Joe haven't spoken since."

"I wish I could help Strong rekindle his family relationships. You say he's brusque?"

Lizzie fished out an olive from the pick Emma had relinquished. "He's been that way since...the time he got beat up."

"I know about that. The boy named Charles. After that, Strong wouldn't use the name anymore."

"Right. I was little, but it's a family history, you know what I mean?"

Emma didn't know but didn't want to stop Lizzie. "Uh huh."

"Well, when Strong couldn't practice piano because of his broken fingers—"

"Wait. He played piano?"

"He was so good the teacher told Mom he was a prodigy. But when he couldn't practice, he lost his love for the piano and never played again." Lizzie released another olive from the pick. "He still enjoys classical music."

Emma suppressed the developing smile. *Oh, yes, he does enjoy classical music.*

Lizzie nodded. "Vivaldi, right?"

Emma's smile went full-blown. She summoned her game face. "I wonder if he ever plays piano."

Lizzie shook her head. "He hasn't that I know of. I think he gave it up because when he got better from the injuries, he started working out. He said he'd never let someone hurt him again like that. And he would do what he could to keep others from getting bullied, too. I think that's part of his secret stuff."

"But, what about his father and brothers?"

"Oh. Yeah. Well, Strong was Mom's first, and she favored him. Mama's boy, you know? It's okay; we accept it. But when Dad cheated on Mom, Strong went nuts."

"Nuts? Strong negotiates—he mediates as a profession."

"Yeah. Go figure. He can't mediate for himself. And I pity anyone who Strong thinks is going to hurt him or someone he loves. I don't know what he said to Lars about me, but it was enough for Lars to back off. And you see how big and strong Lars is." She laughed and puffed up her cheeks, posing in a muscle-man stance. She said in a Russian accent, "Tough. Like Bull."

Any reservations Emma had about getting close to Lizzie were gone. Lizzie's imitation of the Russian bull gained her complete confidence. She'd made a friend, the first since Abbey left. Someone to talk to!

"You can't completely know someone even if you are with them for a long time."

"True. I don't know everything about David, and since he has that quiet Asian-type personality, it will take me longer. But I know enough."

"Thanks for saying that. It's true, and I'll try to remember that when I don't understand Strong. I'd like to meet more of the family."

"Well then, you should start with Becky. She's a lot of fun, and then maybe we can get Joe and Strong together." She rolled her eyes. "Oy! I'm such a Yenta."

"Yes, you are, and I'm glad of it. I'll help in any way I can. You'll introduce me to Becky?"

"You betcha. She'd love it."

In spite of Strong's demand not to bring his father into their lives, she had to know more. "How about your dad?"

"Strong would be pissed, but you're a free person. Sure. You should meet Becky *and* Daddy."

On the way home, Emma stopped on the side of the road. A skinny dog paced back and forth, terrified of the traffic whizzing by. She opened her car door and called to the pitiful dog. His face came to life, and he wagged his tail. "Come on, boy. In the car." The dog jumped over her and onto the passenger seat.

Strong was already home when she pulled into the driveway. He came out and stood by the Fiat.

Emma rolled down her window. "Remember when you said having a dog might be a good idea?"

He nodded.

"Well, I found him on the highway, dazed and confused. I think someone dropped him off. I named him Lucky."

"Lucky…like me," Strong said.

Emma left the car and clicked her tongue for Lucky to follow. She brought him into the kitchen, took a pound of hamburger out of the fridge, and gave it to him in small bits. He ate most of the pound.

Emma stroked the dog. "You need a bath, but I think you've had enough trauma for the day." She sighed and whispered, "I understand, Lucky."

The dog sniffed around the kitchen and settled on the rug in front of the sink. He fell asleep immediately.

Strong kneeled next to the black and white dog and petted him while Lucky's rib-cage rose and fell. "Nice dog." He rose and dusted his hands. "I've got work to do."

CHAPTER NINETEEN

On Monday, Emma took her unfinished work to the courthouse. The Mocha Amazon sat at her desk. Susie looked up as Emma approached her cubicle.

"How is Antwan?" Emma asked.

For the first time, Susie's look did not show the usual defiant glare or any expression with a "dare me" insinuation. Her shoulders sagged. "They think he'll live."

Emma bit her lip. "That's wonderful. I'm so sorry about his injuries. He's a nice guy."

Susie nodded and looked away. After a few moments' composure, she engaged Emma. "What can I do for you?"

Emma held out her file, thick with work. "I'm a little behind."

Susie's gaze moved from the file to the glittering rings. She grabbed Emma's hand. "What the hell?" The bug-eye was back.

"Strong and I were married last week."

Susie rocketed from her chair, knocking over her "beware" sign. It clattered to the floor. She whispered, "Emma," in panic mode. "Get away from him. I have money. I can help you. You have to get away."

Emma pulled her hand back and took two steps from Susie. "Get away?"

Susie held her finger mid-air and pointed to Emma. "I knew there was something dark about him. I've checked him out. He's a government assassin. Save yourself. Leave. Now!"

Emma back-stepped from Susie until she'd left the cubicles and ran to the elevator. The whine in her head blocked noises as she headed to her Fiat, parked where the rest of the peons left their cars. Robotically she inserted the key and drove, not remembering her payment to the parking attendant, the traffic, or her way back to the office. Her phone chimed, but she couldn't answer—she couldn't think. She'd retreated to the protective state she'd developed while living with Aunt Hester and Uncle Gene.

She sat in the parking lot of the Latito Development Corporation building until she could think, take control, and stopped hyperventilating. Smoothing her skirt and holding her head high, she entered the building. Joining the people at the bank of elevators, she wiped her face clear of expression. A quiet ride to the top floor completed her calm. The elevator doors slid open, revealing the modern décor.

She entered her office and realized she didn't want to be there any longer. She made her decision, gathered her things, and headed toward Mr. Latito's office, not stopping for his secretary to announce her. He barely had time to look up. She slapped the files on his desk and said, "I quit."

Before Mr. Latito could put words to his surprised expression, she turned heel and walked out.

Back in the protective state until she reached her car, she didn't regret the decision, but it hadn't provided her with relief; her stomach twisted, and her neck felt wooden. Guilt from not giving a reasonable time as notice assailed her. She reached for her phone to ask Strong to come home early because she needed his arms around her, his shielding atmosphere. The phone showed a message—from Strong. With trepidation, she summoned the recording.

"I have to go right now. Sorry. I love you."

For a moment, she thought her state of mind made his voice sound grim. She listened again. It wasn't her interpretation of hearing it through her unnerved filter. It was real. His tone.... Hard? Cold? Ruthless?

Seeing an opening in traffic, she pulled across the lanes into a parking lot and put her head on the steering wheel. "Strong isn't an assassin," she said, and repeated it harder.

The phone beeped with a text. It came from Lizzie. "Wn cn u meet me 4 dnr?"

Emma didn't use texting shorthand but admired Lizzie for her ability. She closed the message, sniffed, and spoke to the steering wheel. "Yes. I can meet for dinner. My schedule is open. I'm alone because my husband...," a wave of gloom took over, "is away on...business. Business?" *Don't do this.* She willed herself away from sliding into another spell of deep focus.

She replied to Lizzie's message, saying she was free because Strong was out of town. Within a minute, Lizzie's text suggested meeting that evening. Emma was glad for the invitation.

That evening at six, they met at a diner. Kate and Lizzie waited in a booth with another woman. Emma reached the table and paused, waiting for the introduction.

Lizzie smiled wide. "Emma, meet Becky Manning, Joe's wife."

Becky, red-haired and freckled, extended her hand. "I'm glad to meet you, Emma. I hope we can be friends." She cast her eyes to the table for a moment. "Maybe we can do something to make our husbands friends, too."

Perfect. Emma liked Becky. She slid into the booth next to Kate.

Kate took Becky's hand and then Emma's. She squeezed gently and sighed. "Thank you, girls. I didn't know if anything could bring us together as a family again, but now I have hope. Maybe the boys can be happy again."

A lump formed in Emma's throat. She barely remembered family contentment. The experience with the Ludwigs had been unpleasant, and she'd tried to forget those feelings. Was this her chance to be part of a loving group? She would do her best to make that a possibility. "Kate, thank you for having a wonderful son. He's made me so happy. I can't describe it."

"I'm glad, Emma. I know what you mean. I was happy like that." Kate didn't completely control her sadness but managed a small smile. Her voice became solemn. "Hold on to that feeling, honey, and don't let anything destroy what you have."

"What you're saying is hold on to my man *no matter what?*"

Kate looked down at her hands. "I'm a fine one to give advice."

"I appreciate your advice, Kate. I value it. But, how big a leap is it from *give* advice to *live* advice?"

"You're right. Maybe I should live my own advice. Thank you."

In a rare serious moment, Lizzie hugged her mother. "Oh, Mom. We're going to fix things. Will you be part of it?"

Lizzie's gaze sought Becky's, and then Emma's. Both women nodded at Kate.

Kate took the paper napkin from the table and wiped a tear.

They ordered and enjoyed their meal with insertions of small talk and Emma's announcement about resigning. The meeting, albeit low-keyed and studded with quiet thoughts, gave Emma the feeling of belonging.

After the meal, Emma returned home, glad to have Lucky waiting. Walking the dog was new to her. The crisp air put a spring in her step. Goblins and paper skeletons decorated the front doors of the neighborhood houses.

Lucky didn't need the leash. He didn't get more than a few feet from her, frequently turning his face to her and wagging his tail. "I know, Lucky. I know what you would say if you could talk." His eyes did speak. "I love you, too," she whispered.

She got ready for bed, dreading the return of the solo status. The worries she'd suppressed earlier overwhelmed her thoughts. *Where is he? What's he doing? Is he in harm's way? Is he...? No. Stop it.*

She kicked off the blanket and went into the kitchen. Chamomile would not work that night. She wished for something stronger. Padding to the bathroom, she rifled through the prescription bottles Abbey had left. "Ambien," she said, shaking the bottle to hear pills. She paused, then tossed it in the trash. "I can't start that."

A soft noise caught her attention. Stepping out of the bathroom to hear better, she recognized the twirp of her phone.

A text message! At ten o'clock. Who could it...? She ran to her purse and pulled the phone.

The message read, "Everything okay here. Don't worry. Will be a few more days. Love you. Strong."

She put the phone to her cheek. The message worked better than medicine. Giving Lucky an extra ear-noogie, she went to bed and fell asleep.

The next morning, having quit her job and with no plans for the day, she called the local veterinarian and asked to bring Lucky in for an exam. Because the office had a cancellation, she took him right in. He had no owner's chip, and other than being skinny, he was okay. On the way home, she promised Lucky to remedy that situation.

Life was good—she had a husband and her first family addition, if only a dog, to spoil. If she could do something to help Lizzie repair relationships, life could be even better.

Emma busied herself with storing Strong's clothes and items he'd brought from his house. She looked up recipes on food websites, excited to be a housewife. Two days later, Lizzie phoned asking to meet for dinner, saying Dave was on call. Emma was grateful because Strong had not yet returned, and she didn't like eating alone.

"I've asked Daddy to come. You wanted to meet him?" Lizzie said.

"Oh, yes. Great."

The restaurant specialized in St. Louis style ribs. The smell reached the parking lot, starting Emma's hunger before she entered. Inside, Lizzie, and martinis crowded with olives, waited. Within a few minutes, Lizzie pointed to a man entering the place.

"There's my dad," she said, and popped an olive into her mouth.

The man looked like an older version of Strong, hair a little thinner and grayer, and he wore it longer, at the edge of needing a haircut. His suit, a bit loose, was worn in spots.

Lizzie waved, and the man nodded.

He came to the table. "Hello, dear daughter. And who is this lovely thing with you?" His words were slurred, and he spoke with a slight Irish accent.

"Emma, this is my dad, Charles Rockford Manning, Rocky." She thumbed Emma. "Daddy, meet Emma, Strong's wife."

Rocky hailed a passing waiter and asked for a glass of single malt. "What's that you say?" It had taken a moment for the idea to gel. "Strong's *wife*?" He spoke to Emma. "You are married to me boy?"

Lizzie put her hand to the side of her mouth. "His Irish comes out when he's excited or drinking. Both, tonight, it seems."

"Well, Mrs. Manning, I am astonished to meet you." He seized Lizzie's martini and took a gulp. He downed the rest of the drink, saving the lone olive. "Man-O-Jesus! Strong's found him a woman. And a fine one, y'are, too." He took the second drink sitting in front of Lizzie. "I hope ya can weather that storm, young woman. Got your work cut out for ya."

"She's doing fine, Dad."

He engaged Emma with his gray-blue eyes. "My boys won't share breathin' air with me." He held Lizzie's drink and toasted to Emma. "It's nice to meet you."

Lizzie took back the empty martini with the single olive. "Dad, Perry is okay with you."

"Perry? He endures me." Rocky took a long sip from another martini and exhaled. He regarded the glass at eye level. "And me lovely Katie, gone from me arms."

"Oh, brother," Lizzie said. "Dad, are you working?"

"I'm doing a few things here and there—wills, trusts, nothing I can ruin."

Lizzie slipped an envelope into his hand.

"Thanks, darlin'. You're my good girl, the only one who still cares about me."

Lizzie smiled to Emma. "We'll see about that, Daddy. We're working on it."

"Tis true?"

"Think positive," Emma said.

Rocky's malt arrived. They all ordered the restaurant's special rib dinners. Emma kept quiet and observed her father-in-law. He appeared worn and sad, reminding her of Lucky when she first saw him by the roadside. Had Rocky been abandoned like an unwanted dog? Lizzie cared. Kate hurt from the man's absence. How much should she interfere? Emma had no experience with family matters. She trusted Lizzie and would take her cues from her new sister.

When they were done, Lizzie had the waiter bring a "to-go" meal and gave the bag to Rocky. He kissed their hands and departed.

"Well," Lizzie said, "you've met my dad."

Emma didn't know if she should make comments. She settled on, "Yes. I have."

Lizzie laughed. "Uh huh. You're going to be just fine!" She twitched her lip. "As long as Strong doesn't piss you off so much that you—"

Emma put her hand over Lizzie's. "I can't think of anything that would affect our relationship." Susie's face flashed into her mind. She gritted her teeth and banished it. "I love him."

"Strong is lucky," Lizzie said, stabbing at the last olive in the remaining martini.

Emma chuckled to herself. Lizzie had just compared her brother to his dog.

Lizzie handed Emma a card. "This is my brother Joe's number. I'll leave it to you to decide what to do."

Lizzie paid the dinner bill, and they both left the restaurant.

The next day Emma called Joe at the office number. "Joseph Manning?"

"Yes, who's calling?"

"I am Emma Manning, Strong's wife."

The phone echoed with a long silence.

"Last week, I met Becky. I enjoyed our meal."

"I heard about it," Joe said. "Becky says you're nice."

"She's great. I'm so glad I got to meet her. I'd like to meet you, too. Would you be willing to come to dinner at our house? Strong is out of town right now, but if he is okay with it, would you be, too?"

"I don't know. There's a lot of water under that bridge. I would have to think about it."

"That's fair," Emma said.

Joe gave a short, derisive laugh. "You think Strong will be delighted over this idea?"

"I think Strong is an intelligent and good man. If it's the right thing to do, he'll want it."

"Hmm. I haven't got a comeback for that. I'll consider it. It was, uhm, interesting talking with you."

CHAPTER TWENTY

Lucky barked, taking his role as watchdog seriously. Emma checked the peephole just as Lars knocked a second time on the door.

"Quiet, Lucky. Stop. Sit." She'd been working with the dog during the time she had been home. He sat, and she opened the door. "Hello, Lars. What can I do for you?"

He put his hand on his heart. "Ask not what my country can do for you; ask what you can do for your country." He bowed his head to exaggerate his speech. "Nice dog. Strong asked me to look in on you. Everything okay?"

"Yes. I miss him. I wish I knew where he was and what he's doing." She didn't think she should mention his text. "But, I'm okay. Thanks."

"My pleasure."

"How come you didn't go with Strong?"

"It's not a rescue mission. I can tell you that. He's in Peru doing mediation — only partly secret. He's the best at it, and when he's done, each side will think they won. And you know what's ironic? He gets paid twenty times more for negotiating than we do for a mission. Go figure. He rarely gets shot at or has to pee on a tree when he mediates."

Emma smiled in pride. "He's really that good, eh?"

"He got you, didn't he?"

"It wasn't like that, Lars. It is more like I got him."

"*That* is his great skill. He made you feel like you caught him."

"But, Lars, you don't know. It wasn't like that at all."

"Whatever you want to think, Emmakins. Would you like to go to Catalano's for lunch?"

"I would!"

At the restaurant, after a few rounds of small talk, she suspended her promise not to talk about Strong's secret work. She asked Lars about their missions. Lars stepped carefully but answered a few questions with vague answers.

"What is Jo Lynn like?"

Lars thought for a moment. "She's a chameleon. All of us assume roles, but she...she doesn't reveal her true colors."

"Is Strong a chameleon?"

"Not really. Strong's talent is for blending, becoming transparent. You wouldn't notice him at an airport. Strong blends. Jolly is a shapeshifter."

"From what I've seen, I think you can be a chameleon by your voice, your accent, and your dress. How about Aphrodite?"

"Now there's a mystery. She never changes, yet she is always what she needs to be. In the years I've worked with her, slept, ate, dressed, bathed...I know very little. She keeps it that way."

"You've slept and bathed together? That's rather intimate."

"It sounds that way; however, one does not get intimate with Aphrodite. She's barely over five feet, but she's stronger than any woman I know. Stronger than some men. I wouldn't want to fist-fight her. She might win. Look, I know what you are pussyfooting around for. You need to ask Strong. Put it to him straight, and don't let him lawyer out of the questions."

"Am I that easy to read, Lars?"

"Easy? No. Predictable? Yes. Any wife would want to know about her husband's work."

"I want to know, but I can't ask Strong too many questions. I told him I wouldn't."

"He understands your curiosity. He won't hold you to your promise. If you don't ask, you won't learn. Strong, as you must realize by now, is not one to volunteer information. And something else...." He sipped at a large glass of milk. "I'm his best friend. I've known him for years, and we've been in some close calls, but…he's still unpredictable."

Emma had to strain to keep from going into her deep thought at that comment.

Lars took another sip. "But I trust him with my life. I *have* trusted him. That won't change." His eyes bored into hers. "And you can trust him, too."

That remark sent her right into the thought-coma she'd circumvented earlier. She barely noticed Lars excuse himself for the men's room.

"Emma?"

Lars was back, shaking her arm.

"Oh, sorry. I was thinking."

"I see that. Look, I took too long to say this, but I apologize for my behavior the other evening. I couldn't process the fact Strong had married you. I mean…that's an example of his unpredictability. I don't want you to think I'm not happy for him…and you. I just…well, damn! Strong—in love—married. It's the last thing I expected."

Emma toyed with the sprig of parsley left on her plate. "Do you know how the other team members feel about it?"

Lars looked away, staring out the window for a long moment. "About like I felt, initially. They'll get used to it. We trust Strong's judgment. If we can't accept his decisions, we won't work as a team." He picked up his glass and air-toasted it. "And we are a very, very good team."

Emma twirled the parsley. "So you and I are good?"

He nodded emphatically. "Very good." He smiled. "How's Lizzie?"

Emma laughed. "Crazy and wonderful."

He raised his eyebrows wistfully. "Yeah, that's Lizzie."

CHAPTER TWENTY-ONE

The only sounds Emma heard were the dog's toenails clicking on the kitchen floor tiles. When she looked up from the magazine, Strong stood there like a wraith. He moved behind the chair and held her shoulder. With his other hand, he grasped her hair and bent her head back.

Looking down, he said. "I am going to fuck you so hard."

"No way. I can't get up."

He crossed his arms and stepped back. "Why not?"

"Because now I'm sticking to the seat."

"Oh yeah?" He pulled her up and against the wall.

"Is this your favorite position?"

"They're all my favorite positions," he said before biting her neck.

She turned her head to accommodate him. "If someone saw you yank my head back or slam me against the wall, it would look like violence, like you're hurting me."

"But I'm not. Are you hurt?"

"No. It's amazing. How do you do that?"

"Control, baby." His nimble fingers slipped her blouse buttons apart. "Absolute control."

"Welcome home," she said.

Her clothes disappeared as if they had been mist. When she opened her eyes, he was naked, pushing at her.

Lifting her feet off the floor, he held her by one hand. The other caressed her body, eliciting moans and sighs when her mouth was free of his kisses.

It didn't take long before she needed him inside her. He took the cues and parted her legs with his knee. The wall made hollow thuds as they knocked against it in a rhythmic motion.

No scream that time for her, but a grinning moan, followed by his throaty groan. He let her down and, with his arm around her waist, took her to the couch.

"Did I say welcome home?" she gasped.

"I think so," he answered in a hoarse whisper. "It's the best welcome I've…," he took a breath, "ever had. Thanks."

She buried her head into his chest. "You're welcome," she mumbled. "*So* welcome." She giggled. "My pleasure."

"I noticed," he said, and kissed her hair.

They napped on the couch with Lucky on the rug beneath them.

Later that afternoon, as Emma, happier than she could remember, fixed dinner, Strong read the paper at the kitchen table. She didn't want to ruin the fine mood between them and debated if this was a good time to discuss what she and Lizzie had been up to. She started a conversation. "How did the negotiations go?"

He let the corner of the paper fold inward, showing half of his face. "Lars told you?"

"It wasn't secret, was it?"

"Not totally. I can tell you some things. An American construction firm is doing government business in Peru and ran into some legal problems. It took longer than it should have because the CEO is pretty stubborn."

"But you fixed the problems?"

"I did, and more time means more money for us. We got it settled." He let the corner down a few more inches, his eyes narrowing. "Anything interesting happen to you while I was gone?"

She couldn't believe how he read her so easily. She might as well tell him. "I met Becky Manning."

Strong snapped the paper corner up but didn't comment.

"And, I talked to Joe on the phone."

The paper fell a half page, showing his entire frowning face. "Joe Manning?"

She stepped closer to him. "Yes. I asked him if he would be interested in coming to dinner. Becky agreed it might be good to get you two together."

Strong took his time folding the paper, his facial expression showing his struggle to keep from blowing. He left the kitchen and went into his office.

CHAPTER TWENTY-TWO

Emma caught up with him in the bedroom and spun him to face her.

Strong hadn't seen that look on her face before—a mixture of defiance, understanding, and pleading. A burn started inside him. She shouldn't have interfered in his family troubles. "Don't meddle, Emma. Pestering Joe will make him as angry as it's doing to me. You could hamper or prevent any hopes of rebuilding a relationship. It will happen when it happens, and you could screw it up."

Things regarding his family resided in a stormy and unclear portion of his mind. He didn't want to deal with it. He'd worried that Lizzie and Emma would form a team, a tough and unyielding union able to attract support from other members of his family. He wasn't sure what he could do about it.

She looked up at him. "I'm not sorry. I want to help."

"Your help is detrimental. Don't make things worse."

"It's my intention to make things better. Your family is mine now, and I treasure being in it. I had no family after my parents died. I'd appreciate my folks under any circumstances. And you should, too. Don't shut people out."

He didn't have a proper response, but it called for one. "Damn that Lizzie."

"Shame on you. She loves you. And she loves—"

He held up his hand. "Enough. I don't want to argue with you."

"Then don't."

A new pride formed regarding his wife. He loved her quiet

dignity, her values, and other qualities he'd seen in her. This quality, this new backbone, could run counter to what he wanted, but it suited her. The annoyance kicked in. She and Lizzie needed to mind their own business.

As if she read his mind, she put her arms around his shoulders. "It's my business, too," she whispered.

He quashed his first impulse to pull away and leaned into her hug. "I need some time," he said, making his voice as gentle as he could. "Plus, I need to do some work."

"Okay," she said sweetly. "I'll call you when dinner is ready."

He nodded. He wished he had his gym equipment here. He could use twenty minutes with the punching bag. His next house would have a large room completely outfitted with the best equipment. His next house. With what he'd gotten from the acquittal bonus and the fee for the South American negotiations, they could buy a nice house. Maybe Emma would like to design one and have it built.

He sat on his swivel chair, the one he'd brought from his old place. "Look at me," he said aloud. "I'm thinking about a house with big rooms, a house to please my wife." He shook his head as if he had just been knocked out and had come to. "My wife." He rifled through his papers and chuckled. "My meddlesome wife," he said, then let annoyance join the emotional stew.

The long-healed scar showing through his short haircut itched. He didn't mind having it—it was the memory of how he got the wound that made him shudder. That had been a close call. One of the Black Rose's men had thrown a knife, and his split-second impulse to move saved his life as the blade grazed his head. The second man had thrown a knife at his thigh, penetrating the bone. Strong relived the pain. Aphrodite had taken both men down with perfectly aimed shots. A foot shorter than Strong, she'd managed to use her headband as a tourniquet and drag him through the woods to a hollow place under a log. Safe in the hole, she radioed for help. They had completed their mission but almost lost him.

He shuddered again, that time for Emma. Not regretting the

marriage—he loved her, and he'd never felt like that before with a woman. But that close call worried him. For her sake.

Dinner went quietly. Emma refused his clean up help, suggesting he go back to his office to work on his backlog. His legal job provided a cover more than a profession. The country needed his services, and he wouldn't let them down. If he counted on religion, he'd believe the woman working in the kitchen had been a heavenly gift. It didn't matter how he merited her. He had her and would give her everything he could. He hoped it would be a long life together.

They made gentle love when they went to bed, each professing their affection for each other.

CHAPTER TWENTY-THREE

In the morning, after Strong left, Emma called Joe. "Joe, I hope I didn't cause trouble when I asked you to meet with Strong. Please forgive me. When I talked to him about it, he said if I pestered you, it would make matters worse. Please! Can you put this aside and forget I interfered? The last thing I want is to mess things up."

"I am not pestered or annoyed. With Christmas coming, I think this is the right thing to do, Emma. Would Strong come to dinner at my house? We're putting up our decorations, and I think it would be good to have a holiday dinner."

"I can't ask him, Joe. He'd think I was interfering again."

After a short silence, Joe said, "I'll call him."

"Oh, Joe." She let out the breath she held. "Thank you."

"I'm pretty sure I should be thanking you."

"See if you still want to thank me after you call him, okay?"

He laughed. "I think my brother is lucky."

"Thanks." She noted that this was the second time someone compared Strong to his dog.

Chapter Twenty-Four

Evelyn came into the office. "You have a call. It's your brother."

Strong picked up the phone. "Perry, what can I do for you?"

"It's Joe. I spoke with Emma and—"

"Uh, I'm sorry about that." Strong kept his voice flat.

"No, no. She's right. It's been too long. Brother?"

Neither man spoke for a long pause.

Joe broke the silence. "Will you come to dinner next Saturday night? I'll ask Perry, Lizzie, and Mom. We'll make it a holiday dinner party."

Strong hesitated. "We'll come."

"Great. Do you need directions?"

"I remember how to get there. What time?"

"Seven. Strong? Thank you."

Usually quick with responses, Strong fumbled over his words. "Uh, uh…you're welcome. Thank you for asking us."

In the evening when Strong came home, Emma wasn't there. He worked at the computer, and when he heard Emma in the kitchen, he washed up in the bathroom and went into the kitchen.

She stood in front of the sink, washing lettuce. "I had to run to the store. Dinner is ready in a few minutes."

"Joe called me today."

She looked at the floor. "Are you angry?"

"No. I accepted a dinner invitation for Saturday."

She flung her arms around him. "That's so good!"

Holding onto her arms, he pushed her just far enough away to make serious visual contact. "Do you have some news for me?"

She engaged his stare. "I don't think so."

"You have nothing to tell me? Nothing new?"

"I can't think of anything." She looked puzzled. "Have I done something else to upset you?"

"You weren't going to tell me you're pregnant?"

Emma broke free from him and turned the water off in the sink. "I would love to tell you that. But it isn't true. I tested right before I went to the store."

"I know. I saw the test strip in the bathroom trash."

"Well, then you know it said negative."

"It indicated positive, Princess." He took her hand and led her into the bathroom. He showed her the strip now resting near the faucet.

"It was negative. What happened?"

"Maybe you didn't give it enough time to work."

She put her hand over her mouth. "Oh, Strong."

He pulled her hand from her face. "It's what you wanted. Right?"

"Yes. Oh, yes! You're okay with this?"

"Sure. Whatever you want. Things can come at a person fast."

"Too fast?"

"No, just the right speed, Princess."

"Strong, my dreams are coming true."

He put his arms around her. "I'm glad you feel that way. Life with me can be rocky."

Her eyes glazed over like she did from time to time, deep in thought.

"Earth to Emma," Strong said, that phrase being the one he used when she looked inward.

"Sorry. What?"

"Well, I thought this would be a good time to talk about houses. This one isn't ours, and the one I own won't do, so we need a new one."

"What about money?"

He laughed. "I need to get you involved in our banking. I'll be glad to turn those duties over to you. Sarah has been managing my funds."

"Sarah? She's been doing your finances?"

"She runs the office when I'm gone. I needed her to step in for me in money areas, too. I trust her implicitly. But, I hoped you'd be willing to take the responsibilities. I mean, you don't work now...."

"Okay. But back to my original question. What about money in regards to a house?"

"I believe you'll be pleasantly surprised. And you can have whatever you want. The only thing I insist on is a gym." He held up his arm and flexed his bicep. "I don't want to get all mushy."

She kissed his bicep. "Not possible. But, you want *me* to find a house?"

"Or have one designed. There's a certain architect who owes me fees."

She sniffed. "Some felon you got off the hook?"

"Whereas all of my potential clients claim to be innocent, I support the ones I believe *are* innocent. So, yes. I got him off the hook."

"Really? That's not usual, is it? For attorneys to be selective about their clients, I mean."

"I could be wrong, but I think it's usual for attorneys who had the shit beat out of them when they were young. I like underdogs. Innocent underdogs."

"Oh, honey. I'm so sorry you got hurt."

"Hey. It made a better man out of me."

"Did it? But it kept you from being a concert pianist."

"Lizzie. That woman!"

"Who loves you. Who loves the whole family. You are lucky to have her as your sister and your supporter."

"What?" he said, curious at her facial expression.

"Uhm, maybe we should change the dog's name."

"Because I'm so lucky?"

"Yes."

That half-smile formed on her face, the special one he loved, the one that made her more than beautiful—even if she smiled because she'd just compared him to their dog.

CHAPTER TWENTY-FIVE

Snow swirled about as Strong and Emma waited on the front step. Joe and Becky opened the door together.

"Welcome," Joe said. He extended his hand. "It's good to see you, brother." Strong, with only a slight hesitation, took it.

Becky kissed Emma's cheek and hugged Strong. Lizzie, Dave, Perry, and his wife, Christine, sat with Kate around the fireplace.

Becky brought a tray of fancy glasses. "Eggnog? The cherry tops are 'with.'"

"I'll have a 'without,'" Emma said, taking a glass from the left.

"Is the 'with' brandy or rum?" Strong asked.

"Brandy."

"I'll have at least one," he said.

The ring of the doorbell surprised them.

"Who could that be? Everyone's here," Joe said.

Lizzie looked at Emma. Becky rolled her lip as she sprung up. "Not exactly," she said and ran to the door.

When Rocky came into the room, the only noise was the background music of "Walking in a Winter Wonderland." He stopped where Lizzie sat.

Strong gave Emma the "You knew about this, didn't you?" face. She returned with the "Yes, and I'm not sorry," expression.

"Daughter," Rocky said, shaking his head. "You invited me here, but I see I'm not welcome. Shame on you for making us uncomfortable."

"Dad," Lizzie grabbed his arm.

He wrenched free from Lizzie's grasp. "Before I leave,

though...." He walked to where Kate sat. "I must take this opportunity to speak to you." He went down on both knees. "I am so sorry. I was a fool, an idiot, an imbecile. I didn't know that my whole family would be here, but I want you to know that since Lizzie asked me to come, I've not had a drop of liquor to show how much I want to change things. Will you at least hear me for a few minutes?"

Kate nodded and stood up.

"We can talk outside," Rocky said.

Joe stepped toward his father. "Dad, don't take Mom outside. It's cold. You can talk in the den."

Strong flew out of his seat to stand between Rocky and Kate. "He needs to leave. Right now."

Lizzie stood. Her husband grabbed her arm to keep her in place, but Lizzie pulled away from David's grip. She moved Strong aside, away from his mother and father. "They have a chance, Strong. Just because you can't forgive doesn't mean Mom has to live alone. She's miserable, and so is Dad."

Strong folded his arms stiffly over his chest. His face turned red.

In a gentler voice, Lizzie said, "Give Mom the opportunity to throw him out, okay?"

Emma regarded the expressions of the guests in the room. They all fixed their stare on Strong. She took her place next to him and pulled at his hand. He straightened his shoulders and returned to his seat, saying nothing.

Lizzie mouthed, "Thank you," to Emma.

"Strong," Emma whispered.

"Not now," he answered without moving his lips. His face muscles grew so tight he talked as if his jaw had been wired.

"Uhm, Emma? Christine?" Becky said, "Would you mind helping with the table? And you too, Lizzie?"

Emma knew full-well they needed no help in the dining room. The Joseph Manning's had a maid and a cook. "Of course," she said, and quickly exited, leaving the three Manning brothers alone in the living room with nothing but the sounds of the crackling fire.

While Rocky and Katie talked, Becky, Emma, and Lizzie stood in the dining room and pretended nothing important had transpired. The maid set the extra place at the table. The quiet in the rooms became electric when the door to the den opened. The two who emerged looked relieved.

Joe spoke. "Come to the table. We're waiting for you." He stepped between them, and taking each by the arm, he guided his parents into the dining room.

Rocky held the chair for Kate, and when she sat, he put his hands on her shoulders. "Family, your mother has graciously given me another chance. I know that won't set well with a few of you. But I promise I will never hurt her again. I won't touch spirits, and I will work to restore my good reputation in the profession."

"Mom!" Lizzie said.

"Are you sure?" Perry asked.

Kate looked up at Rocky. "I'm sure. I've been alone too long. We're going to try. We'll be crowded, but your father is moving into my apartment tomorrow."

"Strong, your house is empty," Emma said. "They could live there."

Strong rolled his eyes. He sighed and gave a look of painful, distrusting defeat. "Yes, I guess they could."

"Thank you, son," Rocky said. "I thank you all, and especially you girls who cooked this up. I've been miserable, and now I have my family around me."

Dave stood up and held his glass high. "Here's to changes. Family changes."

They all said, "Here, here!"

Strong rested his chin on his hand, captured by deep thoughts. He rubbed Emma's arm, straightened his back, and stood. He held his glass up. "Here's to diaper changes. That will be our family change."

It took a second to register.

"Emma!" Lizzie said. "Are you pregnant?"

Emma smiled. "Uh-huh."

Dave pointed to her. "Then get your pregnant ass into my office at eight o'clock sharp Monday morning."

The announcement broke the tension. The family members sitting at the table exchanged looks. Joe asked the maid to bring in the food.

CHAPTER TWENTY-SIX

"I'm so glad you got back with your brother and father."

Strong kept his eyes on the road, but in the darkness of the car, Emma could see his tight features. "Who said I got back with anyone?"

"That was the whole point of the dinner."

"Maybe for you, Lizzie, and Becky."

"What about Joe? And your mother? What is your problem? You've been pissy all night."

"What's my problem? Are you kidding? You had no business meddling in my family's affairs."

She barely contained the burn, an instant flicker that flamed into an inferno. Tight words pierced the air inside the car. "I thought they were *my* family now."

Even in the dim light of the dashboard, she could see the death grip he had on the steering wheel. "I have no control over what Lizzie does, but—"

Movement worthy of a superhero brought her hand to cover his mouth. "Don't finish that statement." After a pause, she removed her hand. "You don't have control over me. I'm naïve in certain areas, but I'm no puppet." Her voice trailed off. "Never again." She shuddered, feeling the revulsion from the resurging memory of her years slaving under the Ludwigs' domination.

Lightning could have crackled in the charged air between them. He stared ahead at the snowy road; she settled back into the seat. Her hand caressed the soft leather; the plush of the material reminded her of how good her life was and how much she loved Strong. The thoughts drove away the destructive memories.

She closed her eyes and thought about the life growing inside her. This time next year, she'd have her baby, the first step to what she'd always wanted—a family, close, loving, and supportive. Strong would come around. He'd have to.

"Strong, those people we just left are your family. You love them."

"Whatever."

"Strong!"

"Hey, things don't just change in an instant because three women cooked up a scheme."

"Cooked up a scheme? You agreed to have dinner there. Joe wanted you to come."

"But neither of us wanted Rocky there. That was pretty sneaky of you women. And now he'll be in my house."

"I…can't believe you. I just can't believe it." She put her arms around herself and hugged. Snow illuminated the streets as the car headed home.

"I'm in no way taking Rocky's side, but—"

"Rocky? You mean your father?"

"Yes. My father. The man who…. Shit…who didn't care who got hurt with his lust. Lizzie lied to get him there. Joe didn't know…our *father*…was coming."

"It's Becky's house, too. She can invite guests."

Strong took his eyes from the road and glared at her. "I don't want to discuss this. I'm done."

"After you've had your say, you are done. Very convenient. I'm not done with the subject. How do you think your mother feels about us inviting Rocky? What about his apology to her and everyone? Does that have some worth to you?"

"No. I think Mom will be sorry she's allowed that sonofabitch…." He glared at Emma. "Nope. I'm not going there. Let's just ride quietly." His mouth pressed into a hard, straight line.

"You want quiet? Sure. I can do that." She stared out the car window, pulling her self-hug closer. Tears welled up, but she wouldn't let them spill. Her internal wound, the years of being abused by Hester and Gene, had not completely healed. Strong had been her elixir, that which would lead her into loving light and happiness. Had their plan backfired? Did bringing family members together cause a rift between her and Strong? The kind of rift that love could disappear into?

In the dark silence of the car, she slipped into the unpleasant memories of her teen years. She heard Hester scream obscenities because rice had burned. She heard Joey's cries after each smack of Uncle Gene's belt because Joey hadn't cleaned the blades of the lawnmower to shiny satisfaction. She felt the sting of the whistling fly swatter —

"Emma!"

They were home. The car had stopped. She felt the heat from his face, a few inches from hers. She took a staccato breath.

He held her. "It's okay. Sorry I yelled at you. I don't know what gets into me."

She pushed her face into his shoulder. With barely audible words she said, "I love you."

"I know." He pulled strands of hair from her cheek. "I shouldn't have upset you." He got out of the car. Leaning into her side of the car, he gently helped her up and held her face in his hands. "You are the most important thing to me on earth."

"You're not mad?"

"Of course I am. But I love you above anything. I hope you can love me in spite of some of the things I do."

She wondered what he meant.

CHAPTER TWENTY-SEVEN

At breakfast on Monday, Strong said. "How about contacting some real estate agents? Tell them what you want. Narrow the choices, and I'll look at them with you."

They had been quiet for most of the weekend. The conversation felt good.

"Okay. I'll do that today."

He kissed her at the door and stepped onto the porch. He came back, took her into his arms, and kissed her hard. "You know how much I love you."

"You're not angry anymore?"

"Not really. You're right. We're going to be a family. It's important for kids to have good relations with their and aunts and uncles. And cousins. Plus, it's up to Mom if she wants to get back with...*him*...Dad."

Emma hugged him. Calling Rocky "Dad" represented a big step toward family accord.

"Oh, Strong. Thank you."

He kissed her again. "See you this evening."

She fired up the computer and found several real estate offices nearby. After the third call, an agent told her to come right over.

Within the hour, she'd found ten listings that looked promising. The agent told her he would set up appointments during the week. By the following Friday, she narrowed the choices to three. That Saturday, Emma and Strong looked at them together and decided on a large new house that sat on the brow of a hill overlooking a park. It had a finished walk-out basement, which could easily be converted into a gym. The huge three-car garage offered space for their cars and room for a workshop if Strong wanted one. He negotiated the price as a cash deal, and they could move in almost immediately.

With her world moving like a blur, Emma hardly knew where to begin. She asked Kate to help, and the two of them consulted decorators and contractors.

Kate thanked Emma constantly for including her and also for helping to bring Rocky back into the fold. Joe had allowed Rocky to do some work, providing a salary. Kate said the work helped restore Rocky's dignity. Kate proclaimed it a miracle that Rocky hadn't touched a drop of alcohol.

David Chu had become Emma's obstetrician. Outside of morning and sometimes afternoon sickness, the pregnancy caused no problems.

After they moved into the new house, Emma suggested Strong invite his team to dinner. He resisted at first, explaining that they didn't see each other socially, but Emma wanted to meet the people who often held her husband's life in their hands. He finally agreed. They set a date for an early dinner party.

The Saturday of the dinner, Emma stressed out, making sure everything was perfect. She fussed about the kitchen, checking on the food and regretted she hadn't bought good china. She had borrowed Kate's set.

Strong put his arms around her. "Need my help?"

"Do I look okay?"

He laughed. "Of course you do. What's the big deal?"

She had asked herself that same question earlier. She and Lars connected, but she worried about the women of the team, and after seeing Jo Lynn, even from afar, she felt a bit intimidated. "I can't wait to meet Jo Lynn."

He looked out the window. "You don't have to wait; she's here."

"Welcome," Emma said before Strong introduced her. "I have been looking forward to meeting you, Jo Lynn."

Jo Lynn's face didn't reveal a hint of emotion. "Hello." She extended her hand. "Aphrodite will be late."

Lars peered from behind Jo Lynn. "Hi, Emma."

"Wine?" Strong offered. He shook his finger at Emma. "None for her. She's pregnant."

"You're expecting?" Jo Lynn's unflinching expression matched her question.

Emma flushed and nodded. She thought Strong had told them.

"I prefer milk," Lars said.

Two wines and two milk glasses clinked together as a toast to the good news.

Lars chugged half of his glass. He wiped the white mustache and sniffed. "Whatever you're cooking smells good."

"Beef Burgundy. It has another hour or so. I hope you're not too hungry," Emma said.

Jo Lynn took hold of Strong's forearm. "Since we have some time, let me show you what I brought. Can we set up in the garage?"

Strong's eyebrows came together. "Shouldn't we wait for Aphrodite?"

Jo Lynn crossed her arms in front. "Her loss for being late. Shall I set up the demo now?"

"Okay," Strong said. "I'll move the Caddy."

Lars downed the rest of his milk as Strong and Jo Lynn headed for the garage. As he put his glass in the sink, Emma grabbed the counter for support. She wavered and hung on.

Lars's hand shot out to catch her. "What's wrong?"

"I'm sick." She pointed to the hallway and managed to say, "I need—"

Emma leaned against Lars and became limp.

He picked her up. "I'm putting you in bed."

Emma nodded against his shoulder and threw up. Lars padded down the hall to a guestroom and placed her gently on the bed. "Do you have something to take?"

She spoke between spasms, dry heaves. "In the kitchen medicine cabinet. Above the stove. Brown bottle. Ten drops in some water."

Lars threw her a towel and ran into the kitchen. In a few minutes, he helped her sip the medicine.

"Thanks," she said weakly. She saw the mush on his jacket. "Oh, God, Lars. I'm sorry. I'm so sorry."

Lars spotted the mess on his black jacket. He dabbed at it with the towel.

"We'll get you a new jacket."

"Don't worry about it. I've ralphed on a few people myself. Are you okay?"

"I think so. It happens so fast, I never know when I'm going to puke."

Strong came into the bedroom. "What's up?"

Lars brushed at his jacket. "She heaved."

"Oh," Strong said.

Emma backed up against the pillows. "I can't finish cooking. It's the smell, it...."

Strong shrugged. "We'll go out for something,"

Lars stood up. "Jolly and I will get take out. You stay here with your wife."

Strong sat on the bed. "Are you okay?"

She fluffed the pillow behind her. "I am now. I'm so sorry."

"For what?"

"Getting sick."

"Not your fault."

She let out a sigh. "Did it ruin what Jo Lynn wanted to show you?"

He moved strands of hair stuck to her cheek. "It's not that important. Jolly can show us later."

"Jolly," Emma said. "Cute nickname. She's pretty."

"She's okay."

"Come on, Strong. She's a knockout."

"Okay. She's really pretty. But that's not why she's important."

"What does she do that's so important?"

"Everything. She's smart, quick, good with a knife—well, most weapons—and she can take care of herself in hand-to-hand."

"How about Aphrodite?"

"Our bomb specialist? She brings a lot of skills to our group. We can all do the same things, but each of us are extra good at certain things."

"What's special about you?"

"I have good taste in women."

"Women?"

"Uhm," he kissed her nose. "Woman." He got up from the bed and extended his hand. "Think you can get up?"

"I'm okay. What did you send them out for?"

"Pizza. Is that okay?"

She put her hand to her mouth and ran to the bathroom. "No."

CHAPTER TWENTY-EIGHT

A sonogram showed Emma she carried a boy. Keeping with the family tradition, they would name him Charles Whitstone, but call him Stoney.

When her labor pains started, David stayed the whole time with her in the hospital. The birth went without complications, and in two days, she returned home.

Strong didn't enjoy entertaining, but occasionally Joe, Perry, and their families visited. He had not yet warmed up to his father. Emma and everyone else let the matter cool, deciding that an old wound needed more time.

A few weeks after Stoney was born, Aphrodite visited with a baby gift.

"Cute kid," Aphrodite said.

"Want to hold him?"

Aphrodite's brows came together. "Can I?" Emma handed her the baby. "Kinda nice. Cuddly. I'm probably not going to have any of my own." She pushed her nose in the child's golden curls. "Smells good." Aphrodite looked at Emma with serious eyes. "I'm not gay."

The comment took Emma by surprise; she couldn't think of a good response, and Aphrodite waited for one.

"It doesn't matter."

Aphrodite nodded. "You're a nice person. I like you."

"Thank you. You're a nice person, too." She sighed. "Jo Lynn doesn't like me very much."

"Yep," Aphrodite said. "You took Strong away from her. She's still mad at him for it."

Emma's heart did a flip-flop. "They had…an affair?"

Aphrodite raised her brows and pursed her lips. "Don't know if you could call it that. Jolly likes to have control of things, including Strong, but you took that away. You're the best, and worst, thing that ever happened to him."

The comment felt like a slush of ice water in her face. The baby cried, giving Emma the distraction she needed. She took the baby back. As she jiggled him, she forced herself to ask the obvious question. "What do you mean?"

Aphrodite shrugged. "You gave Strong a heart. But now he's vulnerable. It's not good for a warrior to be vulnerable. He knew that and chose you anyway."

Her visit from Aphrodite provided her with information—some that pleased and some that worried her. She filed it away in her mind.

Emma threw herself into her new role as mother. She loved being a mom, as well as a wife. She hated when Strong had to leave, even the times he worked as a mediator. The five-hundred dollar an hour fee did not make up for his absence.

Emma saw Lars frequently, but rarely Aphrodite and Jo Lynn. Strong said Aphrodite liked Emma a lot. In fact, both he and Lars had been surprised with the warmth, something they hadn't seen from Aphrodite before. The absence of Strong's comment regarding how Jo Lynn felt confirmed what she already knew, but Emma let it be. She had a lot to think about, and worrying about a coworker wouldn't be one of the worries.

CHAPTER TWENTY-NINE

When Stoney was three months old, Strong invited Jo Lynn and Lars over to discuss a few new grown-up toys Spence had given them. Aphrodite was out of town. The two team members arrived within minutes of each other. Strong escorted Jo Lynn into the house as Lars struggled with boxes from her car trunk.

Jo Lynn put her purse on the kitchen table and stuck her head into the living room. "You redecorated, Strong. Real fancy. Things must be good for you in the land of crime."

Strong scratched his nose and chuckled. "Always. It's a reverse cliché—crime does pay."

Lars hefted the box onto the countertop. "Here you go, Jolly."

Strong peered into the box. "What have you got to show us?"

"Wondrous things," she said with an awed tone.

"How about lunch first?" Lars said.

"Yeah, let's do that, and then we'll play with the toys." Strong brought out multiple items from the refrigerator. He grabbed soft drink cans and a half-gallon of milk and set them next to the deli items. "We're on our own for a little while. Emma will bring the baby out when she's done feeding him."

"I can't wait," Jo Lynn said in a nasal twang. "As soon as we've eaten, we can set up the demo in the garage." She picked up two slices of bread. "You'll love what I've brought." She stabbed meat and cheese to go between the bread. "There's a position transmitter so small it fits in an earring back. They've ordered religious medals for you two containing transmitters. It is as if God Himself is listening."

Emma came in with the baby. "As if God is watching?" She

sang, "His eye is on the sparrow, I know He watches me."

Jo Lynn rolled her eyes. "Cute." She looked at Stoney. "Cute," she repeated.

Strong wiped crumbs from his hands, took the baby, and held him in front of her.

Jo Lynn regarded the child. "I have to admit, he's adorable." She brushed the baby's cheek with her finger. "I'm not so good with babies, but can I hold him?"

Emma picked up a paper with the diagram of the tracking device. "I wish I knew more about technology; this looks interesting. I would like to participate in your conversations, but unless you talk about diapers or breastfeeding, I'm afraid I'm not in your league."

Lars looked up. "Did I hear someone say breasts?"

Stoney began to cry, and Jo Lynn made a face. "Maybe he's hungry." She handed him to Emma.

"Can't be," said Emma. "I just nursed him."

Lars held his glass. "More milk!" He poured another glass. "Here's to breasts and milk," he toasted. "I wonder how much difference this is," he pointed to the half-gallon, "From what this is." He held the glass near Jo Lynn's breasts.

"Don't look at me," Jo Lynn said, pulling away and scowling at Lars. She sent a quick glance to Strong.

CHAPTER THIRTY

Emma caught Jo Lynn's eye movement at Strong and gave full attention to it. She didn't like what she saw, reading Jo Lynn's look as lust—familiar lust, like something went on between them. Her stomach did a flip flop. Strong spent time away from home with that woman. Emma tried to stop the thoughts that surged into her mind—the images—but they piled up, filling her head with misery. "Let your heart be your best council," her mother had said long ago. But her heart had just processed an unspoken but very real communication between a beautiful woman and Strong. Emma wanted to cry, or shout, or kick Jo Lynn in the shins. Most of all, she wanted Strong to come to her side and tell her everything was all right. Emma pulled from her thoughts when Jo Lynn spoke.

"Listen up," Jo Lynn said as she put her paper plate on the counter. "In addition to the transmitter, I have a scope with a laser target that I need to assemble in the garage. It simulates the new weaponry we're trying out for Spence. You'll want to see it. Strong, bring this box out to the garage and help me set up the demo."

Uninvited to the garage, Lars put his plate in the trash and his empty glass in the sink.

Emma came next to him. "Would you like to see how it tastes?"

"What?"

"Breast milk. You can taste it if you want."

Lars flinched. "From one of the bottles in the fridge, right?"

"No, straight from the cow."

"I couldn't; it wouldn't be cool."

"Nonsense," Emma said with a serious look. "I don't mind."

"But Strong, man, he wouldn't dig that at all."

Emma's eyes narrowed. "I've never asked Strong whether he slept with Jo Lynn on a mission since we've been married. I suspect they have because I know they posed as a couple for their cover. And you know what? She wouldn't think twice about my offer. Why should I? Think it over while I put Stoney to bed."

Lars was still in the kitchen when Emma returned.

"Okay," he said quietly.

She motioned with her hand. "Come with me."

Emma sat on the bed and pointed to a chair. Lars moved the chair next to the bed.

She exposed one breast. "It won't need much pressure." In a short time, Emma tapped his head. "That's enough." She put her hand on her chest. "Whoa, I'm embarrassed. It wasn't supposed to feel like that."

Lars pulled at his pants. "I know." He undid his belt. "I'm sorry, but this is killing me." He turned away and unzipped his pants.

"You better take care of that in the bathroom." She looked up as he opened the bathroom door and saw his erection. "Oh my God, Lars!" She started to laugh. "You're enormous. I'm glad Strong has a good sense of self, or he'd be intimidated!"

Lars spoke as he shut the door. "He's never seen me like this."

"Better keep it that way," she said louder so Lars could hear her. She buttoned her blouse.

Strong came into the bedroom. "What's going on? Where's Lars?"

"He's in the bathroom."

"What is he doing in there?"

The toilet flushed.

Emma passed Strong on her way to the kitchen. "I would guess he's using the facilities."

In the kitchen, Jo Lynn leaned against the counter with her arms crossed in a state of advanced annoyance. Strong followed

Emma and, within a minute, Lars came in as well.

Emma picked up the sandwich items and headed for the refrigerator.

"Uh-uh," Strong said, and stepped in front of her. "What was going on between you and Lars?"

Stepping around him, Emma put the food away and conspicuously unhurried, she sat at the table. "I'll make a deal with you. You tell me if you have been intimate with Jo Lynn on a mission since we've been married. Then I'll tell you what happened in the bedroom." She pointed to Lars. "And you are not to say a thing."

Lars tilted his head and smiled. "Whatever you say, Emma."

"I'm out of here right now," Jo Lynn hissed.

"Goodbye," Emma said maliciously sweet.

Lars walked to the kitchen door. "Yeah...I think I'm out of here, too."

Strong and Emma stared at each other in silence.

Pointing his finger, Strong said, "I don't like this. I need to know."

"You don't like it! I'm supposed to stay at home while you play couples with Miss Goldiecakes and like it? You want the information? You know the terms."

Strong's jaw twitched.

"Don't forget," she said in an unaffected voice, "that your parents will be here at five."

"Why are they coming?"

"They're babysitting Stoney tonight while we go to that new law firm's party."

He grumbled a soft acknowledgment.

Emma got up. "I need to do some work." In a more serious tone, she added, "You think it over."

CHAPTER THIRTY-ONE

It was quiet in the car on the way to the party—no CD, no radio, no conversation. After a few miles, when they stopped for a red light, Strong looked at her.

"All right. I'll tell you. One morning on a mission after you and I were married, I woke up, and Jo Lynn was straddling my morning erection. It happened so quickly I couldn't—well, didn't stop it. It was nothing important, just automatic."

Emma put her hand to her cheeks. "Oh, Strong," she exhaled and looked out the side window.

"Okay. Now, tell me about you and Lars."

She shuddered slightly. "Pull over. Please," she choked. "I let Lars taste my milk."

He hit the steering wheel. "That bastard."

"Wait a minute! It's all right for you to stick your dick into Jo Lynn, but Lars is a bastard for putting his lips against my breast? I don't think so."

"I'm going to pound him."

"No, you're not. It was my idea. And Jo Lynn is never setting foot in my house again."

He put the car in park and turned off the engine. The mediator voice took control. "Emma, we need to get over this. I have to work with those people, and you have to get along with them."

She shot him an angry glance.

"Look, let's pretend we didn't tell each other. When they are around, we'll act normal, and they won't be uncomfortable. It's the best way." He waited. "Emma?" He touched her hand again, more firmly. His next "Emma," became an order.

"You won't screw her again?"

"Don't say it like that. Look, she's saved my life twice. Our relationship is...complex."

"You won't screw her again," Emma demanded. She wiped her eyes with the back of her hand. "I don't feel like going to a party. I want to go home."

"Yeah, I don't feel like partying, either. Ems? We need a blank page."

"What's that mean?"

"It's what the team does to focus, clearing, kind of a *tabula rasa*. We'll blank-page it, and it never happened. Okay?"

"Okay," Emma said softly. But it had happened, and she wasn't experienced in putting things out of her memory. The pain of his admission and the fact he hadn't promised to not do it again lingered, hotly lodged in her mind.

When they came in the side door, Kate and Rocky were in the kitchen with Stoney.

Rocky did a double-take at them. "What happened?"

Emma looked at Strong and bit her lip. "We had a disagreement. You don't have to stay tonight. We're home."

Kate shifted Stoney a bit. "I want to stay and take care of him. Please."

Emma put her purse on the counter. "I think I'll lie down for a little while."

As Strong headed toward the study, his father grabbed him by the arm. "I know you still can't abide me, and you haven't asked my advice, but son, whatever the problem is, go fix it. Don't let any problems interfere with your relationship. Nip it in the bud."

Strong shrugged off Rocky's grasp and closed the door to his study. After an hour, he went into the darkened bedroom. "Emma, I know from your breathing you're not asleep. I need to talk with you." He stripped to his shorts and got into bed. He moved next to her and tried to pull her close.

"Don't," she said.

"Then let me put my arm around you."

"No, don't."

He put his arm around her. "Emma, I made my father miserable for several years because of his dalliance. You had the perfect opportunity to let him know I did the same thing. You had a powerful weapon, and you didn't use it. I know you love me, and I thank you for that."

She didn't respond.

He kissed her ear gently. "I love you. Only you, Princess. And you continue to show me how lucky I am to have you."

"You won't screw her again?"

"Never."

"All right. Let me sleep. I haven't had a full night's sleep since Stoney was born."

Strong kissed her shoulder. "Goodnight, my princess." He waited. "You could say goodnight, my chieftain."

"Good night, Strong."

He waited, holding his breath.

"My chieftain."

Chapter Thirty-Two

Emma thrived with motherhood, and Strong doted on his eighteen-month-old son. One afternoon while Strong did push-ups with Stoney on his back, Emma opened an invitation that arrived by mail. Normally Strong didn't enjoy social engagements, but he explained this one was different because Deputy Secretary Roland Spencer would be there, and it was time Emma met him.

"So, he said you had to go, right?"

Strong stared at her for a long second. "You know too much about me."

She returned his stare. "Not enough. I think you still have a few secrets."

"Maybe." He broke the stare and smiled, his way of trying to change the subject. "Are you wearing the red dress you bought on your shopping trip with Lizzie?"

"That was supposed to be *my* secret."

"Ah, Princess! As if you could keep anything from me. Can't happen."

"Maybe," she said, flinging his word back to him.

That evening, cold raged outside, but inside the country club, the fire blazed. Jo Lynn and her escort were the first guests they saw.

"Hey, Jolly," Strong said as he guided Emma toward the fireplace.

"Hi, meet Ralph. Emma and Strong," Jo Lynn pointed for her date's enlightenment. Jo Lynn did not take her eyes off Emma's cleavage as she spoke. "Nice dress, Emma."

"I like yours, too," Emma said, not breaking her smile.

Strong nudged Emma out of the room. Lars, handsome in his tux, stood arm-looped through the waist of a blonde whose resemblance to Marilyn Monroe was obviously planned, right down to the tiny cheek mole. Strong stopped in front of them. Lars's grasp upon his date slipped as he did a double take. "Emma! My God! You…. Whoa, that dress. Whoa! Uh, Strong and Emma Manning, please meet Charlemayne King."

Emma extended her hand. "Great name, like the ruler Carlos Magnus?"

"No," the Marilyn clone said. "Like Charlemagne, the old king guy." She reached into her purse and took out a package. "Gum?" she offered.

"Oh, no," Emma said. "I might forget I was chewing and pop it while being introduced to someone important."

Charlemagne looked at the package in her hand. "Oh, yeah, that's true." She snapped it back into her bag.

Strong took Emma's hand to move. Lars mouthed the words "Thank you" as they passed.

Strong whispered, "Some strip club is minus their headliner tonight."

"Come on, Strong. She might be a Ph.D., you don't know."

"Yeah, right," Strong said. "Right." He stepped behind Emma and whispered for her to look at the people near the far wall. "You need to meet Roland Spencer."

Spencer saw them and came over.

"Spence, this is Emma."

The gray haired man looked her up and down. Although short of stature, Spencer stood as someone familiar with power, accustomed to giving orders. "Well, well. Mrs. Manning, what a pleasure to finally meet you."

Emma let him take her hand. "Am I supposed to know you, Mr. Spencer?"

Spence's lips curled at the edges. "Indeed not, dear lady. But I know you, and now that we have talked, many questions are easily answered."

Emma didn't move but stayed casual and said nothing, her

face blank.

"Ah," Spence continued. "Perfect." He nodded to Strong and swirled his drink, thinking. He nodded again and left.

Strong put his arm around Emma. "Beautiful and smart." He kissed her bare shoulder.

"But I didn't say or do anything."

"That's exactly the point. I knew you'd pass with flying colors."

"Pass what?"

"We'll talk later. Spence is the high government honcho. You know, my part-time job?"

"I thought you were in charge."

"I am. But Spence is the Man, meaning deputy secretary. He was impressed."

"Do you think he checked me out? You know, background and so forth?"

"Princess, he knows your first dentist visit and your grades in elementary school. And then there's the personal stuff."

A few hours into the party, Emma headed for the ladies' lounge. Lars caught up with her. "Emma, you look unbelievably gorgeous. Your hair...wow. Your dress...it isn't what you normally choose. Beautiful."

"Thanks, Lars. Lizzie picked it out. I must get to the bathroom right away."

"Are you okay?" he said, more alarmed than he should have been.

"I'm fine, but it's Stoney's feeding time. I need to use my, uhm...." She broke into a smile and shook her purse. "I can't use my device anymore. You know, my Lactation Accumulation Removal System, or LARS for short." She waited for his response.

He turned red. "God," he mumbled and stepped away. She laughed softly to herself and then felt a surge of guilt. At that moment, she realized how much she liked him—and Lizzie, her two best friends.

After she returned from the restroom, Strong suggested they leave, as attendance had begun to thin. Emma waved her fingers goodbye at Lars and Charlemagne. Jo Lynn stared without making a gesture.

While they waited for the valets to bring the Escalade, Emma shivered.

"Here." Strong unbuttoned his jacket.

"It's all right. It won't be long."

Strong wrapped the jacket around her arms. She huddled against his chest.

"I love you," he said, placing a kiss on the top of her head.

"Thank you," Emma said.

Before Strong put the car in gear, he looked directly at her. "Are we okay? You and me?"

Emma gave a nod. "We're okay."

When he stopped for a red light, he leaned toward her. He started to speak but checked it.

Emma stroked his cheek. "I know, honey. We must be careful. I wouldn't want to live without you."

Strong faced forward and tapped the gas pedal. He made a non-word sound, meaning "me, too," and swallowed hard. "I have to go on a mission. Tomorrow."

Chapter Thirty-Three

Strong stretched to turn off the lamp that hung from a hook on the tent's top brace. The tent flaps made a move not caused by the wind. He reached under the bedroll for his revolver.

"It's me," Jo Lynn said.

"Don't sneak up on me that way. What do you want?"

She slipped in next to him, ran her hand down his belly, and put her other hand on his groin. "Oh, oh, I found a live one! You don't want to waste a perfectly good hard-on, now do you? You get hard faster than any man I know."

Strong inched up until he sat against the canvas wall. He reached to turn on the lantern. "A blessing and a curse. What do you want, Jolly?"

Her fingers circled the lump under his fly. "I have my hand on your cock, what do you think I want? I'm tense. We had a rough time. Make me feel good."

A rough time didn't even scrape the surface. He understood her motivation but stopped her hand. "Jo Lynn."

"We need to turn out the light, though, to prevent shadows."

"No, thanks. Get some sleep."

"*What* is your problem?"

"I'm married for one. I'm not interested for two."

She twisted her hand from under his and pulled his zipper. Bulging underwear filled the gap. "Uh uh, this says you *are* interested. So how about a quick one?"

"No means no, even if it's the man refusing."

Jo Lynn sniffed. "I don't believe this."

Strong grabbed her wrist tighter than he had to and moved

it from his groin.

"Hey!" She protested. "That wasn't necessary."

He leaned toward her. "Obviously, it was. I'm not having sex with anyone but Emma."

"No one has to know."

"I'd know."

"You did once before." Jolly made a questioning face.

"That was a mistake. And it caused trouble."

"Trouble? How did she find out?"

"I told her."

"What an asshole. Are you crazy?"

"Maybe, but I'm in love, and I only want to be with her."

Jo Lynn moved away so fast she shook the tent. "She's made a pussy of you."

"No, she's made a husband of me."

"A husband. How quaint." Her face softened, her smile forming the way she did when working a mission. "Come on, big boy, a quickie, a meaningless screw? What's wrong with that?" She tossed her head and laughed.

Strong shook his head. "A meaningless screw? It means something if it hurts a relationship."

Jo Lynn crossed her arms in front of her. "Man with the steel heart. Where is all this love stuff coming from?"

He thumped his chest. "Steel to other people, but not Emma. And not my kid."

"Fine," she said, lingering at the tent flaps. "I'll see if Lars can get up for a quick fuck. He's bigger than you anyway."

"Mazel tov, Jolly. You and Lars have fun. We move at dark thirty."

The flaps blew from the zephyr that rattled the nearby branches. "Asshole," she muttered.

"Good night to you, too, Jolly."

She sneered and backed out of the tent.

Hadn't the team had enough grief? "Blank page," he muttered, shutting his eyes. After a few minutes, he reached for the switch but decided to pee. As he passed the tent Jolly and Ditey shared, he saw both of their shadows against the light. Lars's tent was dark; Jolly hadn't availed herself of his large services. The still night carried the low conversation from the women's tent.

"Give it up, Jolly. You can't have him."

"What are you talking about?"

"Strong. Off limits."

"You're crazy."

"Oh, no. I recognize the look. You snuck over to Strong, and he rejected you."

"Oh, really? You know the look, Miz Af-ro-dyke-ee?"

"Ooooooh, name-calling! I must have hit a nerve. You have it bad, Jolls."

The quiet pause meant Jolly had no quick come-back.

Aphrodite's voice turned serious. "Look, Jo Lynn. He's married and has a kid. He's not available and is not likely to be. You don't want him for your husband, but you don't want anyone else to have him because then he's not available for your needs. Gotta be a thorn in your side."

"That's none of your business."

"Whoa, now. It's the kid thing, isn't it? Oh, brother. You are jealous of Emma. She not only has what you want, she has his kid, too." Aphrodite softened her words. "Hey, that's not so outrageous. Most women think about having babies at some time or another. Even me. Yes. Oh, it would be in a doctor's office with a long needle, but it's something I consider. Occasionally."

"That's a laugh. You? Pregnant?"

Strong warred with himself over listening to their conversation. He was lead and needed to know if the team had contention, but did he need to know if the problem was him? Yes. He did need to know. This mission had been horrendous. They were already on edge, and any dissension could ruin their mojo. He stepped closer to the tent.

Aphrodite's voice, although soft, sounded clear in the night air. "You could do it, too. As a specimen, Manning is great. Smart, sturdy, healthy. Take your lust for a guy out of the picture, and you'll see lots of men have DNA worth using. Look at Lars.

Handsome, robust, and nice. Okay, you're not interested in Lars, or you haven't been that I've noticed. But get over Manning. He has a wife. Leave him alone. Hear me, Jolly?"

Strong stood immobile, listening for Jolly's reply. He heard nothing.

After a few moments, Aphrodite continued. "Poor Emma. She worries about Strong facing dangers on the missions. She doesn't know about the real danger, does she?

"Shut up, Ditey."

"I'll shut up when I think Strong is safe. From you. On your word."

"He's safe. On my word. Go to sleep."

"Good. Nitey-night."

Strong had heard enough. Was Aphrodite right? What did Jo Lynn want? Surely not a baby? He swallowed hard. Aphrodite had always been the voice of reason. But that was for missions. How about this problem? She'd stuck up for him. And Emma. His regard for Ditey went up a hundred notches. Where did Jolly sit on his list of admiration? She'd given her word, but that could change. He couldn't think about that now. Their mission, although appalling, had been successful, and now it was over. In the morning, they'd rendezvous with the chopper. If everything went right, this time tomorrow, he'd be home. He'd make sure things went right.

Finding a tree, he relieved himself and returned to his tent without making a sound. The nylon zipper quietly brought the tent flaps together. It took a few minutes longer to relax than usual. He would figure a way to solve this problem, like he had resolved all previous problems with the team. But this one…this problem had a different nature. It would work out. If it didn't….

CHAPTER THIRTY-FOUR

In the dark before dawn, they loaded their gear and waited for the chopper. Strong silently chanted, "Blank page, blank page." The thwak-thwak song of the far-off rotors readied him. After making sure everyone was aboard, and his mind cleared, he took his place next to Lars inside the lifting craft.

He leaned against the metal side of the helicopter and held the non-thinking state until they reached the base. From there, he and Lars hitched a ride to Fort Wood and then a private plane to St. Louis, arriving after midnight.

Strong tapped the digits into the front door lock. He entered the house and input the second series of numbers on the panel next to the door, deactivating the alarm. With light footsteps, he walked to the bedroom and placed his duffle next to the open door. Emma always left it open when she went to sleep so she could hear Stoney. She didn't fully trust the baby monitor.

A shaft of light from the hall outlined her contour as she lay asleep on the bed. Should he wake her? The need to touch her, to feel her warmth answered the question. Crawling under the sheets on his side of the bed, he spooned her and ran his hand over her nightgown. Flannel. He loved flannel. Much sexier than lace. Soft and clingy, the flannel beckoned tenderly, an invitation. He ran his hands over her covered breasts and nuzzled her ear.

"Mmm," Emma murmured sleepily, rolling over to face him. "What a nice surprise."

His hands caressed her breasts.

"Find something you like, big boy?"

"Here's something *you* might like," Strong said, pulling her hand down to his thickened groin.

"Indeed," she whispered as she fondled him.

In a flash, he pulled the nightgown up and over her head, bringing her arms with it. Wrapping the gown around her wrists, he pinioned her against the mattress and kicked her legs apart with his knee. Her quick breaths urged him on. He pressed his lips hard against hers and found his way between her legs. She groaned with the first thrust. They slammed hips over and over until she broke free from his kisses.

"You're too rough." Her voice became harsh. "Finish."

"But, you need —"

"Finish. I don't want mine."

"Emma...."

"Go on."

He thrust less vigorously and then groaned. He moved to lie on his side with his cheek against her shoulder. In the quiet, he pushed up and walked firm steps on the carpet to the bathroom.

Hot water. He needed to loosen his muscles, to relax and keep away the visions of the mission. "Blank page," he mumbled. Steam roiled within the glass shower, the pulse-head making needle points on his back.

Emma opened the door. Clouds of steam churned out. "Can I join you?" Her arm recoiled at the first encounter with the shower. "It's too hot. You'll scald yourself." She snaked her arm behind the stream, turned the control to the other side, and waited a few seconds before testing the water. Together, under a cascade of warmth, he gripped her tightly for a long embrace.

Strong turned off the shower. She grabbed a thick towel and dried his back. He faced against the tile and let her dry him. "Blank page," he whispered to himself.

Leaving the towel behind, she took him by the hand and led him back to bed.

"Bad mission?"

Words failed him. He nodded.

She pushed his head under her chin and kissed his forehead. "Honey." She ran her finger around his ear and whispered, "My precious lamb."

Precious lamb? That's what she said to Stoney when she had nursed him. Baby talk. Why not? Needing tenderness, he relaxed into her breasts.

"Can you tell me about it?"

Squelching the worst of the memories, words came in his cracked voice. "We lost men."

"Oh, no! Not Lars?"

"No. Not from my team. The Bearcats. Their leader, Brent Coleman, we called him Alley Oop. He just got married. Jesus… his wife. Shit."

"Tell me what happened?"

Strong sat up. Emma fluffed the pillows against the headboard, and they leaned back together.

He put his arm around her. "We were in Colombia, out in the jungle surrounding a compound. Thirty hostages. From Intel, we knew exactly where they were. We could see the building—a small one facing us. We found a clearing about twenty feet wide that led directly to the area. Alley Oop said he'd take his team through the clearing and be our cover. I didn't like it. I said it was too easy, that we needed to approach in a different direction. Oop said, 'didn't we need some easy now and then?' He motioned for his team to follow, and they traveled the edge. But it was a trap. The clearing was mined." He choked on his words. "They—all of them—blew up." Mentally he said, *Blank page.*

Emma pressed hard against his chest.

He swallowed twice. "That brought a few of the guards from the building out to check. My team circled, and the third team covered us."

"What happened?"

He wasn't going there. She didn't need details of slaughter and carnage. "The Tigers had the cover." That would have to do. "We moved into the building." Expelling a long breath, he stiffened. "The hostages were little kids. Those bastards raided a nursery school from the nearest town and used the kids to keep the locals under control. They held the kids in the counting room."

"What's that?"

"Where they kept the money. American dollars. Stacks and stacks of bills, some three feet high. And their counting machines. And those kids...dirty, hungry, crying."

"But you saved them, right?"

"Yes. We got them out." His tone lightened. "But not before Aphrodite had them stuff their pants with as much money as they could handle."

"Isn't that against the rules? Is she in trouble?"

"For us, it's against the rules—big trouble. But I never saw a rule that says someone else can't take it. And I didn't try to stop Ditey from helping those kids. Why not? Our orders were to torch the place before we left."

"You mean to burn all that money?"

"Yeah. It's just paper. It doesn't mean anything."

"But to those kids—"

"It would mean everything. And they deserved it after what they went through. Those kids...little ones, some not much older than Stoney."

Emma snuggled under his chin. "But they're safe. Because of you. Stoney is safe. And you are too, home, next to me."

"But not Oop. Tomorrow a chaplain and an officer will knock on Mrs. Coleman's door...."

Banishing the images, he leaped out of bed and strode heavily toward the baby's room. Emma joined him at the small bed.

"I thought about you and Stoney as we took that building," he whispered.

"It's only natural."

"But it shouldn't be. It has to be about focus. We shouldn't be thinking about our families. It leaves us vulnerable. That's why Oop wanted something easy. So he could get home, back to his wife." Strong took her by the shoulders. "It could have been me. Oop lost focus."

"But you didn't. You.... How did *you* know not to use the clearing?"

"Gut. The feeling…gut instinct. Oop didn't listen to his gut."

"And you did. You're not losing it, Strong." She tapped the hard muscles of his abdomen. "It's still there."

He sighed; his shoulders sagged. "I hope so. I can't let my family interfere with my job. But I can't let my work interfere with my family because it's also my job to keep you and Stoney safe."

"You will. Me, and Stoney…." She patted her own abdomen. Her mouth broke in a wide smile."And the new one."

CHAPTER THIRTY-FIVE

Strong's eyes flew open at the sound of Stoney's call. Glancing over to Emma next to him, he took a long look at her peaceful face. How had he been so lucky?

Emma stirred. She yawned, fluttered her eyes awake, and sat up.

"Hi," he said.

"Mmm. It's good to have you back home." She scooted to the edge of the bed. "I've got to take care of Stoney." Her hand shot out and grabbed the headboard for stability. Putting her other hand to her mouth, she garbled, "Ohhh."

Strong tensed. "What's wrong?"

"Bathroom," she demanded.

He held her over the toilet. Her body shuddered, accompanied by a heaving sound — no denying — morning sickness.

He gave her a towel. "I'll take care of Stoney."

"Thanks," she managed to mumble before dry-retching into the towel.

In his room, Stoney had pulled himself up and over the crib's bar. He dangled over the side.

"Oh no you don't, little buddy."

Stoney's eyes widened. "Daddy!" He let go of the bar to reach out.

Strong caught him before he fell and held the boy aloft with one hand. Stoney let out a cascade of rippling laughter and grinned as he came slowly down into his father's caress.

"Daddy!" He pulled back and shifted gears, looking at Strong, eye to eye. "Hungry."

"Yeah, okay. Let's get you changed. And we'll give Mom some ginger ale. She drank a lot of that for you."

With Stoney in his highchair picking Cheerios off the tray, Strong hurried into the bedroom with the ginger ale. The memories of the mission were behind him now. He had his family to take care of.

When Emma recovered, Strong brought Stoney into the bedroom and tossed him on the mattress for a quick bounce. The boy demanded another one-armed soar and got one.

Emma pulled the toddler into her arms. "I'm better. I know you need to go to the office."

"I can't leave until I know you're okay."

"I'm fine. I'll have a few pukes each day. You remember."

He did remember. Demands of his job warred with his desire to spend time with his family. How fast things had changed. Living a double life and having a wife and child had not tripled but quadrupled responsibilities and worries.

Emma tapped his shoulder. "Really. We can manage just fine. Go."

Guilt never stayed too long with Strong. In military style, he sorted the needs and how to meet them. Within twenty minutes, he slid into the plush leather seat of the Escalade.

Sarah's car was nosed at the parking lot's cement barrier. Good, he thought, she's already there and made coffee. The smell of the fresh brew led him directly to the small kitchen in the office. Sarah, her face barely clearing the counter behind her, beamed as he entered.

"Welcome back," she said. She grabbed his special cup, its place of honor next to the pot. It had "Manny" written in black script across the white wall. She poured the steaming richness into the cup. "By the way, Evelyn won't be in until eleven. Doctor's appointment."

"Thanks." He took a short sip and blew on the rim. "Ah, just what I needed."

Sarah moved her head in the direction of her office, making her shiny curls bounce. "Come with me, okay?"

Strong followed his cousin, noting she wore high-heeled shoes. Sarah always dressed professionally but usually wore low shoes. The heels accentuated her slight limp, but her height increased. He took a seat and pulled it next to her as she hopped up on the rolling chair.

"So," she said with one eyebrow cocked, "safely home from your...whatever it is that you can't tell anyone about."

He controlled his surprised flinch. "Hey."

She flicked her hand in the air. "Come on. I know you and Lars gad about on some secret mission-type stuff."

He pulled back against the chair and folded his arms. "I'm glad you realize it's a secret, and I can't tell you. But I trust you."

"Of course, and you should. But if you ever need any assistance...."

"I would definitely ask you. Now let's get down to business."

"Yeah...I have some personal business for you."

"You do?"

"Yep. Right before you left on your secrecy thingie, I met a man. Not a dwarf, a regular man. Okay, he's short, but taller than me, see—"

"Why are you telling me this?"

"Shut up and listen. Okay, this man's name is Leon Circle. He's a really nice guy." She raised her palm to stop his question. "I'm getting there. Don't hurry me. So, he's really good in bed, and...."

No! Sarah in bed with a man! He didn't want to hear this. Why not? Other than being a dwarf, she was a normal woman, besides being the smartest person he'd ever known. Why shouldn't she have a lover? He tuned back into her words.

"I'm in love, Strong. Leon wants to get married. He's Jewish but not practicing, and I don't care anyway. You know I don't have a preference in my route to the Higher Power."

He understood that perfectly. He'd been raised Catholic but hadn't been to mass in years. Occasionally Emma went to the nearby Methodist church, but he didn't attend. Sarah and he hadn't spoken about it, but he knew they were on the same page regarding religion.

"So, anyway, Strong, I'd like you to meet him, and—"

"What have I got to do with it, Sarah?"

"Okay. Bottom line. I'm pushing thirty, my biological clock ticks faster than other gals. I'd want a kid right away. Putting political correctness aside, I want my kid to have a better chance to be normal, not a dwarf. "

Strong ran his fingers through his close-cropped hair. "Jesus, Sarah."

"I want your take on him. Will you meet us for lunch?"

"Today?"

"Leon said as soon as you got back here, he wanted to meet you. He's available at your convenience."

"You want me to vet him?"

"Yeah. Not like Lars does. You know...gut reaction." She gave him a look that said she knew he made a lot of gut decisions during his secret work.

His jaw stiffened. "All right." What else could he say? Sarah had saved his business for him when he took missions or foreign mediations.

"Good. Now we can get down to law business."

From a wide drawer, she brought out a stack of files. Organized to the max, she had them alphabetized. She pulled one from the middle and tapped it. "I was ready to hand this one over to Joe. The counsel demands you sit second chair. You weren't here, and I can't do it."

Strong pulled his chin. "Joe? He hates appearing in court worse than I do."

"I know." Sarah cast her eyes to the wall quickly and back, engaging Strong's gaze. "You know who's as good—well, almost as good as you, and who *does* like the courtroom hubbub? And has sparkly eyes and a delightful if not laid-on Irish accent?"

Strong stood up like a wooden nutcracker, stiff and staring. "Don't even think about it!"

"I have thought about it, Cuzzie, and if you continue to be away for weeks at a time, I can't cover for you in court. Oh, I could lay out facts that would shake a jury into reasonable doubt like Tinkerbell shakes fairy dust, but we both know any jury would be so focused on my size and my Minnie Mouse voice they wouldn't hear me state those facts. Remember, in his day, Uncle Rocky had juries eating out of his hand. He needs to be employed, too. What do you say?"

"I say no. Look, I'm going back to my office. All of that stuff," he pointed to the stack of files, "is on my computer, right? Let me study it until lunch. After our little date, I'll have a list of questions."

"Chicken-shit," Sara said, smiling. "Okay. Lunch at twelve. Ralph's?"

Strong closed his office door and read through the computer files until Evelyn knocked on his door. "Strong? Lizzie wants to talk to you. Can she come in?"

Strong went to the reception area and escorted Lizzie back to his desk. "What can I do for you, sis?"

"I need your gut reaction to something."

"You do?" Shit, he thought. Was his gut about to be stretched beyond capacity for feelings? He had had enough gut decisions on his mission. Now his cousin and his sister demanded his opinions, his gut services.

Lizzie leaned toward Strong. "You know I want to have a baby...."

He leaned back in his chair. Shit. Shit, shit, shit.

CHAPTER THIRTY-SIX

The bridesmaid dresses Sarah picked strained Emma's ability to keep quiet. Huge roses, dahlias, and giant, unrecognizable florals, red and pink on an ivory background, screamed curtains instead of evening gowns. Although Lizzie hadn't voiced a negative opinion against the choice, Emma suspected Lizzie held her tongue because she respected Sarah so highly and felt happy Sarah had found love. Sarah ordered extra material so the dressmaker could fashion a maternity outfit for Emma.

"Sarah looks like a bride doll I had when I was little," Emma whispered to maid-of-honor Lizzie.

"Yeah, she's adorable. And Leon can't take his eyes off her. Isn't that cute?"

Emma caught Strong staring at her from the audience as he stood for the bride's entrance. He winked. His new charcoal-hued suit softly reflected the lights from the hotel's wedding chapel. His wink turned into a smile. Sometimes he could be so handsome. Her heart did a little skip. They had been married four years, and he still thrilled her. As their shared stare continued, she ran through a list of feelings—thrill, love, gratitude, and a smidge of self-deprecation at being so excited in her physical reaction to this man, the one who loved her.

At the rabbi's prompting, Sarah's little voice squeaked a low "I do," and the music played. The audience headed for the reception while the bridal party stayed for photos.

For the reception, Sarah and Leon had spared no expense, and the champagne that literally flowed from a fountain came from France, bottles and bottles of it. Emma broke her no-alcohol-while-pregnant rule to sip one glass as a toast, and it was delicious.

Emma danced with Strong, her belly keeping them apart. She danced with Rocky, Lars, and David Chu, who seemed distant. He was a quiet man, and Emma couldn't read him. What did that matter? she asked herself; he was a good doctor, and Lizzie seemed happy with him. Lizzie would have been a lot happier if she could conceive. Emma chuckled to herself. What an irony — married to a fertility specialist, and Lizzie couldn't get pregnant. Sarah had decided she wanted a baby as soon as she and Leon set the wedding date. Although no announcement had been issued, the way Sarah went around smiling and the questions she'd been asking about pregnancy made Emma suspect there'd be a little one before they ate the top of the wedding cake on their first anniversary.

Emma's labor went without a hitch. They named the baby Katherine Elizabeth — after Kate and Lizzie, the women who made Emma feel like part of the family.

The morning she was to be discharged, Sarah, home from her honeymoon, visited. "Hi, kiddo."

"Hi, Sarah. I know it's a stupid question, but how was the honeymoon?"

"Fabulous. And look at you — a new mom again." She strained to peer over the plastic bassinette. "Really cute. And most babies aren't. But this one…looks like…."

"Kate," Emma said. "She has Kate's eyes. That's her name, Katherine Elizabeth."

"Nice sentiment. Can I ask you some questions?"

Emma smiled. "Sure. Can I guess?"

Sarah stared for a second. "You know, don't you?"

"I think so. But ask. I'm an expert now."

Sarah pulled a chair next to the bed. "I only take advice from experts. And I trust you completely."

A little wave of warmth spread through her. That was a real compliment. "Thanks," was all she could manage.

Sarah started with small questions — morning sickness — and

moved all the way to when the sex stopped. Emma answered as completely as she could, adding that some of the questions should be given to the gynecologist.

"David Chu is excellent, by the way," Emma said.

"As a doctor, I agree."

"What do you mean?"

Sarah let out a little breath. "He's a good doctor. I'm not sure he's a good man."

"Sarah!" Emma had never heard Sarah slam anyone. "I like him. Lizzie loves him."

"But does he love Lizzie?"

"I'm not going there," Emma said.

"Well, I'm not going there either, then, and I won't be using him for my doctor."

Emma ping-ponged Sarah's words, trying not to go deep into one of her thought comas.

Strong could be arrogant, but most of the time, he stated facts as they occurred to him. Relating his regard for Sarah, he'd once said, "I'm usually right, ninety percent of the time. But Sarah... when she makes a statement, you can take it to the bank. Her fail rate, I would bet, is less than one percent. Like Ivory Soap, ninety-nine and forty-four one hundred percent purely correct." High praise indeed, coming from Strong. So what did Sarah suspect about David? *Not now. Drop it.*

"Uhm, Sarah, I need to get ready because I'm being discharged, and Strong should be here shortly."

Sarah looked at her tiny fingers for a second. "About that... he's not coming. He asked me to get you."

What had been confusion bouncing in her brain became anger. "He's not coming! I don't believe it. I just had a baby and—"

Sarah's tone turned soothing. "He asked me to take his place because I already know he's into something secret, and I don't demand explanations. I take it you don't usually demand them either, which is why you are so perfect for him."

Emma let her head fall back on her pillow for a short spell.

Then she sat up. No good would come if she threw a fit. "I'll just be a minute. Then we have to wait for the nurse to bring in the wheelchair."

Sarah nodded. "Look, Strong has a really good reason not to pick you up himself. He's a fine person. Only a few people hold my high regard. You and Strong are on the short list. I'd do anything for either one of you, and Emma, if you ever need me, ask. For anything. You understand?"

"I understand," Emma said.

CHAPTER THIRTY-SEVEN

"Listen up," Roland Spencer said as the plane left the runway. "You're dealing with really bad characters on this mission. Be extra cautious and keep looking over your shoulder. We're liberating an item this time, not a person. I'm not sure what it is, only that it's contained in a black leather case. The Mings," he showed them several 8 x 10 color photos of an Asian man and woman, "are trying to get it. They've killed multiple times to get the thing, so it has to be important. It's up to you four to find that case. It's top priority; we think national security. You are going to Cameroon. Here...." He passed each one a packet. "After you've finished reading, you will be anthropologists, PhDs. Lars, you are Jonathan Brick; Jolly, you have become Remelie Scott; Aphrodite, you'll be Carman Diaz. Meet Serge Wooten." He pointed to Strong.

Spencer erected an easel and stuck a thick pad of giant paper on the ledge. "There are other teams from a Dutch university working in the jungle. Make friendly with them—good for your cover." He pushed packages with passports, wallets, and other identifiers toward them. "Here are your documents and your identity descriptions. You have ten hours to become experts."

Strong waved his hand. "Any idea what the thing is we're after?"

"Maybe health related. Very nasty."

Strong pulled at his chin. "Mings, eh?"

"Yeah," Spence said. "Every rock we turn over has a Ming slide out from under it."

The team read, slept, and read again. Experts, all.

A week later, the American team sat around the campfire at the Dutch scientists' camp. They shared dinner, and after eating, they passed a large bottle of wine. A joint made an appearance and did the circuit as well. As with the wine, Strong politely refused as it passed him by.

"When you find the proper size ape colony, what will you do?" Strong asked Dr. Ischian, the lead scientist.

"First, we'll pick a female and anesthetize her for blood samples. Then we'll tag her and try to get as many female samples as we can. We are doing pheromone studies and are hoping to develop a pill that will stimulate captive ape males to mate. The way the wild populations are waning, the only ones left in the world might well be the few we have in our zoos."

Aphrodite took the final large swig from the wine. "Absolutely!" She wiped her mouth with the back of her hand. "Pheromone levels are important. Take humans, for example. Say you have a young male who isn't thinking with his dick, goes about daily life happy and productive. Then he meets a female, ultra-oozing with pheromones. She can turn him around pronto. Next thing you know, he's Tarzan in bed, when it wasn't *his* hormones doing the work."

"Yeah," Strong said. "Happens to me all the time."

Jo Lynn sent a sharp elbow into Strong's rib. "You're an asshole," she whispered.

When the fire died to glowing embers, the Americans said goodnight and left for their own camp. In Strong's tent, he said to Aphrodite, "That was brilliant, you know, the stuff about pheromones and how the stronger partner can stimulate the weaker one."

"Aw, shucks." Aphrodite yawned and stretched. "I extrapolated on the information Spence gave us. Actually, I made it up."

"Wow, you made it up? It sounded right on. I was impressed. So were the Dutch. Good work." Strong unzipped his bedroll. "Time to go nighty-night. Sweet dreams."

Aphrodite stiffened.

Strong stopped zippering. "What is it?"

"How much do we know about the local apes?"

He thought for a second and shrugged. "Only the bit that Spence read to us on the plane. Uhm, I can remember that African apes don't have tails."

"Uh-huh." Aphrodite sucked her cheek. "The Dutch bought that shit I said about the ape pheromones. I was just pulling that out of my ass. We could fool regular people, but not experts. Dr. Ischian and friends never questioned our knowledge. They aren't anthropologists. I think they are what we are."

Strong ground his teeth as he glimpsed the truth of Aphrodite's gut feeling. "God, you might be right. Give me a minute. Kasmian Ischian said he would share research, but other than pheromone blood levels, he never quite said what the research was he would share. They hadn't found an ape colony because they *weren't looking* for one." He pointed to Jo Lynn. "We need more information. Dr. Ischian has been eye-banging you since we met. Use it to the best advantage."

Aphrodite patted Jo Lynn's shoulder. "It's what you do best, girl. In fact, you've been eye-banging him, too. He's your type...." She pulled her head back and stared at Jo Lynn. "Wait a minute! You've already...hmmm."

Jo Lynn folded her arms in front but didn't say anything.

"Good," Strong said. "Work on him, Jolly. Find out what they're up to."

She rolled her eyes. "My pleasure."

"Right," Strong said.

It wasn't first light that awakened them. Sharp cracks of weaponry punctuated the quiet of the morning, followed by a nerve-tingling pause. Strong and Lars grabbed their weapons like a well-rehearsed ballet. Strong motioned to Lars to follow. They crept low to the ground to a position where they peeked through cracks in the dense foliage. They could see the tents of the next camp in the shallow basin below. Four Asians rifled through the items strewn about. After a few minutes, the Asians left.

Jo Lynn and Aphrodite silently joined them, and they

headed out as a team. Double checking that none of the assassins remained, Strong jerked his head toward the ransacked camp. The Dutch team lay unmoving and bloody. Jo Lynn stepped over the gory bodies of the team until she stopped and stared at one of them. Dr. Ischian moaned.

"Kazzie." Jo Lynn squatted next to him. "Tell me what you came for. Really."

He opened his eyes, and the look of understanding crossed his face. "Remelie, find the case." A trickle of blood ran from the corner of his mouth.

"What's in the case?"

"Serum," he winced.

"Who are you?"

He took a breath. "I'm an anti-bioterrorist from Holland. The Mings are testing a terrible virus. The case holds the only known cure. The world will be held for ransom."

"Why didn't your country work with us?"

"We didn't know who to trust."

"How did you know about this?"

Ischian groaned, coughed, and choked on the blood oozing from his lips. Aphrodite took off her headband and wiped his mouth.

The man strained for breath. "We found out…because one of the…testing victims had a natural immunity and escaped." His eyes closed.

Jo Lynn held his head in her lap and stroked his cheek.

Ischian opened his eyes. "The guy found a group of real anthropologists…they took him back with them."

Strong squatted over the man. "Is it airborne?"

"Waterborne…very deadly…very fast." His voice became a whisper. "Get the case, Remelie. Ming Wanfu and Shawon are looking for it in the village. We just found out that the village doctor has it. Code word is Walloon."

Ischian's head went limp in Jo Lynn's arms. His blood-soaked shirt ceased its movement. Strong raised the man's weighty shoulders and pulled Jo Lynn upright. He shook his head, allowing a few seconds of sadness before clearing his emotions. They had to get to the village.

Getting the case from the doctor proved no problem, with him suspecting it was something dangerous and glad to be rid of it.

Strong contacted headquarters asking for a chopper. The team laid low in the jungle near the clearing where the chopper would land before sunset. Jo Lynn kept the case close to her body while the others circled her with guns drawn. By the time they heard the hum of the far-off helicopter, daylight had softened. They'd had no food or water that day.

Strong sensed they weren't alone and whistled the birdcall they used to convey the need for extra caution. When the copter approached, shouts from the surrounding bush preceded shots from the Ming Alliance, who had heard the chopper, too. All the team members took bullets when they made their break for the clearing and the descending craft. None of the hits prevented them from reaching the chopper as it made its touchdown in the clearing. A hail of bullets barraged the helicopter as it lifted, pinging on the metal sides.

They were flown to a hospital in Younde, where Strong lay on a cot awaiting his turn for the French doctor. Strong insisted Aphrodite's neck wound be treated first. Strong bled internally from a bullet that nicked his femoral artery; blood accumulated and coagulated in his groin. He had almost bled out by the time he received treatment. The army sent a medical C-130 to get him and deliver him to a special facility near Washington, D.C. The other team members were treated at a German base, and in two weeks, Jo Lynn, Aphrodite, and Lars were released. Strong recuperated slowly, and even though he had only seen his daughter Katherine on the day she had been born, he refused to go home until he was completely healed. The specialist in D.C. said he might be sterile from his injury.

CHAPTER THIRTY-EIGHT

Six weeks after Strong left, Emma got a call from Roland Spencer saying he was sorry he hadn't called her before. She shouldn't worry, her husband was safe but wouldn't be home for a while. He gave no details about when Strong would return or his state of health. After two months, she still had no word.

Because Sarah no longer signed checks, Emma came to the law office every week to discuss financial accounts. She noticed a payment to Lars.

"Evelyn? Can you explain this debit? I know Lars gets regular pay, but this one is for expenses."

"He's been doing work for Sarah. I don't know anything else."

Sarah had her office door closed while she conferred with a seamstress regarding maternity clothes. Emma waited for the dressmaker to leave.

Emma tapped at the open door. "Sarah?"

"Come in."

Emma sat on the chair, still warm from the dressmaker. "Lars is back?"

Sarah nodded. "He returned last week."

"Did he mention Strong? Maybe he knows something."

"I only spoke with him on the phone to give him instructions. He didn't say anything more than Strong hasn't returned. While we're talking about the office, do you mind if I hire Rocky for some court appearances?"

"I don't care. Strong won't like it, but he isn't here."

Emma left Sarah's office and called Lars from Strong's desk.

She demanded he meet with her. He chose Ralph's, the private room.

Emma waited in the room Strong used, eyeing the steaming plate of raviolis. She thought back to her introduction to the room and the tasty morsels. The memory produced a mixture of emotions, the most powerful one being worry.

Lars entered, limping.

"What happened to you?"

"Nothing to worry about."

"I assume you've checked this room for bugs, so tell me what is going on. Why are you home but not Strong? You've been avoiding me. And tell me why you are limping."

Lars sat and pulled a dish in front of him. "The room is safe." He spooned some sauce on a plate and stabbed a crispy appetizer. "I'm sorry. I have been avoiding you because I can't tell you where we were or what we did on our mission. Please don't ask. All I can say is I was injured and am recuperating."

"Strong? Was he injured?"

Lars looked away. He moved his gaze to his plate and then to her. "Yes. But I don't know the details. When I left…." He didn't say where he left from but paused. "Strong is alive. I'm not sure what he's doing, but he will call you —"

"I'm his wife, Lars. I don't like this evasive crap. I have a two-month-old child that he hasn't seen since she was born."

Lars sighed. "I know. It can't be very good for you. But take comfort in the small facts, okay? He's back in the United States, and he's alive."

She left Ralph's feeling more dread than she'd felt before. Kate had volunteered to watch the kids for the day, saying how much she enjoyed caring for them. Having a day off gave Emma an opportunity to speculate, and that made her worries increase. She returned home and allowed Kate to stay for the afternoon. The baby was sleeping, and Stoney played with Lucky in the back yard. Emma took a nap, something she rarely did.

A month later, she got a phone call from Strong, quick and to the point, saying to pick him up at the airport the next morning.

Emma waited with the children at the closest place the TSA would allow. She laser-eyed each passenger until she saw him. He looked fine, no worse for wear. He smiled and hugged her. Strong picked Stoney up, put the boy's arms around his neck, and carried him piggy-back style. Katy cried, not recognizing her father, but he added her to his load in a tight hug, and the four of them walked close all the way to the car. Emma drove. On the way home, Strong said very little about the mission that lasted so long. One thing he did say was that he wouldn't take any missions for at least another year and that he planned to buy a plane.

Emma thought the combination of the two statements sounded strange, but that was the Strong brand of conserved words. She didn't care about the details. She was glad to have him back and double-glad to know he wouldn't be in harm's way — at least for a year.

They clung to each other all night, enjoying quiet sex at first. They rested and repeated the love-making more actively in several positions. Neither one wanted to sleep; they made love for hours.

CHAPTER THIRTY-NINE

The next morning, Strong put down his coffee cup at breakfast. "I'm buying a newish Lear 70."

Emma stared across the table. "Just like that? Aren't those planes expensive?"

"Uh, huh. This is a steal at three million."

"That's rather out of the blue. Don't you want to do some research?"

Strong's face showed no change, but his eyes said he knew everything he needed to know.

Emma couldn't keep her face emotion-free. "Is that what you did while you were away? Look at planes? Take your time to decide what you want? I've kept our finances, and you never ask, so how do you know we have enough to cover the price?" Her pent-up worries pushed the boundaries. "I was here worrying about where you were, what had happened. You're home one day, and you've made arrangements to buy a plane!" Katie stopped nursing and cried. Lucky, sensing the tension, curled up under Emma's chair.

"Just because I don't ask doesn't mean I can't check the accounts, Emma. I know we can cover it and all the expenses attached. I'm sorry about being gone so long. There were some things…I had to get right before I could return. I used some of the time to think about planes."

"You could do research and use the computer, but you couldn't contact me?"

Strong left his seat and stood behind her. She ignored him and repositioned the baby.

He kissed her head. "Sorry, Princess. I'll be at the office." Squatting, he ran his finger over Katie's cheek, then reached over and ran his fingers through Stoney's hair. "I'm really glad to be back." He left.

Emma finished nursing Katie and lay down on the bed next to the baby. She sorted out her feelings and squelched the anger. Strong was home and appeared fit. For that, she said a prayer of thanks. For the time he had been gone, when she felt helpless and worried, she couldn't dismiss the anger. What had he been doing? Well, besides looking for airplanes. She called Stoney in for his nap and put Katie in her crib. Having one of those rare moments where both children slept could have provided her with a nap, but she was too keyed up.

Three days later, Strong took a flight to Tampa, Florida, where he picked up the Lear jet and flew it back to St. Louis. He rented a hangar at a small airport. The purchase of the plane did not sit well with Emma. She declined to join him on a quick family trip to try the plane out.

CHAPTER FORTY

Life settled down to a normal pace, and after having Strong home for a year, Emma relaxed without worry about him going on a mission and eased into a sense of security. But the security waned when Strong was called on an assignment. Uncharacteristically he sat with her on the bed an hour before leaving.

"I don't want you to worry. I'm being called to Colombia regarding a kidnapped American engineer, meaning hostage negotiation. It may take a few weeks."

"Just you?"

He nodded.

"Tell me the truth, Strong. Is it dangerous?"

He pursed his lips. "There's always an element of danger. But kidnapping has become almost routine. As long as the company is willing to pay the ransom, and if the kidnappers are experienced, meaning they're in it for the money and know what they're doing, it can be handled easily and quickly."

She hung her head and then looked at him. "That sounds like a lot of ifs." She took his hand. "Here's an 'if' for you. If you get hurt, I want you to come home and let me take care of you."

He eyed her for a quiet moment.

"Can you promise me that?"

He glanced away. After a few seconds, he looked at her. "All right. If I'm injured on this mission, which I don't think will happen, as soon as I can travel easily, I'll come home." He rose and packed his suitcase.

Had he just used his double-speak with her? She sorted

his words and reviewed the way he'd delivered them. "On this mission," meaning just this time. "As soon as I can travel easily," translated to what? She followed him out of the room and into the nursery where Katie lay staring at dangling angels and stars rotating to a chiming song, and Stoney slept. Emma stood in the doorway while Strong picked Katie up and played with her. He kissed Stoney's cheek.

He joined her in the doorway. "I love you. Sometimes I can't believe my life—having you and the kids. How did I get so lucky?"

Emma had been ready to argue his promise, but she couldn't. He was who he was, and she had to accept it. She pushed her face into his neck after the goodbye kiss.

Later that afternoon, Lars visited.

"Strong asked me to keep tabs on you."

"Really? Why?"

"He doesn't want you to get too upset. I'm supposed to keep you—"

"Mollified?"

Lars grinned, his flawless smile beaming. "Mollified. I'm not certain I can get you to change your name to Molly, but…."

"Have you always been this charming, Lars?"

"Charming? Me?"

"Why don't you have a significant other? You could have your choice of almost any woman."

Lars looked off into space. "The two women who meet my requirements are taken."

"Two? I know you cared for Lizzie, but who's the second?"

"The lovely wife of a good friend."

Emma let that confession pass. "You didn't like me very much at first, did you?"

"Not very much, no," Lars said. "When Strong told me about you, the only thing I could think about was what it would do to our team. Of all of us, Strong is the most detached. I couldn't fathom him being in love, much less getting married. I didn't understand."

"But you understand now?"

"Yes indeed."

Emma looked at Lars, half smiling, half questioning. "What made you understand?"

"Two things. The first was when we were in the parking lot at Catalano's that night he told me you two were married. He said having you made him value a future. For Strong, that was some statement."

"Whoa." Emma appreciated the importance. "And the second thing?"

"When you barfed on me. You were so vulnerable it made me realize how frail we all can be at times. Being the kind of person you are, I knew why Strong wanted to take care of you and how important our work is. You made me value a future, too."

"Pretty heady stuff, Lars. I don't know what to say."

"You know how I feel about you, Emma."

"I love you, too. Lars. You and Lizzie are my dearest friends."

"Thank you," he whispered. "You and Strong are my family."

Emma swallowed hard. These people, Lars, Lizzie, Katie, Rocky, and Sarah, had become her family. She embraced the feeling, the one she had wanted so very badly, the one she had been deprived of when her parents died and she had been sent to live with the Ludwigs. She'd lost her last connection to family when her brother Joey ran away from the abusive situation.

That night, after putting the kids to bed, memories she'd suppressed for years popped into her mind like the Whack-a-Mole game at an arcade she'd seen. She had mastered the art of whacking those moles. Memories like the wooden heads bursting through the holes of the game darted again into her mind. The loss of her parents; moving to the Ludwigs' home; Aunt Hester applying the stinging flyswatter; having to refuse dates in high school, including the prom; working for hours to afford her college expenses; and now, the worry of whether her husband would come home injured, or come home at all. She whacked each one as it presented and wrangled with the recollections until way into the morning.

When Katie cried the next morning, Emma had handled the past and allowed her life to fill her mind.

Two weeks later, Emma accepted a lunch invitation to meet with Lizzie.

Chapter Forty-One

When Emma arrived at the restaurant for lunch, Lizzie was pulling off the first olive from one of the sticks in the martini. "Daddy said he might stop by. This is his favorite restaurant."

"How are the olives here?"

Lizzie counted the short skewers soaking in the drink. "Fair. Their glasses aren't wide enough to get more than five olive spits. I'll have to manage."

"I've just weened Katie. I can have wine.

Lizzie took another olive. "Ah, what mothers sacrifice for their children!" She chewed. "I'll gladly give up my marinated olive habit when I have a baby."

"Of course. You'll make a wonderful mommy."

"Yeah," she swallowed. "I wonder when that will be. If I don't take pretty soon, I'm afraid my eggs will dry up."

"Silly! Your eggs will be fine."

Lizzie eyed the half-empty skewer she held. "Hmm. If the skewer holds four olives and two are gone, is the skewer half full or half empty?"

"Half full."

"That's you, Emma, thinking positively. Strong is so lucky. He gets to do what he wants, and you take care of everything. You know, you are one of the few housewives I know who doesn't bitch about not having a career or about having to give up doing interesting things because of the needs of the family."

"What do you mean?"

"Well, you do it all. No housekeeper, no nanny; you hardly ever go out to do something fun. I mean, how often have we been able to have time together lately? And you don't complain about it. You never whine about not being successful or feeling unappreciated."

Emma's eyes filled as she mulled over Lizzie's statements. How could Lizzie not see the whole picture? The comment hurt her, and combined with the worry and concern over Strong being gone, she lost her composure. "All I ever wanted was a family to take care of. I thought I *was* successful."

"Oh, of course, you are. What I mean is—"

"What you mean is, I should have been a lawyer, or a spy, or a doctor. That my tits have stretch marks from babies chewing on them, and that my fingernails have the lasting smell of baby shit embedded in the tips."

"Emma! No! That's not what I meant."

Rocky approached their table. Emma wiped the run of black mascara down her cheek. Lizzie pressed the table linen to her eyes.

Rocky leaned close to the table. "Man-O-Jesus. What's Strong done now?"

Emma pulled her finger under her bottom lash, smearing the black on her hand. She sniffed. "Why do you think Strong did something?"

"Well," he slid into the booth next to Emma, "when I see family women cry, I know either Strong or I did something. And I've been very good lately." He crooked his finger for Lizzie to move closer to him. He put one arm around her and the other around Emma.

Lizzie blew her nose into the white table napkin. "Oh, Daddy, it's me. I didn't mean to hurt Emma's feelings. And Emma, I didn't mean your life is boring because you stay home all day and don't do any fun things."

"Daughter!" The brogue infiltrated his speech. "You've said enough."

"I'm sorry." She reached for the martini glass and started to sip the martini.

"No!" Rocky grabbed the glass. "Don't turn to that when

you're stressed. Believe me!"

"Oh, Daddy, I don't know the right words to make this better."

"You'd best not say any more, girl, lest you dig it deeper. You're a fine girl, ya are."

"Emma," Lizzie said. "You're a great mother. That's your career. That's what you do."

Rocky took the linen from Lizzie. "Elizabeth, stop. Get you home now."

"Okay. I know." She buttwalked on the seat to the end, then leaned close to Emma. "I'm going, but Emma, you still love—or like me, right?"

Emma pulled the napkin across the other eye, making a matching black streak on that side. "Of course. You can't help it if I am a loser. It's not your fault."

"But Emma—" Lizzie said.

"Go home, me lass. Git."

Lizzie left.

Rocky took the napkin and gently cleaned Emma's mascara clots. "Here now, girl. What's this about? You think you're not successful?"

Emma nodded.

"My porcelain angel, if you sat on your arse and never lifted a finger for the rest of your life, you'd still be the most successful person I know. You have brought a broken family together. You've made a human out of my iceberg son and given me what I wanted most in the world. You have given back me Katie." The accent was in full swing now.

"It wasn't me. It was Lizzie."

"Not so. Lizzie's been tryin' since all this shite went down. She couldn't do it. But when you came around, all things got together. It was you, young woman, who got it done. And look at me son. He's happy. Well, sometimes, that is." He hailed a waitress. "Bring us some coffee and a chocolate thing." He patted Emma's hand. "Ladies need chocolate in tough times."

"I guess. But, look at Lizzie—the doctor. She's successful."

"And if ya look at her, what do you see? She's a grand gal and bright as a new penny. Ah yes, sometimes words fail her, but in her heart, she would rather be doing what you do. Why do you think she went into pediatrics?"

"She loves children."

"Yes, she does. And she loves you, too. She'd rather be takin' care of her own babies. And let me ask you this. Would you rather be doin' something different? Think about it. If you wanted to be a lawyer, would Strong support you?"

"Yes."

"He would hire a tutor so you would ace the LSAT, then he would make an anonymous donation to the law school of your choice to see you were admitted, wouldn't he?"

Emma nodded.

"And say you wanted to be a nurse. When he knew who was in charge of applicants, he would have Lars investigate until he came up with some dirt, and press that person until you were on the top of the waiting list."

Emma bit her lip and started to laugh.

"So what I'm saying is, you're doin' what you want because if you wanted a career, you would already be workin' it. Right? Last time I looked, you were drivin' a fine car. You live in a lovely home." He picked up her hand. "You're not wantin' for fine gems or the best of what can be purchased. Ya have fine kids and an appreciative man. So who's successful?"

Emma held the napkin to her nose and gave a blow. "Me."

"Okay, then. And don't you go holdin' that stuff against me darlin' Lizzie. She gets word-muddled sometimes, but she's got a heart as big as the sky."

"I know," Emma whispered.

The waitress brought a huge slice of chocolate cake.

"Now eat your dessert, girl." Then he added in a low voice. "I could do with a stiff scotch for sure." He smiled at her. "But I know better, so don't worry. Here, let me try a bite of that."

Emma appreciated her father-in-law and wished Strong could warm up to the man. She'd deal with Lizzie later when the sting of the words had waned.

Strong returned that night in good health and twenty-five-thousand dollars richer.

CHAPTER FORTY-TWO

The phone identifier said it was Strong. "Two things, Emma."

"Hello to you, too."

"Hey, I just left home an hour ago. But hello, my dearest."

"That's better. So, what's number one?"

"First, I've been asked to mediate in Buenos Aires next week, and from reading the background information, I'll probably be there for a few days. It's strictly business, so come with me. Mom would love to look after Stoney and Katie."

"That would mean your dad would be here, too."

"Yeah," he said, the word turning to ice. "But I won't dwell on that if you agree to go with me to Argentina."

"I'll talk with your mom, but it sounds good. Number two?"

"Dinner out tonight."

"O-kay! We haven't been out to dinner for weeks. So, yes, yes, yes. Fancy?"

"Ralph's."

"Ralph's?"

"Do you want to go out or not?"

"A barbecue place?"

"Suddenly, you don't like barbecue?"

"I still like it. If you have a taste for smoky meats, I'm good with it."

"Ah, my girl. See you around five-thirty."

Odd, she thought. Strong owned a quarter-interest in Ralph's so he could use a private room to consult. The place had excellent barbecue and good service, but he'd never gone there just for the food. Would they sit in the dining area or use the reserved room?

She chuckled softly, imagining Lars's weekly inspection of the reserved space, checking for listening devices.

Her visions of Lars using some kind of monitor in the private room dissolved when the phone rang. Kate. Wow, fast. Kate said she'd be delighted to watch the kids. The invitation to Buenos Aires had become a done deal within five minutes. Emma put away the phone and checked the play area.

Their formal dining room had changed, outfitted with mat flooring, children's toys, and a sturdy barricade. Stoney concentrated on a wooden puzzle with Lucky at his side, while Katie sat and batted animal-shaped pendants that made accompanying sounds. A series of "baa-aa's" indicated the eighteen-month-old enjoyed whacking the dangling lamb cutout.

Emma let herself through the gate. She sat on the mat next to Katie and twirled her daughter's dark curls. Emma had been concerned that Katie rarely spoke, but Lizzie assured her the child was normal, probably highly intelligent, and the reluctance to speak had nothing to do with the sign language lessons Emma provided each day.

Using hand gestures, Emma signed to Stoney. *Let's do some hand play.* That's what she called the lessons. Both kids caught on easily. Emma often communicated with them in Amslan. She added a new word each day and sometimes a new alphabet letter. On occasion, Katie would repeat a word or a letter, enough to convince Emma the toddler could talk—when she wanted to.

After the lesson, Emma relaxed on a large beanbag with the two kids. She caressed them, saying in a whisper that she had what she'd always wanted—a home with children and a husband who loved her. That Strong loved her she never doubted. Her love for him exceeded what she thought capable of when as a girl, she'd dreamed about marriage. She had a perfect life.

At five that afternoon, Kate arrived. "Rocky won't be here until later. He's so happy working in Joe's office. I hope Joe will partner with him again."

What Kate didn't say, and didn't need to, regarded Strong's relationship with his father. Both women hoped someday the bond would grow from strained tolerance to father-son love. Except for Strong, the rest of the family had welcomed Charles Rockford Manning back into the fold.

When Strong arrived home, Emma greeted him wearing a slate blue silk dress, her body fragrant with the subtle scent of Joy perfume.

He swept her in his arms. "You're beautiful."

"Thanks, but you're prejudiced."

"Nuh-uh. Okay, I am. But it was your beauty that caught my eye when I first saw you." He chucked her chin. "I didn't know how lovely you were inside." He gave her a squeeze and pulled back, meeting her gaze. He spoke low so only she could hear. "I don't have to compliment you to get in your pants."

She laughed, but couldn't chide him. He knew she loved him deeply and desired his lovemaking. The thought of his touch sent internal shivers racing in all directions, but mainly to nether regions that quivered in anticipation. How lucky was she?

Within a few minutes, they kissed the kids and left in the Escalade.

At Ralph's, like always, an aura of smoky goodness drenched the parking lot launching appetites for all things hickory. The hostess beamed when she recognized Strong and addressed him like visiting royalty. With a cheery "Come this way," the young woman led them past the dining room and into the back area. She swept her arm to the door marked "private." Strong touched the glass handle and the hostess left with a nod.

Strong paused at the door. Emma's heart skipped a beat, but she wasn't sure why. Something in his eyes sent a message. Something or someone waited beyond that door. She grasped her clutch purse in an iron grip. He pressed a kiss into her cheek and opened the door.

Inside, a man stood. Recognition slowly materialized. He looked a lifetime older, his face seamed with lines. Disbelief stunned her. She hadn't seen her brother in seventeen years.

He took steps toward her. "Emma."

"Jo-oe-y," she said, her astonishment spreading his name

into three syllables.

He stopped short of her, remorse cutting his features from internal wounds that hadn't healed.

Emma quickened her pace and threw her arms around him. "I'm so glad to see you."

"Really?" He held her eyes for a moment, then broke contact.

She pushed her face into his shoulder. "Of course."

He pulled away and dropped his chin on his chest, his face wrapped with regret.

"Joey?"

"I've dreaded this moment. Emma, I'm so sorry. Can you forgive me?"

"Certainly. But what am I to forgive?"

"I left you with those horrible...monsters."

She grabbed his rough hand. "You had it a lot worse than I did. I was glad you were free. I prayed you were all right, that you made a good life for yourself."

Strong stepped close. "I know you two have a lot to talk about." He pointed to a table laden with covered dishes. "Have dinner. And after that," he pulled two suitcases from under the table. "Have these. I'll check on you later." He left.

"I think we should sit down," Joey said.

Emma swallowed hard and nodded. Joey held out a chair, and she sat. He took a place across from her, but neither one reached for food.

Joey avoided her gaze. "I got your address from Mrs. Schwartz after you left for college."

"I know," Emma said. "She told me. I figured you'd get in touch when you were ready."

"I was never ready. I couldn't.... Not until I got this letter." He took a folded paper from his shirt pocket and handed it to her.

She read the letter with Strong's letterhead, an invitation for dinner with Emma, and instructions to pick up a pre-paid rental car.

Emma returned the paper. "Never mind about the past. You accepted, and now you're here. Tell me what happened after you left. Your life."

Joey took a box from a nearby chair and pulled out a thick album. "My wife Helen put this together. She's good at this kind of stuff." He opened to the first page. "There's nothing in here about me before I met her. I moved to Chicago for work. We got together when I was seventeen, and we married the next year. See?" He pointed to the first picture showing two young people smashing cake into each other's faces.

Emma leafed through the pages while Joey narrated his adult life captured in photos. The last page, a formal picture of a well-dressed family, hid the blue-collar truth of his lifestyle.

Emma took an electronic tablet from her clutch and showed Joey photos of her kids. She gave a brief rundown of her life since he had left the Ludwig home when she was eleven.

Strong popped into the room. "You haven't opened the suitcases." He put one in front of Joey, and then the other he lowered to Emma. "Go ahead."

Joey opened his, but Emma couldn't see the contents. At Strong's prompting, she opened hers. Inside, neatly arranged, were stacks of bills held taut by paper bands. Emma examined a bundle. They were all hundreds.

Strong sat down next to Emma. "Five hundred thousand dollars each. Courtesy of Hester and Eugene Ludwig."

Emma's face burned. "I don't understand."

"Insurance money. Your parents' policy paid out one million dollars. Your aunt and uncle took it. Now they've given it back. Read their letter."

Joey pulled an envelope from his stacks, opened it, and read while Emma scanned her letter. "Emma and Joseph, your parents had an insurance policy. Here is the money."

Joey's gaze alternated from the letter to Emma and back several times.

Strong stood. "Maybe you two need a little more time." He left.

Emma slammed the suitcase shut. "I can't believe those two. No apology. No shame. I want to hear that they're sorry for the way they treated us. I don't want this money."

"I want mine," Joey said. "Now I can get a truck I'm proud to put my carpentry business sign on. Helen can get some nice clothes. Maybe my kids can go to college."

"Well, then," Emma said, pushing her case closer to him, "take mine."

He shook his head. "I don't want your share. Find a good use for it."

His cell phone rang. His eyes apologized for the interruption, and he answered. When he closed the call, his expression sent deep regret. "My son, Daniel, just broke his arm playing football."

"You have to go," Emma said. "I understand. We'll get back together, right?"

He nodded, adding, "Absolutely. Yes." He held his suitcase firmly.

She walked him to the door. "Next time, I'll have an album for you." She kissed him and gave him a tight hug. "I love you. I can't wait to meet your family and for you to meet my kids."

"It will take a while for all of this to sink in," Joey said. "By the way, you look beautiful. I hope you are happy."

She cast a look back at the suitcase, the one full of hideous memories. "Yes, I'm happy." She then added a note of cheer. "As long as I don't think about some things."

CHAPTER FORTY-THREE

Working for eighteen hours without a break the first day, Strong advised Emma not to wait for him to see the sights of Buenos Aires. The mediations weren't going well; the United States' mining firm executive had exceeded the Argentine government's representative in stubbornness.

Being close to their hotel, Emma walked the few blocks to the Eva Peron museum, spending the entire day there. The city's mixture of contemporary and Old World architecture surprised her, appearing as a blend of Paris and Miami. Mansard roofs were everywhere, with heavily carved stucco and waving palm trees in a warm, humid climate.

Their hotel sported a soccer theme, puzzling Emma until she learned how important football had become to the Argentines. Huge TV screens hung about in the lobby with past winning games playing twenty-four hours. The basement offered a collection of sports memorabilia that meant very little to an American woman. She enjoyed seeing the doors of the rooms— each featured a player in a full action pose. Their room's door showed a wild-haired, handsome athlete in mid-air, having just kicked a ball.

At breakfast on the fourth day of their trip, Strong said he'd made some strides toward agreements, and perhaps they could conclude that day. Then he would be able to show her the sights and be her guide. He described Iguazu Falls just over the border to such a degree, she really wanted to see the place.

Strong kissed Emma's cheek and left her at the table. A little wave of nausea gave her a clue to what she already suspected.

She wouldn't sightsee today. She'd noticed a pharmacy a few blocks away from the main thoroughfare. Even in Spanish, she could recognize the positive or negative sign of a pregnancy test.

That afternoon, after seeing the plus symbol on the test, Emma reclined in the cushy chair situated in front of the large window that overlooked the city. It really did look like Paris.

The knock on the door startled her. Strong's warning echoed in her mind. "Don't open the door to anyone. Housekeeping has been told not to bother us if the *Do Not Disturb* sign is on the door." The sign was there when she'd entered.

After the second knock, Emma approached the door. "Who's there?"

"I need to talk to you," came a woman's voice in an Asian accent.

Emma tossed answers around in her mind.

"Mrs. Manning?" the soft, muffled voice behind the soccer player door said. "Mr. Manning has sent me to fetch you. It's his birthday."

His birthday? That was their code. "What about a birthday?" Emma said, using the correct response.

"July fourth. Party time," the voice said, sounding strange from the accent.

Hearing the correct code, Emma peeked through the peephole, which revealed a small, elderly lady, appearing anything but threatening. Emma unlocked the door.

The elderly Chinese lady's head barely reached Emma's shoulders. With a serious expression, she gestured. "Hurry, Mrs. Manning." She spoke with slurred "r's" and "l's," in almost a comical way. "Your husband needs you. I've come to bring you to him."

"All right. Let me get a few of my things."

"No time to waste. Come now."

Emma grabbed her fanny pack sitting on the coffee table containing her money and identification before stepping out of the room. The elevator door waited open, beckoning. For a petite, older person, the lady moved quickly. She extended her hand with a small tattoo and grabbed Emma's wrist to hasten her past the front desk and out the glass doors into the street. The pace picked up as they rounded the side road, down a slight grade, and into an alley that emerged on an empty street, quiet and unattended, unlike the area they had left.

"You must hurry," the lady said, with the last word sounding like hully. "Mrs. Manning. I've lied to you. I need you to help me. Your husband has made a terrible mistake. He won't listen to us. Let me show you something, and maybe you can convince him not to kill me and my family."

"Kill you? Your family?"

The lady stopped and faced Emma. "Yes. That's what he does. But this time, he's wrong. I'll show you everything. Then you talk to him." She grabbed Emma's hand and picked up the pace.

Emma halted. "I don't understand." She tried to pull her hand away, but the tiny woman had a vice grip that wouldn't budge.

The Chinese lady pulled on Emma's arm. "You will come." She added, "please." She pulled harder.

Emma resisted. Her heart pounded.

"Let her go!" The words echoed, bouncing off the buildings flanking the narrow alley. It took Emma a moment to recognize Strong's voice. "Stop right there," he commanded.

The woman flew behind Emma, her head peeking out behind Emma's shoulder.

Strong charged up the grade from the far end of the alley, wielding his Walther PPK. He stopped, aimed the pistol, and fired. A gust of air breezed past Emma's neck just before she heard the gun's report and the *splot* of the bullet hitting flesh behind her. The Chinese woman went down.

"Strong!"

He sprinted to her and grabbed her arm, jerking her away from the still body on the sidewalk. Pushing and then and pulling her out of the alley with a firm grip, they moved at unnatural speed. At the next thoroughfare, one cab passed, then another.

"This one," he said, meaning he never took the first cab available.

When the cab stopped, Stong thrust her into the back seat. "There's a plane waiting for you. Jolly's there. Go home. I've got to clean this up. I'll be home later." Giving the driver a wad of American dollars, he spoke directions in Spanish.

The cab sped off. Emma turned to see out the cab's back window as Strong disappeared back into the alley. She slumped on the seat, unable to summon calm. Her emotions failed her. No tears, no shaking, no thoughts. Numbness.

In an untold amount of time, the cab turned into a small airport. A plane similar to Strong's Lear waited, its metal steps outward, beckoning. Jo Lynn leaned against the fuselage. Emma couldn't bring herself to call the woman Jolly because there had been nothing about the woman that registered as fun or even warm.

The cab jerked to a sudden stop, its tires squealing on the tarmac. Jo Lynn strolled to the car, her motions in casual opposition to the previous event.

"Come on, Emma," Jo Lynn said, pulling the door open.

Now Emma's emotions kicked in. She could barely emerge from her seat, her legs not giving full cooperation. Her shaking hands grabbed the handrail on the plane's steps. She continually swallowed, as if the bad taste from what had just happened could be displaced. Zombie-like, she forced her legs to move up and through the open door. She sat in the closest seat.

A man in a pilot's uniform pulled the steps up and fastened them. "Seat belts," he said as he moved to the cockpit.

"Howdy," Jo Lynn said in a flat tone as she slid into the leather chair opposite Emma.

Emma had no words. The sound of the engine winding up for takeoff drowned out any conversation anyway—fine by her.

When the engines became quieter, Jo Lynn said, "Strong called and told me to look after you, so I'm your company for... hmmm, ten hours or so. I guess you need a drink."

Emma waved away the drink offer. "I'm pregnant."

"Yeah?" Jo Lynn smirked. "Figures. Perfect mother and all.

We have milk aboard. Lars isn't here, so you might as well have it."

Emma shook her head. "No, nothing, thank you." She stared out the window. Clouds sped by as the plane gained altitude.

"Had a pretty bad day, eh?"

Emma continued to watch the gloom of white and dark billows. She bit her lip. *Bad day?* She'd just seen her husband shoot an elderly lady, one who had stood only inches away. The thought produced a spasm in her stomach, followed by nausea. She put her head against the jet's plastic window.

Jo Lynn unsnapped her belt and went to a refrigerator in the craft's kitchen area. She returned to the seat across from Emma and sat a Coke down on the small table that separated them. "Never seen someone die like that before, I guess."

What kind of a question was that? "You have?"

Jo Lynn took a long pull on the Coke. "Yep." She blotted an errant drop at the side of her mouth with the bottom of her palm. "Part of the job."

"Job?" Emma tried to relax, knowing stress wasn't good for the baby, not to mention herself. "What are you saying?"

"I'm saying...but wait.... Strong is allowed to tell you since you're his wife. Maybe I shouldn't discuss this. He should tell you. It's his responsibility."

Emma tightened. "Strong said he negotiated, mediated, and worked with the three of you to extract people from danger."

Jo Lynn chugged the Coke until empty. "I guess he forgot to mention a few things."

As the blood drained from her face, Emma's nausea increased. "Are you saying that your team kills people?"

A smile formed on Jo Lynn's face as if a pleasant bit of news had come her way. "Well...not the team exactly."

"Strong? Is he...?"

"Tsk, tsk, you don't know what else he does?"

"Are you saying that your team, Theta Mu, is an assassination team?"

"I'm not saying that at all. Look, we really do rescue people, but our missions are multi-purpose. We do what we're told. However, only alphas have the license to kill. The rest of us are a support team. And who do you think our alpha is?"

"No! There's no such thing as a license to kill. That's only in books."

Jo Lynn shook her head and toyed with the Coke bottle. "You really are naïve, aren't you? Don't be a fool. Every major country has agents with a death pass."

Emma dropped her head on her chest, bidding the nausea to abate. A few deep breaths helped restore her composure.

Jo Lynn used the bottle as a pointer and waggled it at Emma. "Government assassins are one thing, see. They are given missions to take out bad guys. Remember Bin Laden? In that case, the directive was given to a group, basically whoever saw the bastard first — and they could take out whoever stood in the way. But the death pass? That person can choose at will. No questions asked." She sat back, easing into the leather seat.

Emma appreciated Jo Lynn's pause until she realized it served to let the thoughts sink in. "I don't believe it. Strong wouldn't just kill someone."

Jo Lynn sat forward, threw the empty bottle in the air, and caught it by the neck. She tossed it two more times, like the coin practice. She put the bottle down firmly. "What did you see within the last hour or so? Think about it."

Emma shook her head resolutely. "No!"

Now Jo Lynn used her finger, pointing inches from Emma's face. "I guarantee if someone held a gun to your head and told Strong to give up 'the plans,' and those plans threatened our country, he'd refuse. Or more likely, he'd whip out his own gun and shoot, sending the bullet through you into the bad guy's heart."

Emma shot up from her seat. "Stop it. I have to lie down."

As Emma opened the lounge door, Jo Lynn said with a laugh, "Don't worry; you're safe. You're not on the hit list." She chuckled. "But I wouldn't make him too mad."

Emma closed the door with a slam and locked it. She flopped

on the soft bed and pulled the blanket over her. She wouldn't be able to sleep, but maybe she could get some rest. She tried to force the conversation out of her thoughts. Knowing that would be impossible, maybe she could think it through rationally. How would she do that? Her mother's advice from so long ago emerged. "Weigh what you know against what you feel and let the answer slowly surface. Let your heart be your council."

She had some information locked in her heart, and then there was the information residing in her mind. Her heart told her Strong would never hurt her or the children. But the words in her mind...what had his father said? "...my iceberg of a son." And Lizzie's description? "...my icy brother." What about Susie when she found out they had been married? "You've hitched yourself to a government killer." The Ludwigs? Antwan? It couldn't be... but, what had she seen hours ago? And even though Emma knew Jo Lynn disliked her...well, why would she lie? Especially about something like that?

There would be no sleep, but she could rest...and think. Could she sort this out? Jeeze, she hadn't told him about the new baby. Why should she? Her path was clear about what she had to do. Strong was a killer. No matter that he loved her and the kids. No matter that she loved him, she couldn't live with an assassin. Hard as it was to believe, she'd seen it for herself. Her mind would not allow her heart to be the best council.

She knew what she'd seen, and Strong knew her. He'd understand why she had to flee. He wouldn't like it, but if she stayed away long enough, maybe he'd accept it. How could she get away long enough for him to understand that she'd left him? Gone from him. Forever. She relaxed into the pillow, taking cleansing breaths.

How did someone disappear and not be found? She'd recently read something. What was it? Right, a spy thriller. The hero stayed off the main roads to avoid cameras. What else could she put into play? When in public, wear hats and sunglasses. Pay cash for everything, use a non-traceable cell phone. What did they call it? A burner? Get a new computer and use public WiFi.

Blend…she reviewed what she remembered of the book's details.

The hours ticked by as the jet engine whined. During some unnoticed instant, her mind snapped, changing her. At an earlier time, hours ago, even, what she thought about would have challenged her morality. As her plan formed, each idea, like the heads in the Whack-a-Mole game, rose, and she came down on them so hard with her hammer, they would not surface again. She'd do what she had to for herself, her children, and her future child.

What she most needed was time away, long enough to leave the old life behind and forge a new one. The kids were young enough, and didn't she have cash? Her belief in divine intervention doubled. The irony could have been humorous if it wasn't so drastic. Strong had muscled a million dollars out of the Ludwigs. Her stomach cringed. Did he threaten them with a gun when he demanded the money? She couldn't summon that image. But the face of that Asian woman…. The gasp of the poor little old lady before she collapsed…. *Stop.*

Her plan was made, and it was dangerous to think further. *Blank page.* Hadn't it served Strong well in his reprehensible career? How could someone kill so coldly and wipe away guilt with two words? From now on, she would employ the power of the mantra, too.

Once she had her plan formed, *blank page* took over; no more contemplation necessary. The change inside her had shaped her into someone new, and she accepted the challenge—she'd leave and find a new life. Away from St. Louis and her home. Away from Strong.

When the plane dipped downward, the knock on the door came as no surprise.

"Ten minutes to touchdown," Jo Lynn said. "You know… seatbelts and all."

Emma ran her fingers through her hair to restore what the pillow had flattened. She returned to the passenger seats.

Jo Lynn didn't lower the magazine she read until the jet hit cloud bumps in the plane's descent. She tossed her reading aside and made eye contact. "We're setting down at a private airport close to your house."

"Is your car there?"

Jo Lynn raised her eyebrows. "No." That one word represented a thousand, starting with, *What do you think I am? Some lackey who chauffeurs inferiors around? Do you think I'm here to serve you? You, the bland wife of the man I used to screw?*

Emma looked away to stem that unspoken conversation. Jo Lynn would never look down on her again.

Jo Lynn cleared her throat. The disdain faded, replaced by a superficial and well-practiced sweetness. "There'll be a car for you and one for me when we get there." She peered out the window. "In about two minutes."

Having had enough of Jo Lynn, Emma didn't respond. She'd also had enough of whatever secret force her husband served on as alpha. But what about Lars? She had no beef with him. Lars was a good guy, the kind of friend one rarely finds. Lizzie still held him in esteem. Her head ached. Lizzie! They had parted under strained conditions. But Emma couldn't let anyone, Lars, Lizzie, or Strong, prevent her from what she had to do.

The tires chirped on the tarmac, and the craft roared in complaint as the pilot retarded the engines. The jet slowed and made a turn onto a runway. Although drizzle on the round window obscured details, clearly, they headed for a hangar. Two dark sedans illuminated by parking lot lights coughed steam from their exhaust.

The plane came to a stop, and the pilot wordlessly let down the metal steps. Emma said nothing as she exited and headed for one of the sedans.

A man wearing dark pants, a white shirt, and a dark tie jumped out. "Mrs. Manning?"

Emma nodded. The man opened the back door. She whispered *blank page* to herself and slid into the back seat. The driver pulled smoothly out of the airport and onto a perimeter road. She recognized the main road when they turned onto it. How could an airport be so close and she didn't know about it?

How did she not know a lot of things?

In fifteen minutes, they turned onto the street that led to her home. The driver helped her get out, and she muttered a soft "thank you."

Emma keyed in the numbers of the front door and, after stepping in, hit the button on the alarm system. At nine, the smell of fresh coffee surprised her. Rocky liked his evening decaf. In the kitchen, Emma found her mother-in-law pouring a cup.

"Oh, hi," Kate said. "I didn't expect you back so soon."

"Change of plans," Emma kept her voice evenly modulated, controlling her emotion. "Strong stayed in Argentina. I'm not sure when he'll be back."

Kate held her cup up. "Want some?"

Emma nodded. In the ten hours she'd been on the plane, the only thing she'd consumed were a few bottles of water. Hunger hit, but she had other things to do. Food would have to wait.

Kate handed her the coffee. "Did you have a good time in Buenos Aires?"

Emma stared at her reflection on the surface of the full cup. "Not really. Strong worked the whole time, and I got lonely for the kids."

Kate cocked her head, smiling with understanding. "I'm sure! They're wonderful. Such a joy to be with."

"Thanks for caring for them. I don't worry a bit when they're with you." *What the hell am I doing? There's no time for chit-chat.* She put the cup down untouched. "I'm home now, so you and Rocky don't have to stay."

Kate's eyebrows came together. She lowered her cup to the counter with a thud. "What?"

"I'm back. You and Rocky can go home."

Kate's face wrinkled with questions. "You want us to go. Now?"

"If you don't mind. And would you mind taking Lucky with you? I'll get him later." She hated lying. What did "later" mean?

Kate rose and stiffly went into the living room. The drone of the television ended, and low conversation hummed. Emma didn't hear the words, but the tones were clear. She had little time. They had to go.

Rocky approached Emma, his customary eye twinkle gone, and in its place an air of disbelief. She cut him off before his first word. "I'm tired. I want to be alone with my children." No apology, no explanation. Had some of Strong rubbed off on her? Of course, and she needed to draw on it for what she had in mind. Lucky waited at her feet. She pulled his leash from the hook near the back door and attached it to his collar. Emma pressed the nylon handle into Rocky's hand without a word.

Rocky and Kate left. The sound of the garage door closing let Emma breathe normally. In the kids' bedroom, she bent over them where they slept peacefully. She'd have to wake them, but first, she had to pack, including the suitcase full of money. How ironic. Now she had a good use for it—her getaway.

The packing didn't take long, just a few things crammed into a canvas bag. They'd buy what they needed on the way. On the way to what? She'd let the details unfold and deal with the decisions as they came. When the car was ready, she shook Stoney gently until he stretched and yawned. She pushed his blanket into his arms. "Come with me." He tagged along as she carried sleepy Katie to the car and fastened them into their seats. The garage door opened, and she backed out, not sure of where, but sure that she had to go.

CHAPTER FORTY-FOUR

Before she turned onto the interstate, Emma stopped at a Wendy's drive-through. Not a fan of fast-food, she considered this meal as survival rations.

On the road, she wouldn't let herself think too hard. She took a bite of a burger and said, "Blank page." With each bite of burger, fries, and soft drink, she whispered her new mantra, hoping her mind would stay blank — enough to keep her going.

Dawn shone yellow light into the car, and the sign "Chicago" meant she'd officially left her old life. The three of them ate breakfast at Rose's Diner on Highway 90. She studied an atlas and decided which direction to take. She knew the car could be traced by photos taken at each collection station. No problem — she wouldn't be using the interstates any more.

Her brother's house was nearby, and being Saturday, he might be home. She called him, and he invited her over. Good. He had a laptop she could use for now.

Joey welcomed them with smiles and hugs. She couldn't prevent the warmth she felt meeting his family. Things were good for him, and she wouldn't worry about his life again. She didn't let on she and the kids had left St. Louis. Emma regained a tight hold on her emotions, so the irony of her reuniting with Joey and meeting his family coming at the worst time possible wouldn't send any warnings.

The steel in her spine, however, met a serious challenge when Joey told her word had come to him that the Ludwigs had been found murdered. He had no details other than what he'd learned from a childhood friend he'd recently run into. He wasn't exactly sure when they were murdered, but likely around the time they got the money.

Blank page screamed in her brain. She asked Joey if she could use his computer, and then she cut the visit short.

She used her phone to locate a hospital a few miles away. There, across the street at a Denny's, she met the man she'd contacted on Joey's laptop, the man selling his Jeep Patriot on Craigslist. Cash? No problem. Sure, she promised to register the car on Monday morning, with her fingers crossed behind her back. The seller didn't ask too many questions as he counted the bills in his hand. No negotiating—he got exactly the price he asked, plus an extra five hundred to leave the tag on. She had parked the Lexus in the hospital's underground parking area and had the seller meet her at the nearby restaurant. After the sale, she returned to the Lexus twice to get the car seats, the bag of necessities, and the suitcase of cash. Within a half hour, they drove the second car away, leaving the Lexus to be discovered as abandoned. She stopped at a Walmart, threw her old cell in a trash can, and bought a no-contract phone and a cheap tablet. She drove away from the large department store with mixed emotions, the sadness of leaving her good life, and a feeling of independence she'd never experienced before.

Her mantra, *blank page*, didn't always work. While she drove, Emma pictured Lizzie, Strong's sister, but more, Emma's dear friend. Strong would worry when he found them gone, but he'd *know* why she'd taken the kids and fled. And he wouldn't, couldn't, tell anyone. Lizzie, though, she'd be hurt. They hadn't talked since that lunch...how many days ago? A lifetime—the old life for Emma.

At a truck stop in Wisconsin, she bought a card and wrote a quick note. *Lizzie, we're okay. Try not to worry. I have my reasons for leaving.* She gave the stamped card and twenty dollars to a truck driver with New York plates and asked him to post it when he got home. He refused the money, promising to mail it in two days, his expected arrival in the Empire State. She believed him.

They stayed two nights in Minneapolis, where Emma used

her tablet at a café to access Craigslist again to purchase a Chrysler Town and Country. She parked in a covered lot at a mall and worked the previous exchange method.

In an Idaho hotel, she noticed one of the housekeepers had a blackened eye that could not be completely covered by Mary Kay's best. Despite the huge bruise, this woman, named Kerry E. Marshall, had the same height, weight, and coloring as Emma. Emma gambled, telling Kerry she and her kids were fleeing an abusive spouse. She'd hit a nerve. Kerry stiffened and nodded, her eyes taking on the distant look of someone who understood. In addition to the woman's deepest empathy, for three hundred dollars, Emma got Kerry's driver's license and a promise she wouldn't apply for a replacement for two weeks. The next morning, the new owner of the driver's license, Kerry "Emma" Marshall, zig-zagged her way west. Each day they ate at small restaurants, and each night stayed at Mom and Pop motels, paying cash for all transactions.

Every few days, she bought another car. It amazed her how a few hundred dollars got her the current license tag, and no one insisted they go with her to transfer the title.

After weeks of incessant travel and being very tired, Emma took a turn off a Montana state road and got lost. Because it was late afternoon, she pulled the Hyundai Santa Fe into the Mountain View Diner parking lot. She swerved to avoid hitting a little boy. He had the look she'd seen before — at her parent's school for hearing impaired children. She got out of the car and signed to the child. He signed back. Yes, he was lost, but afraid his mother would punish him when she found him. He looked at the diner and signed he was hungry.

She should call the police, but the child had experienced enough trauma. The call could wait until he'd eaten. Emma, her kids, and the frightened boy went into the diner, where after washing in the restroom, especially little Greg, the runaway boy, they had dinner. As the kids finished dessert, Emma dialed 9-1-1.

"Sheriff's office," a man said. "What's the emergency?"

"I've found a lost boy. His name is Greg Morton. We're at the

Mountain View Diner."

"I'll be right there."

"You?"

"Yes. I'm the sheriff, Pete Newell." His tone hardened. "It's a small office. I answer the emergency sometimes. Wait…. How do you know the kid's name is Greg? He's deaf and doesn't talk. What's your name?"

Emma's newly formed veneer thickened. "Are you coming here or not?"

"I'm coming. Don't go anywhere."

Emma reviewed the conversation. Should she really have talked to the law like that? What if he wanted identification? She practiced Kerry's name and address.

Within five minutes, a uniformed man, late forties, walked in, a woman with him. The woman spied Greg and hurried to the table. Greg stopped coloring on the placemat when he saw the woman, and his eyes grew large. Emma asked Greg if the woman was his mom. He shook his head.

The woman squatted down to eye level with the boy and smiled. "We'll take him home."

Emma engaged the woman's gaze. "No. I'm not letting you take him. You're not his mother."

"But I'm the sheriff," the uniformed man said.

Emma pursed her lips. "Badge?" What was wrong with her? In for a penny, her mental voice said.

The woman stood and looked at the sheriff. He tapped the eight-pointed star on his shirt. He produced his wallet and flipped it open to reveal a photo ID.

Emma signed to Greg. Wide-eyed, he shook his head, rushed out of his seat, and almost left her breathless when he pushed his face against her breast. He wrapped his arms around her in a death grip. She patted his head. "He's afraid. Not of you two, but what his mother will do when she finds him."

The woman nodded. She sat next to Emma and Greg. The boy had wedged in tightly.

"I'm Grace Newell." She offered her hand.

Emma snaked hers from Greg's hold and shook.

Grace's eyebrows went up. "And you are?"

What Emma feared—questions. Okay, time to put another marshmallow—Marshall—in the fire. "I'm Kerry E. Marshall. The E is for Emma, the name I prefer."

"Nice to meet you, Emma. Pete is my husband."

Pete didn't ask for her driver's license but tapped a chair in an unspoken request to sit with them. Emma nodded.

Grace touched Greg's shoulder, and he flinched. "I understand why Greg is reluctant to go home. His mother, Molly, has five boys—all of them with the same disability. It's rough on her, being a single mom. The kids are difficult to handle since their dad left. Molly Morton had to come back here to live with her mother. Greg and his brothers attended a special school in Great Falls, but Molly couldn't afford to stay there. Greg is one of my students. I run the only private school in this town. I invited him to attend because the public school just can't get through to him. Actually, I've never seen him so calm." She leaned in close to Emma. "How did you do that?"

"I spoke with him in sign language. He's probably confused because no one communicates with him."

"But you did. Look how comfortable he is with you and your kids—very well behaved kids, too. Such an adorable little girl."

"Thanks. Her name is Katie."

Grace tucked Katie under the chin. "Hello there, Katie-Cutie." She locked Emma's gaze. "Do you want a job? Please? I need someone like you."

Emma swallowed hard. The vibes from Grace sang a favorable song. The small town's sign, "Welcome to Hogan," had called out to her as they passed through, and Emma was tired of running.

Pete excused himself to go to the men's room. Grace stared at Emma for a moment. As if she could read minds, she smiled. "We don't need a lot of information about you. It's a small town. We use our gut instincts."

Where had Emma heard *that* before?

"I can tell you're a fine person," Grace said. "And if you take my offer, we can work out any small details that might be advantageous for you and these darling children. As for me, I could bring the other Morton boys to school. Maybe you can teach all of us sign language."

Emma wanted to trust Grace. She liked what she had seen of Hogan, and the kids needed a place to live.

"I'll sweeten the pot," Grace said. "Pete's mother has a two-bedroom bungalow behind her house that she rents sometimes. We can work out the rent with your pay. How's that?"

The temptation swirled, found its mark, and struck home hard. But a fin crested the water. "I'm pregnant."

Grace didn't bat an eye. "We have a doctor in town and a small clinic. Great Falls has a big, modern hospital." The fin disappeared beneath the waves.

A ray of emotional sunshine warmed her. Maybe she wouldn't have to give Grace and the sheriff the whole iceberg — maybe they'd settle for just the tip. The numbness she'd invited for the last few weeks melted like ice. Mental sharpness returned, honing her *gut feeling,* which mingled with the urge to accept Grace's offer. If she qualified her lies in the order of their wickedness, would this lack of information add to the list? *Blank page,* a voice in her mind said, and a loud and clear command added she should stop thinking and accept. She could leave if she didn't like it. "Can you provide me with a car — you know, as part of my pay?"

Grace's gaze drifted as she thought. "Probably. You'd want to sell the one outside, keep the cash for spending money, and have me get another one. But I'd keep it in my name and cover it under my insurance, right? In lieu of a paycheck."

It sounded like Grace understood her situation and would work around it. But Pete was the local law. "The sheriff won't mind our arrangement?"

Grace smiled. "Our arrangement would be school-related." Her face became riveted, serious. "People around here don't butt their noses into other folk's affairs. And Pete rarely questions my business decisions. Plus, having the Morton boys contained in an educational setting means they'd stay out of trouble. See where I'm coming from? So will Pete."

Emma took a long look at Stoney and Katie. They needed stability. So did she. "I accept."

CHAPTER FORTY-FIVE

"Great!" Grace whipped her cell out of her purse and pushed the speed dial. "Mom? I have a tenant for you. A lady and two little kids. Can she come over now?" Grace's expression could have been one from winning a large lottery. After hanging up, her cheer declined a bit. "You'll have to peel Greg off, I'm afraid. He should go home to his mom."

"You know," Emma said, feeling like she had the upper hand for the moment. "He's had a rough day. Do you think his mother would let him stay with us? I know I'm a stranger, but—"

"Ha!" Grace said. "She'd probably let you have him for as long as you could stand it."

Maybe Emma did not have the upper hand after all. "Uh...."

"Don't worry," Grace chuckled. "You won't have to keep him forever. That family needs to deal with their own problems; we just have to help them do it." She stood. "You can stop for a few groceries and then follow us to Gladys Newell's place. Pete will unload your luggage."

Luggage? Aside from the case of money, all they had were two shopping bags. Emma had been stopping at department stores and buying what they needed for a few days, throwing away what they had used. It kept her unencumbered for the next car purchase. Would that car outside be the last she'd have to buy for a while? She clung to that thought.

With a few items from the convenience store, they drove for ten minutes and left the main road for a side street. She stopped behind the Newells when they turned into the driveway of an unassuming house. The driveway continued past the house, ending at a small building with a vine-laden trellis and a front step mat that said, "Welcome." Emma felt the welcome.

The key was in the door lock, but the bolt hadn't been engaged. Somehow Emma knew a lot of Hogan folks didn't engage their door bolts. This front door opened into a living room simply furnished with a beige couch, recliner, and a small flat-screen television. The place was clean and looked comfortable. Soap and towels in the bathroom provided the finishing-touch.

After putting the groceries in the little kitchen, Pete delivered the cash case and the two store bags into the bedroom with the double bed. Emma had a mini-panic, hoping the latch on the case stayed put. How would she explain over four hundred thousand dollars?

Like the rest of the house, the bedroom was plain. She used her foot to push the case under the bed. She laughed softly to herself. What kind of safety did a mattress offer? Then she smiled wider. That had been the first bit of humor she'd experienced since...when? The breakfast in Buenos Aires, when Strong put his hands on her shoulders and gave her a promising kiss before he left? The same day she allowed that kiss to accompany her to the pharmacy where she bought the pregnancy test? How long ago had that been? Three, four weeks? She didn't know. It had been an era. Wasn't an era an undetermined amount of time that changed history? Her history had been changed for sure.

"Mommy?" Stoney jolted her from the introspection. Grace and Pete waited in the kitchen for her. She brushed aside the remnants of her recent unhappiness as a clock chimed six. Barely two hours had passed since she'd parked at the Mountain View. Two hours that had drastically altered her journey.

Grace looked like she expected conversation. Emma stepped up to the plate. "All of this happened so fast. I'm not sure what I should say."

"Good things often come up fast," Grace said.

Words caught in her throat. Her mom had said that, and Emma believed it. Except...sometimes bad stuff happened just as quickly. *Blank page,* a stern voice told her.

Grace picked up her purse. "I'll get school going tomorrow, and then I'll come here. We can hash out details."

Emma heard the words, but what she hoped they really said was, "We want you to stay here, and we'll make things better." Events that had been turning left had begun to turn right.

She bathed the kids, put the boys each on the twin beds, and took Katie to bed with her. It felt good. No motel road noise, no worries that a front desk clerk would give out information, or any of the other things that had nagged her at night before she went to sleep.

A night bird sang.

CHAPTER FORTY-SIX

At ten the next morning, a car drove slowly down the pavers and stopped at the bungalow. Emma took a short breath before checking through the screen door. Last night in the dark and with all of the happenings, she hadn't taken notice of the kind of car Grace drove, only that it was silver. Two quick toots of the horn from the silver car now parked in the back sounded friendly.

Grace got out and took the few short steps to the back porch. She wiped her feet on the brush mat. "Everything good?"

Emma swung the screen door wide. "Great. Come in. Coffee?"

"I guess a third cup won't kill me," Grace said. "Strong and black. I'm addicted to coffee." She chuckled. "I guess that and loving donuts are the price a lawman's wife pays."

She liked it strong. Strong.... Was Strong considered a lawman? What exactly was his title? She'd certainly paid more than a coffee-and-donut addiction. What price had she paid? What would be the total cost? How about the kids?

"Emma? Are you with us?"

Emma quivered and swallowed, coming out of her deep thoughts. "Sorry. I was thinking."

Grace put her hand to her chin. "I noticed. You okay?"

"Fine," Emma said, and turned to the counter and reached for the coffee pot. "Have a seat. Mind the munchkins, though. A fort, you know."

Stoney sat with Katie under the table, playing with their only toys, a stuffed bear and a plastic alligator. Greg scribbled a red crayon on a Teenage Mutant Ninja Turtle coloring book. Stoney made growling noises and shook the gator at his sister, who ignored him. Although Stoney looked like Strong, it was Katie who had her father's personality, his stoicism. She rarely spoke but missed nothing—her large expressive eyes acted as if she could see right through someone and read their thoughts. Emma had noticed it, and other people like Kate and Rocky said the same thing. Emma let out a little breath. *I wonder what they think now?* What had Strong said about her leaving? Did Lizzie get her letter?

"Emma?"

"Oh, sorry." She smiled, hoping Grace wouldn't ask any questions.

"What do you need?" Grace asked.

"What?"

Grace pointed to the kids under the table. "Crib? Clothes? I notice you only had one suitcase. You must need some things."

"Oh. Yes. I'll need to buy some items."

"There's a Goodwill store about thirty miles from here in Rogers." Grace pointed to the left. "If you go forty miles in the other direction," she pointed right, "there's a larger town, Richford. It has a Babies-R-Us. I can't go with you today; we have state inspectors coming to evaluate the school."

"That's okay. I'll get what I need. Tomorrow I can start work. I'm assuming my children can be there?"

"Sure. We take little ones now and then. Most of the mothers in the town stay home for their kids for the first few years. We usually get them at three or four, but we'll love to have Katie. Does she talk?"

Emma sighed. "She can, but she doesn't unless she needs to say something. She uses sign language mostly. She said 'jack-a-rabba' yesterday when Stoney pointed out one running along the side of the road."

"Odd," Grace said. "They usually come out at dusk."

Odd. My life is odd right now. Emma rinsed a cup from the cabinet and poured coffee. She handed it to Grace and sat at the table across from her...new friend? She really needed one.

Grace took quiet sips. After a few minutes, she put the cup

down. She brushed a fly from her cheek. "The neighbor has ten acres and keeps her horse in a stall. That's where the flies come from. But...." Grace went to a drawer under the kitchen counter and removed a fly swatter. She swatted the buzzing fly and handed the item to Emma.

Emma stared at the thing. She had never held one before— the thing that had been the symbol of her young terror. The old fear died as she gripped the plastic handle. "Thanks," she said.

Grace pushed the chair under the table. "Well, I'll check on you later. I need to take Greg back with me to school. His mom will pick him up this afternoon." She handed Emma a card. "My school number and my cell. Call if you need me. I hope you can start tomorrow, but we can wait. No stress, okay?"

"Thanks, Grace." *No stress. If only.*

Grace left and backed her car skillfully down the narrow drive. Emma gathered the few dishes from breakfast and got the kids ready. They headed right, forty miles west to Richford.

At the Babies-R-Us, Emma ordered a sturdy crib, a changing table, and a child's bed for Stoney, plus a few toys. At a nearby Target, she bought enough clothes to last for a week before having to think about laundry. Laundry! The sign of a stable life. She never thought she'd long for laundry to do, but she welcomed that thought.

Because she paid extra, cash, of course, the store said they would deliver her purchases that night. They'd set the furniture up for her as well. At a large grocery store, she bought a rotisserie chicken and side dishes. They'd eat that night in their new place. *Home.* The word struck her like a knife. She'd left St. Louis, but at some point, she'd have to deal with Strong. If she was gone long enough, he'd get the picture. Maybe he wouldn't press...*Blank page,* her brain shouted. *Not now.*

They were home for two hours when the truck arrived with the furniture. Home didn't seem too bad when she put the sheets on the crib mattress. She would have rather washed them first, but some things had to be done differently. She'd adjust.

CHAPTER FORTY-SEVEN

When Grace called that evening, Emma promised she'd come in the next day to school.

At eight sharp in the morning, Emma and the kids parked at the red brick school. Pushing through the glass front door, Katie pointed to the ceiling and asked in sign language, "What?"

"Ask me with words, Katie."

The toddler pointed again and said, "What?"

"It's a security camera, honey."

An older lady came down the hallway and waved. "Hi. I'm Alice. You must be Ms. Marshall." She looked at the camera Katie still pointed at. "Grace put these cameras in last week to help with our state certification." She bent down to eye level to Stoney. "What's your name?"

The boy looked her in the eye. "Stoney Manning."

Emma stiffened and bent down close to him. "Uhm, Stoney Manning Marshall."

Stoney's face squinched. "I thought I was Charles Whitstone Manning?"

Emma brushed a fleck of dust from his collar and whispered. "Remember when I said you had a new name? For now, you're Stoney Marshall, okay?"

"Okay." He was an easy-going child. No problem. Kate had said he reminded her of Perry, who tried to make everyone happy.

Alice patted his head and turned her attention to Katie. "You've got to be the prettiest little girl I've ever seen." She tickled Katie's cheek. "Have you ever thought of letting her model?"

The idea of putting Katie's face in public now that she was in hiding sent a shiver down her spine. She forced a grin, hoping to conceal her internal thoughts. "Nah. I'm no stage mom."

"She'd be famous," Alice said. "But welcome to Hogan Private School. I heard you tamed our little Greggie. His hands were going like lightning yesterday. I think he was asking for you and your kids. Poor child. He did *not* want to go home with his mother. We could hear him screaming all the way to the parking area."

"Do you think he'll be here today?" Emma asked.

Alice nodded. "He's too much for his mom to handle. He'll be here." She checked her watch. "School starts at eight-thirty. I'd say he'll be here in a few minutes."

Through the glass, they saw an old Dodge truck pull up. Greg got out, and as soon as he came into the office, he threw his arms around Emma in the same death grip he'd used the night she found him.

Alice tousled Greg's hair. "I see you're the flavor of the day, Ms. Marshall."

"Call me Emma. Please." She pried Greg's arms from her waist and signed for him to go to his class. He signed furiously.

"He wants to be with us until the class starts. He wants us to go with him."

Alice bobbed her head. "That would work. Greg is in with the younger kids. The teacher, Miss Adelide, could really use the help. Especially with this one." She tousled his hair again.

Grace came out of her office. "Oh, Emma. Great." She laughed. "I see Greg found you. We really need to learn sign language."

"Well, then," Emma said. "We can start today."

"Perfect. The teachers eat together at lunch. You can give us our first lesson. I've already ordered some books. I'm so pleased! Emma, you are a gift to us."

Emma wanted to say how thankful she was to feel safe and secure in Hogan but held back. She wouldn't give anyone grist for a question mill.

The first hours at school started smoothly. It occurred to

Emma that she fulfilled one of her goals, to follow in her parents' footsteps working with the hearing impaired. It had all happened spontaneously. Divine intervention? Whatever. It took a tiny bit of sting out of her situation.

The day went well, and her instruction at lunchtime brought surprising success. By the end of the meal, the teachers could sign the first quarter of the alphabet. Stoney and Katie seemed happy with their surroundings.

At home that evening, as Emma served dinner, she stopped for a moment and had the kids fold their hands. She said a quick blessing, with thanks for finding the town of Hogan, getting a job, and the ability to take care of herself and her kids. After the "amen," Stoney added, "And God bless Daddy and Lucky, too." Emma couldn't decide what caused her sudden wave of nausea. Could it be the pregnancy or the mention of Strong?

Two days later, Pete drove a two-year-old Honda CRX up to the kitchen door of the bungalow. Without a lot of conversation, Emma handed him the title, still in Roy L. Lubkin's name, addressed in Fargo, N.D. Pete handed her two sets of keys, and after switching the child seats from her Santa Fe to the Honda, he left. She wondered if the Hyundai would end up on the used car lot Grace's father managed in Great Falls, but she didn't ask. Grace had a way of dropping bits of information without a lead-in — or summation. The used car lot had been one of those statements.

Working at the Hogan Private School, being able to trust Grace, and the feeling that she offered an important service, helped Emma settle into the bungalow on Elm Street. The kids loved the school, and Greg's behavior changed dramatically. Grace decided to wait a while before adding another Morton boy to her school's roster until all of the teachers could communicate by sign language.

Emma met the town's physician, an older man, Dr. Carruthers, the following week. His nurse showed her to his office and handed the doctor Emma's one-page medical form.

"Hello," he looked at the form, "Ms. Marshall." He studied

the paper for a short while and smiled at her. "Well, then. I see you're pregnant. Everything else okay?"

Emma sat up sharply. "I didn't say on the form that I was pregnant. How do you know?"

The old man laughed. "When you've seen as many expectant mothers as I have, the signs are there. How far along are you?" He asked the usual medical questions, and like Grace, didn't pry about her personal life. At the conclusion of the interview, Dr. Cee, as the townsfolk called him, examined her and said all looked fine. He explained that he supervised a small clinic in Hogan, but if needs be, there was a first-class medical center fifty miles away in Great Falls.

Hogan represented the best of small towns, full of friendly people, kind, generous, and trustworthy — the kind who minded their own business but were helpful if someone needed assistance. No one locked their houses or cars. Force of habit made Emma lock her door. She stowed her money case under her bed but placed caches of bills all over the small house. She had put at least one hundred thousand dollars under Katie's mattress, but she rarely thought about the money…or how she came to have it.

All of the bases were covered. What else could she ask for? Nothing — most of the time. The hardest part occurred at night before she drifted off to sleep. She missed Strong terribly but tried not to remember his touch, his caresses, his presence. Her waking thoughts could be wrangled, but not her dreams. The erotic dreams were so realistic. She dealt with a recurrent image of her straddling him, coming down slowly onto his erection — her favorite position — the one producing the deepest and longest-lasting orgasm. She heard his words, "Easy baby. Slow. God, oh, yes!" and felt his hands on her hips guiding her. She smelled his rich, pleasant man smell and enjoyed the heat radiating from his muscular body. The dream always concluded with an orgasm, one that lasted for a few minutes, making her call out, waking up with pleasure pulsing through her. The last time she'd had the dream, her cries woke Stoney up, and he came into her bedroom asking what was wrong.

What was wrong? She choked on her answer, garbling the words, able only to escort her son back to bed. Getting back into hers, the place of loneliness where she took her nightly rest, was difficult. Every night alone in her bed brought despondency, but the nights she experienced the dreams were almost impossible to bear.

CHAPTER FORTY-EIGHT

When they'd lived in Hogan for four months, her baby bump became prominent, but no one asked questions. Most of the teachers at the school could communicate effectively in sign. Emma had progressed to lip reading instructions. Grace told her every day how grateful she was for Emma's contributions. The school took on Greg's brother, Stevie, older by two years.

Pete came by often to see his mother and do little repairs on the house and bungalow. Often, old Mrs. Newell invited Emma and the kids to have dinner, especially when Grace and Pete were there. Pete took an interest in Stoney and let him hammer a nail or hold a board to help. One night in the big dining room of the house, Grace invited Emma and the kids to join them for the weekend.

"We're staying at the ranch for a few days; why don't you come with us?" Grace said. "You'll love it there. Too bad you're pregnant; you could go out on the trail."

"You have horses? How big is your ranch?"

Pete shrugged. "I'm not sure, actually. The deed says from one river bank to another on two sides, and from the base of the mountain to the old trail." He scratched his head. "It's not been surveyed for over a hundred years, but I'd say between one hundred to two hundred thousand acres."

Emma wasn't sure she'd heard it correctly. "Hundred thousand?"

Grace laughed. "Most of it's wilderness. We have a big log house with five smaller cabins nearby. People rent the cabins and ride the horses in the wild. We have a manager, but we need to go there and make sure things are going okay. Come with us this weekend. Pete can show Stoney how to ride."

"Stoney is only four," Emma protested.

Pete pulled at his chin. "Yep, a mite old, but if he's sharp, he can still be taught."

Emma laughed at Pete's joke. She really liked these people and trusted them without misgivings.

"Maybe Pete can take Stoney camping," Grace added. "It's primitive, but he'd have a good time."

"Primitive?" Emma asked. "Like sleeping in a tent and cooking over a fire?"

"Nah," Pete said. "No luxuries for us. A blanket, a knife, and some salt."

"And a gun." Grace engaged Emma at full attention. "He'd have his gun with him. You're probably squeamish about having your kid see a gun."

Before she could bid the memory to leave, Emma thought about Strong's gun in the bedside drawer. She'd worried about it constantly, but he always had it with him unless he was in bed. Strong had taken her to a gun range and given her instructions in use and safety. She hit the target more times than not, but it wasn't something she liked. Guns had been part of their life in St. Louis, and although she wouldn't allow Stoney to touch a gun, he'd been aware of them. Strong had discussed the dangers with his son.

"We'll take a rain check on the camping, how's that?" Emma said. "But I would love to see the ranch."

While old Mrs. Newell worked in the kitchen and Pete had taken Stoney outside, Grace grew serious. "Pete really does know his way around the wilderness. When he was a kid, he got into some trouble. His dad figured it was more serious than corporal punishment could handle, so he gave Pete a horse, a shotgun, and a hunting knife and told him to go camping until he straightened his mind out."

"That's awful," Emma said.

"Sounds harsh, I know, but Pete said it worked. Out in the

woods with only himself to depend on, he thought things out. When he came home, he said he wanted to be a law officer. He took classes at the university, and that's where I met him. He's a good man. Our son lives in Kansas City, so it's nice that Pete can have Stoney to occupy his need to be with a kid."

"It's good for Stoney, too," Emma said, "but we'll still wait on the camping, okay?" Emma appreciated the involvement that Pete and Grace offered her and the children.

At lunch one day, Grace asked Emma if there was anything she'd like Pete to get in New York — as a gift or something special for the kids.

"Pete's going to New York?"

"He's flying out tomorrow afternoon to attend a conference. Are you okay?"

Emma thought fast. Her face burned. "If I give him a letter, would he mail it for me?"

"Of course." Grace cocked her head. "You want it post-marked in New York City."

Emma nodded. Could she push Grace a little bit more? "And I'll put it in a big envelope. Pete can't touch it."

Grace cocked her head to the other side. "He can't touch it?"

She'd already gone this far. She rolled her lips, then said, "No fingerprints, please."

"My God, Em, that sounds serious."

Emma looked at her hands and sighed. "It is. Will he do it?"

Grace patted Em's shoulders. "Of course."

Emma raced to her desk and wrote to Lizzie. Being careful not to give any information on their whereabouts, she assured Lizzie they were fine, living in a good place, and covered as many questions as she thought Lizzie might need. She didn't say when she would be back or that she was expecting. She had a little guilt on that one, but best not to stir up the waters. The letter ended with, "I love you, and hope you can understand and trust me that I needed to be away."

Emma got a package of mailing envelopes that had not been removed from their cellophane and carefully put the stamped letter in the envelope. She gave it to Grace, who, by her raised eyebrows and slight nod, let Emma know Pete would mail it as directed.

Grace, how I love you for not asking a lot of questions.

Chapter Forty-Nine

Emma's feet swelled almost every day, even though she carefully monitored her sodium intake. She hadn't gained a lot of weight, but Dr. Cee predicted the baby would go eight pounds, explaining her fatigue. Grace insisted she work part time, but Emma didn't want spare time. She took it easy, staying off her feet as much as possible.

One morning, as Emma waddled down the school's hallway, she noticed Grace at her desk, dazed, holding her phone mid air and staring at the window.

Emma stood in the doorway. "Grace? Are you okay?"

"Yes, and I don't know," Grace said breathlessly. "Sit down." She set the phone in its receiver and studied the papers on her desk absently. "I've just spoken with the CEO of a large electronics firm." Her bewilderment started to fade. "The firm is relocating to Hogan, and they are breaking ground next week. She wants to buy the school for her employees."

A chill went through Emma.

"The CEO said her daughter is hearing impaired, and so is the child of one of the board members. She'd heard that all our teachers know sign language." Grace pointed. "You did that, Emma."

"Are you going to sell?"

Grace relaxed into her chair. "She offered me so much money that Pete and I wouldn't have to wait twenty years to retire. You've seen our ranch. We could live there permanently."

How could Emma refute that? "You will still run the school?"

"No. I like to be the big cheese. You must have figured that out by now."

"If you move to the wilderness, won't you get bored?"

Grace's face softened. "We can fix up the ranch. I've always wanted to do something worthwhile with that property. We could expand, accommodate more people. Have a riding school, a wilderness camp. So many possibilities." She reached across the desk and touched Emma's hand. "You and the kids are welcome there, you know that."

She knew it but staying with them smacked of charity. "What about our students?"

Grace nodded. "I already told the woman if I took her offer, she'd have to let the current students stay on at the same price. She agreed and said if she had to enlarge the place, she would — no problem."

Emma stiffened. The rug was about to be tugged from under her. What could she say? "Good luck with your decision." Emma left Grace's office heavy with dread. A dark cloud hung over her, and she braced for lightning.

She had been to the clinic the day before, and Dr. Cee said she would go into labor within the next two weeks, maybe sooner. She did an about-face and returned to Grace's office. Sticking her head into the door, she said, not asking but stating, "I'm taking tomorrow off to spend the day with the kids."

"Good idea. No problem." Grace's fine mood suggested she had made up her mind about selling the school.

For the rest of the day, Emma considered her future. A big corporation wouldn't accept the arrangement she had with Grace and wouldn't compensate with rent, a car, and free tuition for her kids. They would require a social security number and all the other identifiers easily traced by someone who searched. If Strong still searched….

It had been eight months; did she expect this to go on forever? Maybe Strong had given up looking for her. He had to know by now that she didn't want to live with him and why. He knew her better than anyone and would understand the reason she took the children away. She hadn't let herself think about this because it hurt, but she had to think about it now. Did she want to stay on at the school if Grace left?

She'd hash it out tomorrow, her day off, with the kids in Great Falls. They'd go shopping for baby items and some new toys. They'd have lunch at a fun place. Did Great Falls have a fun place? Except for going out to Grace and Pete's ranch, how much fun had she and the kids had since they'd left St. Louis? How many times had she deflected Stoney's questions about when they'd go back? She'd mull the situation over tomorrow.

In the morning, she packed the car and put the kids in their car seats. The baby moved inside her, making driving uncomfortable. The miles between Hogan and Great Falls seemed to have doubled. Even though the countryside offered lush valleys and stunning scenery, she couldn't fully appreciate the beauty. She had so much to consider. Grace had offered to care for Stoney and Katie when she had the baby and stayed in the clinic. Old Mrs. Newell said she'd help when Emma came back. They hadn't talked about when Emma would return to work. That may have turned into a moot point.

Maybe she should think about getting a new car, putting it in her real name, and returning to St. Louis. Sarah Manning. Yes! Sarah would help her with the legals — getting the house, alimony, and a divorce. *Divorce!* She choked on the unspoken word.

The view from the car window showed the mountain terrain had turned to plains, meaning they were getting closer to the city. It surprised her that she had managed to sort out her future in the hour's ride to Great Falls. She'd have the baby, wait until he or she could travel, and they would return to St. Louis, where she would have her own life — a single life.

Being so large and dealing with swelling feet, she moved slowly that day, but it was a good day, one she would remember as a pleasant time with her two children.

CHAPTER FIFTY

"Just a minute, sir. You'll need to speak with the principal," Alice said, wide eyed.

Strong followed Alice past the front desk and into the adjoining office.

Grace looked up from her work. "Can I help you?"

"Yes," Strong said. "You have two children enrolled in this school, Charles Stoney Marshall and his sister Katherine. I'm their father, and I want to see them. I'll need their address and phone number as well."

Grace, jaw tight, rose. "The identity of our students is held in strictest confidence."

Strong reached inside his jacket and brought out his leather badge case, flipping it open. "Not only am I their father...." Light reflected off the metal emblem. The case slipped from his grasp. He bent down and retrieved it. "I'm with the secret service."

Grace Newell crossed her arms. "I don't care if *you* are Santa Claus. Leave immediately."

Strong didn't budge. Grace didn't stir a muscle. His nemesis had gauged his resources, and the contest notched up to a more intensive level. After a short staring match, Grace reached for the phone. "I'm calling the sheriff. You have five seconds to get out of my office and away from this school."

Strong slipped the leather case back into his jacket. "I don't need you." He left.

Sitting in his car across the street, he watched the building and listened to the conversation sent via the bug he'd dropped under Grace Newell's desk when he picked up his badge from the floor. He saw the woman bend a blind slat and look out the window. She probably figured out he was in the car.

He eavesdropped on the conversation as Grace called her assistant. "He's in his car at the curb, probably monitoring our phones. If we call her, he'll get Emma's cell number. He might be able to trace her movements all the way back to her house. Alice, go to the gas station on the corner and use their phone. Emma took the day off, and the kids are with her. Tell her a man claiming to be her husband is looking for her. Poor Emma. I suspected she fled an abusive husband. That one sure fits the profile."

Strong swore a string of words.

Alice slipped from the back of the school and ran to the gas station. He moved the car to the corner and pointed a device toward the small building. Numbers showed on the digital screen and indicated that Emma didn't answer. It didn't matter. He got what he needed and drove the black Crown Victoria into a church parking lot. He called Roland Spencer, who put an expert into action. Even though the cell was a non-contract phone, within twenty minutes, Strong had an address showing the place of its most frequent use.

Strong parked his car a block from the bungalow. The front door lock gave up without a struggle. He stretched out on the couch, confident Emma wouldn't be too late. She'd get the kids home to meet their bedtime.

CHAPTER FIFTY-ONE

Before sundown, Emma wedged the shopping bag between the back door and her belly to unlock it. "Here, Stoney, take this to the kitchen." She handed him her purse. After putting the bag on the counter, she let go of Katie's hand and closed the door. Katie toddled after her brother into the living room, and Emma flopped on a kitchen chair. As she relaxed, she heard conversation.

"Daddy!" Stoney yelled.

Emma's muscles tightened. Blood drained from her face.

"Stoney! Hey, Katie-bug!"

Strong came into the kitchen holding Katie and Stoney. "Hello, Emma." He stared at her enlarged belly, his expression changing from surprise to relief. "Are you all right?"

Emma closed her eyes tight and shook her head. "No. I'm exhausted, so very tired."

"You don't look so good, Ems." He put the kids down and pulled a chair next to her. "Why didn't you call me? You should have told me about the baby."

She clamped her teeth and looked away from him.

His voice sounded more hurt than angry. "That was stupid, Em, unbelievably foolish and dumb. Why not?"

She put her head back and kept her eyes shut. "I didn't want to hear how stupid and foolish I was."

"Mommy, we're hungry," Stoney whined.

"I know." She touched his cheek. "There's soup in the cupboard. Give me a minute." She sniffed Katie. "You need changing."

Strong kissed his little girl. "I'll change her. And get fresh clothes. Let me take them out. You stay here and rest."

"No! You won't bring them back!"

"What? Jesus, Emma." His voice leveled and became softer. "I'll bring them back. I came for all of you. Look, you're tired and not thinking straight. I'll take them for dinner and bring something back for you. Then we'll talk. I have the plane at the airport. We're leaving tomorrow."

"No!"

His lips formed a thin line. "You and the kids are coming back to St. Louis with me."

With Katie in his arms, he helped Emma up and steered her into the living room, standing like a guardian while she eased onto the couch. She didn't argue as he propped pillows around her and took off her shoes and socks one-handed. "Where do they like to go to eat?"

"There's a diner about a mile south. They think it's fun to eat from the small buffet and the food is good. Take my car; it has the child seats. No sweets — meats and vegetables."

Strong went into the kitchen. Keys rattled from her purse. He came back into the living room and ruffled Stoney's hair. "Where's your bedroom, buddy? Show me where I can change little Katie-bug."

Stoney took his father's free hand and led him into their room. Emma closed her eyes and tried to unclench her jaw. From the back room, Katie's words echoed, "Daddy, Daddy." It had been eight months, and Katie remembered him. The child who rarely spoke didn't stop talking. Words Emma had to pull out of her babbled freely to her father in that sweet baby voice. In a few minutes, Katie wore a new outfit, and Stoney had his hair combed smooth. The children breezed past Emma without a word.

"We'll be back, don't worry," Strong said as he opened the front door. She flinched at the Honda CRX's door creaking open and the thump of its closing.

CHAPTER FIFTY-TWO

Strong fastened the belt on Katie's car seat and helped Stoney into his. He examined the car, marveling at how Emma had eluded him. The trail had gone cold after they found the Escalade in Chicago. He'd interviewed Joey Whitstone, who said the visit had been short with no mention of what her plans were. The two letters to Lizzie from New York had dead-ended, with fingerprints of a clueless truck driver on the first letter and no prints on the second.

When they arrived at the Mountain View Diner, Strong put Katie in a rolling high chair and went straight to the small buffet in the back. He pushed the chair along the serving line, and everything Stoney pointed to went on the trays without question, with a marked absence of anything resembling vegetables. Strong didn't bother taking the food from the trays when they got to the table.

"Hello, Stoney," a lady's voice said. "Hey there, Katie-Cutie." It was Grace Newell.

"Oh, you," Strong said, masking his emotions. He handed Katie a potato nugget.

Grace bent close to Stoney. "Who is this man you're with?"

Stoney gave his chicken wing a fierce pull. "My daddy."

"What's your daddy's name?"

"Strong Manning."

"Where's Mommy?"

"On the couch."

"Why is she there? Is she hurt? Crying?"

"My mommy is tired. I don't think she's crying."

"You're a very good boy," Grace said.

"Satisfied?" Strong asked. She obviously enjoyed poking him in the eye.

Grace put her hands on her hips. "Not really."

"So call the sheriff."

"I did. He was in his unmarked car, keeping an eye on Emma's place. When you took the kids, he tracked you, and there he is now." Grace pointed across the room. When Strong followed the point, he saw a uniformed man entering the dining area.

"That's my husband, Pete Newell, the sheriff."

"Look." Strong wiped his mouth slowly as a device to take hold of his deepening aggravation. "I don't want trouble. I am taking my wife and kids home. Stay out of it."

"We'll see," Grace said, and left.

CHAPTER FIFTY-THREE

Emma tried to nap, but agitation buzzed in her head. She struggled to get up when she heard the doorbell. It rang several times.

"Emma!" Grace increased her volume. "I'm coming in."

"Okay," Emma said.

Grace hurried to where Emma reclined. "We tried your cell and the phone here to warn you."

"I must have been out of range." Emma glanced at the kitchen counter and saw the blinking light of the answering machine.

Grace sat next to her. "Is everything all right? I just saw *him* with the kids at the Mountain View. He came into the school flashing some kind of badge, demanding your address. He said secret service."

Emma shifted and sat up straight. "He showed you his badge? Jeeze, I've only seen it twice by accident. Secret service? He doesn't work for them."

"I couldn't read it, but the picture ID looked like him. He said he was your husband, and at the diner, Stoney said he was their father."

Emma nodded.

"He also said he was taking all of you home. Is that true? Do you want to go? Where is home?"

Emma looked to the ceiling. "St. Louis."

"Are you afraid? Will he hurt you? The kids? Will he bring the kids back from the Mountain View?"

Emma had initially panicked and feared he'd take the kids, but he wouldn't give up on taking her back. "Don't worry. He won't do anything awful." The Asian lady's face popped up — like the ugly Whack-a-Moles she thought she'd subdued forever.

Grace made a face. "We'll stay until they get back. Pete will wait in the car."

A half hour later, Strong brought the kids in.

Grace regarded Strong with an ominous stare. She spoke to Emma. "St. Louis, eh? Do you wish to go?"

Emma put her foot on a stool.

"Emma?" Grace said.

Strong still held Katie. "She wants to go home, damn it." He unbuttoned Katie's jacket. "Bedtime," he said gently. "You, too, Stone-boy." He took them from the room.

"They need to be washed up," Emma said.

"Hey." Grace took back the conversation. "You don't have to go anywhere if you don't want to."

Strong spoke from the bathroom. "She looks like she's going to deliver soon. She needs to be back with her family and her doctors."

Grace increased her volume. "We have doctors here, Mister Secret Service guy, and a big hospital an hour away." She lowered her voice and added, "Forty-five minutes in a flashing squad car." She touched Emma's hand. "Our clinic here is small but adequate. And the big one in Great Falls is top-notch, if you need it. *No one* can make you go *anywhere*."

Strong brought the kids for Emma to kiss goodnight.

Grace caught Strong in her gaze as she spoke to Emma. "You are safe here, Emma. Pete can call out multiple deputies if he needs to. And he will. If he needs to."

Strong swung Katie up onto his arm. "Say goodnight to the nice lady, baby."

"Night-night," Katie said clearly.

Emma and Grace looked at each other.

In a few minutes, Strong returned to the living room. He sat on the recliner and stared at Grace.

"Emma?" Grace asked.

Emma slumped against the back of the couch. "It's all right,

Grace. I'll go back."

Stoney called for a drink, and Strong went into the kitchen.

"Really? You're giving up this easy?"

"It's best for the kids." Emma let out a long breath. "I'd already decided to go back. He won't hurt us."

"Hmph," Grace sniffed. "As soon as you get to St. Louis, I want you to call me. When do you think that will be?"

"Tomorrow afternoon," Strong said as he took the water to the kids' room. "We'll call."

Grace sniffed loudly. "*She* needs to call. I want to hear her voice telling me she's safely home. And I want to hear it again in a week, understand?" Grace fished in her purse for a notepad and pen. She gave it to Emma. "Write down your address."

Emma wrote on the pad. Strong came back to the recliner.

Grace took the pad and noted the address. "I want you to know that Pete has cop friends in St. Louis."

Emma sighed. It had become a pissing contest, and the contenders had similar abilities.

"Good for Pete," Strong said. "I have cop friends there, too. And *other* friends."

Grace whispered into Emma's ear. "If there's one thing wrong, when you call me, wish Pete happy birthday, you hear?"

Emma managed a smile. A birthday code word, like Strong had used. He had found his match. "I'll call as soon as we get there. Thanks, Grace. Uhm, would you like any of this stuff for the school?"

"I'll find a good home for the crib, and the rest I'll distribute or call the Salvation Army."

"Before you give the crib away, take out the money that's under the mattress. Also, there are various vegetable bags in the freezer, but they're really rolls of money. Take it all."

"What?" Grace asked.

"Take it and pay Pete's mother for letting me stay here. Take some for yourself. You've covered so many of my expenses. Give Mrs. Morton money for her boys. They really need it. What's left, distribute to a good cause, and use some for a needy kid's tuition.

Do what you think is best. I know you'll put it to proper use."

"That sounds like a lot of money, Emma."

"It is."

"But you might need it," Grace said.

Strong shook his head. "She won't need it. Again." He frowned.

"Well, I'll distribute some, but I'll put aside some of it, too. Just in case you do need it." She glared at Strong. "Again."

Strong lost the pissing contest. He exhibited a rare "Don't fuck with me anymore" look and said, "Time for you and Sheriff Mayberry to git."

"Emma?" Grace said with raised eyebrows.

"We'll be okay, Grace. Thanks for everything."

Grace chest-clasped her arms. "Give me a call."

Grace stood, and Strong beat her to the door to open it. "Goodnight," he said with an air of finality. But he hadn't won, and it showed on his face.

Grace had the last word. "Good luck, Emma. Send pictures of the baby."

As the door swayed open, she saw Pete standing against the sheriff's car.

"Let's get to bed," Strong said, closing the door. The gravel cracked as they drove away.

In the bedroom, Emma pulled her nightgown from the top drawer. "How did you find us?"

He followed her into the bathroom. "After trying all of the usual methods—credit card charges, cell phone calls—we came up blank. You're impressive, Emma. This town is perfect. It's low tech and small, but large enough for you to blend. Your friend, the sheriff's chick and head dominatrix, ratted you out when she installed a real-time camera so the parents could check on their kiddies during the day. We tried a new face recognition program for children. I used a photo of Stoney and got a hit."

"Oh," Emma said. "The cameras...."

"But *you* are something. It wasn't easy to find you. Using the money from the Ludwigs and paying cash for everything was effective. A cash economy leaves no trail. We found the Escalade in a hospital parking lot. The security cameras showed you entering the hospital and leaving the emergency area, but that was all. The trail went cold. Clever. You had to have a car to get here, so tell me how you managed that."

"I bought cars from Craigslist and deserted them."

"What about that car in the driveway outside? It has a license tag from Montana. Your name never showed up on any registrations or car insurance policies."

"That car outside belongs to the Newells, and they paid the insurance."

"Motherfuckers!"

"Don't say that about them. They are fine people and wanted to help me."

"They thought you fled an abusive husband. Damn."

Emma stared hard at his face, needing no words.

Strong's lip quivered. "Look, I really don't understand why you left. I know you had a horrible experience in Argentina, but Jolly explained it to you on the plane home."

She glared at him, her lips barely moving. "Yeah, she told me everything."

"Let's talk about it."

"I didn't and still don't want to discuss your...work." She clasped her hands over her ears.

"All right," Strong said. "Later, when things settle down."

Emma closed the bathroom door to wash. When she came to bed, Strong was in his underwear. He stood next to the bed. She put her hand up to his face. "Not here. Sleep on the couch."

"No way. I'm your husband. I sleep with you." He switched out the light. "This isn't like our king-size, is it? I really missed you and the kids."

A mixed stream of emotions spiked through her body. She sat up. "Out. Leave. Right now. On the couch."

"Emma—"

"I'm uncomfortable enough." Oh, how she wanted him to hold her. To kiss and cuddle her, to say things were going to be fine.

"Okay." He padded out of the room.

She turned on her side, wedging a pillow for support. It had been so long. She had missed the warmth of his body, the smell of his skin. The urge to call him back and press against him confused her. She couldn't think straight and craved his caress, but the face of the Asian woman flooded her memory. The cough of the silencer rang in her ear. She couldn't let him touch her. She started to weep softly and then lost control. The sobs moved her body.

He returned and sat on the bed. "Emma, it's all right now. Everything's okay." He thumbed her tears away.

Sobbing, she couldn't tell him everything was far from all right. Gaining control, reducing the episode to sniffles, she said, "Don't touch me. Go back to the couch."

He didn't argue; he walked away, leaving the door open.

Chapter Fifty-Four

In the morning, they were solemn as they packed the few things they could take on the plane. At the airport, while Strong completed the pre-flight, Emma searched her purse for the cell phone, but it wasn't there. When Strong came into the cockpit, Emma asked him about it.

He patted his pocket. "Smart. It's non-traceable. Prepaid in cash for, what, six months?"

"Three months. This is the second one."

"What were you planning? Were you going to have the baby and stay in this shit-hole forever? I worried about you. At first, I thought you had been kidnapped, but then Lizzie got your first letter."

"Can I have my cell phone?"

"Later." He put it in a storage compartment. "You don't need it right now."

A chill ran down her back. She had no power over herself or anything. He strapped the kids into their seats and then gently pulled the seatbelt across her expansive lap.

"I can do that myself," she said.

"I don't mind."

"Stop." She pushed his hands from the latch. "Don't touch me."

"What's wrong now?"

She turned her head to the small round window.

"Emma. What is it? What are you afraid of?"

"You," she said into the glass. "I'm afraid of you."

"That's nonsense, and you know it. There's no good reason

to be afraid of me."

"What difference does it make what reason I have? The truth is I don't want to live with you. After we get to St. Louis, find another place to live."

She could sense his coiled-up anger, but his voice remained flat and expressionless in a well-practiced demeanor.

He grabbed the metal buckle and pushed it into the latch. "This isn't a good time for this conversation. We'll sort it out, maybe tomorrow."

"Maybe never," she said.

Four hours later, when they landed, Strong left the cockpit and talked with the hangar manager. Emma found the cell and called Lars.

"Emma! Where are you?"

"I'm at the little airport where Strong keeps the plane. He came and got us. Lars, will you come to the house? Please! I don't want to be alone with him."

"God, Emma. What's wrong?"

"Lars, please. Will you come?"

"You know I will. I'm leaving now."

Strong hopped inside the plane to help the kids out. "Lizzie's coming over this afternoon." He extended his hand to Emma and gently led her down the metal steps. "I'll be back in a minute. I've got some paperwork to file."

A minute? That was enough time. She'd seen the Escalade when they turned toward the hangar. He had brought it back from Chicago, and there it was, parked around the side of the building, steps away. She pulled the kids with her. Strong must have been confident he could find them and bring them back if the child seats were waiting. Well, good. That fit her plan just fine. She hustled the kids into their places and slid into the driver's seat. All the time she'd been away, she still had the valet key in her wallet, the slim extra that Strong made her keep for an emergency. Well, hello emergency. The car started, and she backed out.

At the house, Lars waited, leaning against his bumper. He

watched while the garage door made its way upward and then followed the car inside. A wave of concern edged across his face. He opened the door and stood motionless while he connected the dots. "Where's Strong?"

She undid the seatbelt and struggled to get out. Lars extended his hand to assist. He shot a quick look at her pregnant belly and bit his lip. Turning from her, he opened the back door and helped the kids out. "Hi, there, Stoney. Remember me? And Katie! Aren't you the cutest thing I've ever seen." He picked up both children and turned to Emma. "Strong?"

She rolled her eyes. "If I'm lucky, he's still at the airport." She hurried into the kitchen.

Lars followed. "What's going on?"

Emma took a bottle of water from the fridge and poured some into two glasses for the kids. She drank the rest. "What's going on? I need your help."

"Whatever I can do. You know that."

"I have your word of honor?"

"You don't need that, but yes, of course. What do you want me to do?"

A sharp pain stabbed inside her abdomen. She keeled over, grabbing a chair to keep from falling. Lars put his arms under hers, lifeguard style, and helped her into the chair. She let out a groan as a gush hit the marble floor.

"Emma! What's happening?"

A woman spoke, her volume increasing as she approached. "I think her water just broke."

Lars gulped. "Lizzie! I'm so glad to see you."

Lizzie squatted, eye level to Emma. "Look at me, honey." She took Emma's pulse and looked at Lars. "I'll take her to the hospital in my SUV. You stay with the kids."

"No!" Emma said. "Lars, please bring them with you. Promise to stay with me, and don't let Strong get near."

"What?" Lars said as he helped her up.

"You said you'll help me in any way? Then do what I ask. Please."

"Promise her, Lars," Lizzie said. "Whatever she wants. She needs to be calm. We can deal with this later."

"Okay," Lars said, letting out a long breath. "For now. But—"

"Lars!" Lizzie said. "I need to get her to the hospital. You drive the kids in their car." She took the Cadillac key from the counter and tossed it to him. "Come on, Stoney and Katie, you go with Unkie Lars." She bent and kissed them each on their heads. "Gee, Katie, you were adorable before, and I didn't think you could get cuter. But you sure did!"

Emma hugged Stoney and then Katie. "Thanks, Lizzie." Another pain took over.

Lizzie bent close. "Try to relax. Don't think about *anything*. You're home and safe with the people who love you."

Emma sighed. How could she relax? What did "safe" really mean? Lars wrapped his hand gently around her waist as he helped her to the car. On the trek to the hospital, she called Grace to say she was home but in labor and would call later.

They entered the hospital through emergency. A wheelchair waited at the entrance. Lizzie had arranged for one of the attendants to park her car so she could stay with Emma. Within a few minutes, Kate and Rocky arrived and took the kids. Emma shut her eyes hard at the memory of the last time she saw them— she'd thrown her in-laws out of her house. Words bubbled to her lips, "Kate...."

Kate took Emma's hand and smiled. "We are so glad to see you. Don't you concern yourself about a single thing."

"But—"

"Whatever distressing business split you and Strong apart, please know, we've been to that place, and we understand." Kate cast her gaze to Rocky, who nodded.

"Thanks, Kate." Emma could summon no other words. She sat back in the chair, but a pain stiffened her again. "You'll watch the kids for me?"

"Of course. We'll do anything for you."

Emma looked from Kate to Rocky, engaging them. "Strong is not to take the kids anywhere, or even see them. Understand?"

"But, Emma…," Kate said.

Rocky put his hand on Kate's arm. "We can do that for a few days. Right, me darling?"

"Well, until you've had time to think things over and come back with the new baby," Kate said.

Lizzie, who had been conferring with the charge nurse, rushed back and grabbed the wheelchair handles. "Time to go, Emma. Say aloha for now."

Emma, bracing for a pain, stared at Rocky and Kate. "Remember your promise. Please!"

Kate and Rocky nodded solemnly.

Lizzie pushed Emma toward a set of double doors. "Hit the large button, Lars."

The doors swung wide. Lars took over the wheelchair management and followed Lizzie.

"Is David here?" Emma asked.

Lizzie stopped short. Lars had to pull back to avoid hitting her.

Hands on hips, Lizzie turned, first looking at Emma and then to Lars. "David left six months ago. He moved to Rochester, Minnesota, for his new job at the Mayo Clinic. He is directing a fertility study." The expression on Lizzie's face belied the information she'd just delivered, showing no grief, no sadness, but clearly anger. "I'm not going to go into the details now, but Dave had been lying to me. I don't know why he wouldn't tell me, but I wasn't infertile. He finally admitted he didn't want kids and then said he was leaving. I haven't told anyone until now, but he's filed for divorce, and I'm not going to contest."

Suddenly, Emma sensed vibes from Lars. His "I'm sorry, Lizzie," imparted no sincerity.

"Yeah, Lars." A sparkle formed in Lizzie's eyes. "Thanks." She quickly looked down at Emma. "Dr. Ross is on call, and I think he's great. You can trust him." She looked back at Lars. "I would."

A ten-minute trip through the hospital into the obstetrics area brought Emma and company to an examination room door.

A middle-aged man in a lab coat with "Dr. Ross" embroidered over his pocket met them. Lars waited in the hall. The doctor and two nurses helped Emma remove her clothes and get onto the table. While Dr. Ross examined her and a nurse started an IV, Emma reviewed the last few hours, ending with the conversation outside the door between Lizzie and Lars. Wow, their names even sounded right. They had been a couple, but...Strong! He'd broken them up. Emma burned thinking about him. The burn included her deep feelings and her confusion over those feelings. She hardly noticed the machines that now beeped and chirped or the look of concern on Dr. Ross's face.

"Mrs. Manning?"

That got her attention. "What is it?"

"Your baby is in distress. We need to deliver him by Caesarian section."

Him! She didn't know the gender because she wouldn't go to the big hospital in Great Falls for a sonogram, fearing Strong might be able to trace medical records. Doctor Cee in Hogan seemed competent, and he had always given her the thumbs up.

"Mrs. Manning?" Dr. Ross said. "Is Mr. Manning available? I should talk to—"

Emma interrupted him. "Mr. Manning is not involved, but Lizzie, Dr. Manning-Chu, can be my advocate. Can you ask her to come in?"

It took Lizzie a few minutes to listen to Dr. Ross, nodding continually. She came next to Emma and took her hand. "By the way, I'm back to Dr. Manning. Dr. Ross has told me—"

"I don't care about the details. You'll stay with me?"

Lizzie nodded.

"And Lars, too. Lizzie...please, don't let Strong get near me."

"Oh, honey, that may be difficult, but we'll do what we can. If you are sure that's what you want."

Emma gritted her teeth at the massive cramp that started in her back and waved around her girth. "I'm sure. Keep him away from me."

Dr. Ross stepped close. "We should go right now."

Emma pressed Lizzie's hand into her cheek. "Okay."

Nurses transferred her onto a gurney and rapidly moved her out of the room. Lars caught up with them, his footsteps on the floor providing her with some odd sort of comfort.

"Lars?"

"I'm here, Emma."

"Keep Strong away."

"All right. If that's what you want."

As they pushed her through the double doors of the operating suite, she called out to him. "That's what I want."

***

When Emma opened her eyes, the blurry figures sitting close became Lars and Lizzie. "Thirsty," she whispered.

Lizzie left her seat and bent over Emma. "Here." She put a bent straw to Emma's lips. "Just a little. For now."

Emma drew a mouthful of cool water and appreciated the feeling as it trickled down her throat, quenching the dryness. She licked her lips, better able to speak. "The baby?"

Lizzie grinned. "He's beautiful. And perfect. He looks like you. Eight pounds, twelve ounces, a real linebacker."

"Good," Emma said. "I'd like to see him."

"In a few minutes, honey," Lizzie said. "He's in the nursery. They'll bring him in when you can sit up."

The wide wood door opened, and Strong walked heavily into the room.

"No!" Emma called. She tried to sit up, and her free arm grabbed her stomach where the stitches felt like fire.

"Strong!" Lizzie said. "Not now."

He continued, in slower steps, toward the bed. "She's my wife."

Lizzie stepped between Strong and the bed. "My patient. And I said no."

"You're a pediatrician. You can't keep me from her."

Lars stood next to Lizzie. "I can."

Strong's face screwed into perplexity. "You, too?"

Lars took Strong by the arm. "Outside for a minute. Okay,

buddy?" His eyes entreated cooperation. "Let's go out into the hall."

Strong shook Lars's grasp. "I can take you if I have to."

"It won't come to that."

Lizzie stepped forward and gave Strong a sound push. "Any wonder she doesn't want you around? Look at the trouble you caused in thirty seconds. Give her a break, Strong. Don't upset her. Leave now."

The muscles in Strong's jaw twitched. He looked from Lizzie to Lars and then to Emma. "Well, you can't keep me from seeing my child." He stomped out.

Lizzie rushed to Emma. "Don't worry, honey. Everything's okay. You'll be fine; everything's good."

Emma closed her eyes, and things turned gray.

Chapter Fifty-Five

Later that afternoon, a nurse pushed a transparent bassinette next to Emma's bedside. Lizzie picked up the baby and straightened his striped blue cap.

"Aw," Lizzie cooed. "You're so sweet." She kissed his forehead and waited for Emma to finish raising the head of the bed.

Emma suppressed a groan from the stinging stitches as she got into position. Extending her arms as an invitation, she eagerly reached for her baby.

Lizzie placed the baby in Emma's arms. "I want one of those." She turned to Lars and repeated the statement seriously. "I want one of those, Lars."

Lars slipped his arm around Lizzie's waist and nodded wordlessly, seriously.

Lizzie's phone chimed. She checked the text. "Look, one of my patients has been brought into emergency. The baby can stay here with you, Emma. Lars?"

"I'm here for the duration," he said.

Lizzie walked toward the door, stopped, and then turned. She uttered no words, but her eye contact touched Emma and then Lars. With an odd smile on her face, her look spoke to them, saying, "I love you. Both of you. All three of you."

Emma understood the different kinds of love. Fine dark hair peeked from the little cap. She wondered if Strong got to see Alan Benjamin, the names of her father and Strong's grandfather, the ones she'd chosen for her new baby.

The nurse came in with a tray and put the baby back in the

bassinette. Lars scooted his seat closer to the bed. "Emma? I'd sure like to know why you left St. Louis and why you won't share air with Strong."

"Maybe later. I don't want to think about it. Let me have my way for a few days, okay?"

"Okay. We'll spoil you rotten until you leave here. How's that?"

"Good."

A few hours later, Strong stood in the doorway. He spread his arms as if saying, "I'm just standing here. No problem. I'm not coming in." He stretched his neck to get a look at the bassinette.

Lars let out a long breath. He gently pushed Strong out into the hall and shut the door behind him. She couldn't understand the words, but Lars's voice vacillated between firm and pleading.

Over the next three days, Strong made doorway appearances. On the afternoon of Emma's discharge, he stood with his hands folded on his chest, not entering the room, but watching, trying to make eye contact with Emma.

Lars patted Emma's shoulders and headed toward Strong. Strong wouldn't budge. "I'm taking her home."

"Can't you just leave her alone for a while?" Lars's voice became harsh, demand pulsing the words. "I'm taking her home. Don't go there until she asks for you."

Emma couldn't help but watch the exchange. She'd never seen that look on Strong's face before and couldn't identify the emotion.

With his nostrils flaring, his lips barely moved. "If that's what she wants. I'll leave. For good." He turned and walked away.

Strong wasn't the type to change his mind, meaning she got what she wanted—he'd leave them alone. Emma's heart did a double beat. At that moment, she wasn't sure whether she really wanted him to leave until the Asian woman's face popped into her memory, along with the sounds and the smells of that event. How could she love an assassin? He understood her, so why did he expect her to want him in her life? He must know why she left, why she couldn't be with him.

"Emma? Are you okay?"

She shook her head to come out of her thought-coma. Lars's face peered down at her. "I'm okay." Little Alan made tiny eck sounds. "He won't come to the house, will he?"

Lars shook his head. "Not if he said he won't." He scratched his nose. "I've never seen him look that way."

Tears threatened to spill. Emma steeled her will to stop them. "I haven't either."

Lizzie came in, dressed in a lab coat. In blue embroidered lettering over the pocket it said, "Dr. Manning." The hyphen and the "Chu" had been pulled out, leaving tiny holes and a few threads. She took a stethoscope from her neck and listened to Alan's chest. She smiled. "Uh, huh, still perfect. Ready to go home?"

"Are you coming?" Emma asked.

"Sorry. I'm on duty, and one of my little patients fell from a tree. Head injuries. I have to be here when he comes out of surgery." She checked her watch. "Soon. Daddy is coming to take you back to your house." She touched Lars's arm. "You will stay, right, Lars?" His name sounded like silk on satin as it left her lips.

"You betcha," he said, showing a lot of teeth. He added, "Elizabeth."

A nurse and Lars gathered up what little Emma needed and the load of stuff the hospital had for the baby. Rocky waited at the hospital's covered drive with the Escalade. She got in the back with the baby and Lars. In less than a half hour, she was home.

CHAPTER FIFTY-SIX

Rocky stayed for only a few minutes. He drove back to the place he shared with Kate, and now Stoney and Katie. He'd brought Lucky back. The dog ran tight circles and whined happily. Emma appreciated having the dog there and seeing him again.

She laid the baby on the couch, surrounded by pillows. "The nursery is too far away. I can take care of him here," she explained to Lars.

Lars sat on a recliner next to the couch. "Can I get you anything?"

"No. I'm good. Except...where did I put that baby bottle of water?" She felt around the couch and then patted the pocket of her robe. "Oh, I have it here, keeping it warm."

"Everything's taken care of. Let's talk." He spoke with the same seriousness he'd used with Strong earlier.

She put her head back and stared at the ceiling. "Tomorrow."

"Now."

She gritted her teeth. "I can't believe you haven't figured it out. You know me. I can't live with an assassin. I don't understand how you can be his friend."

Lars pulled his head back in a slight jerk. "Who are you talking about?"

"I'm talking about Strong, the alpha, the man with the death pass."

Lars shot from his seat. "What does that mean? What's a death pass?"

"License to kill."

Lars shook his head. "What are you talking about? There's no such thing as a license to kill. Where's this coming from?"

"From Jo Lynn. But I've had enough evidence that I should have known it myself."

"What evidence?"

"So many things. His threats—like Antwan Givens. The money he got from the Ludwigs—they were murdered. And—"

"Whoa, slow down. The ADA, Antwan Givens? What does he have to do with this?"

"He got shot."

"So?"

"Strong threatened to play dirty if Antwan went after me. We had sort of a date. Then he was attacked."

Lars laughed. "*Sort* of a date? Look, Givens prosecuted a lot of people. Prosecutors stay in the crosshairs of bad guys. But come on, that's not Strong's style. You married Strong. He won. Plus, if Strong had gone after Givens, the man would be dead. They didn't catch the guys that messed up Givens, but it certainly wasn't Strong."

She folded her arms over her chest. "Okay then. The Ludwigs."

"Strong didn't even meet them. I handled that whole deal. I drove to Maryland and spoke to them. I thought I might have to threaten with my usual IRS lecture—I have friends at the service—but they laughed and called their accountant. They won a multi-hundred-million-dollar lottery. They couldn't have cared less. They kept a million in cash in their house safe. The accountant brought me two suitcases the next day. I heard about them getting murdered. You weren't around then, but the cops found out it was four meth-heads demanding cash, and the Ludwigs didn't have any because they'd given it to us and hadn't gotten more from the bank. Nasty, bloody thing that was." He screwed up his face. "You thought Strong...?"

"Yes, I thought it. He's a cold-blooded killer. You can't dismiss what he did...what I saw in Argentina."

Lars stopped pacing and sat next to her, engaging her eyes.

"What did you see in Argentina?"

Her lip quivered; she swallowed hard. "He shot a little Asian lady who was hiding behind me. The bullet went…." She put her finger against her neck to show the path.

Lars's face, tanned and handsome, turned as white as a corpse. His head shook like an old man's tremor. "Asian lady? Tattoo of a rose on her hand, right?" He swept his fingers through his golden curls. "I read that report. It failed to mention that you were on the scene."

"So you admit that Strong kills for the government."

"You've got this all wrong." He struggled for words. "Jo Lynn…." His hands reached into the air as if he were trying to grab an invisible something. "Look. Strong took you to Buenos Aires when he was called to negotiate. There was a 'kill on sight' notice regarding Shawon Ming. We got word that she was stalking Strong and had tracked him to Argentina. I contacted him, and he left the negotiations to get you out of there. Jo Lynn was in Panama, so I had her fly to Buenos Aires to accompany you."

"So? Who is Shawon Ming?"

Lars's eyes widened. "That little Asian lady made Bin Laden look like the Easter Bunny. Take my word for it. She had it out for Strong but could never kill him. She and her thugs tried, but he always recovered."

Emma recalled the time Strong used a cane and the line of stitches in his scalp. "But—?"

"She couldn't get him, but she could get *you*. My God, you have no idea." Lars stopped talking and took a breath, the kind of breath that calms. He shook his head. "What she would have done to you." He shuddered. "My God, Emma. I didn't know you were at the scene—with her."

"She told me to come with her. She had the password."

"Jesus, Jesus! Strong took the only chance he could. I'm sure her gang was nearby, and once they got you…." He shot up from his seat and paced again. "He took a deadly chance and could have shot you, but it would have been much better than what…."

He cocked his head. "Jo Lynn?"

"Said he was an assassin; that he answered to no one regarding whom he chose to kill."

"Jo Lynn." He rolled his eyes. "That answers a few questions. She knew all of this and didn't tell him, and wouldn't help find you. Strong has been nuts looking for you. He didn't go to work, he didn't eat right—"

"He didn't go to the office? All this time? Who—?"

Lars raised his eyebrows; his chest moved from a short laugh. "Rocky and Sarah. They're like dynamos. No one can beat them. It's crazy, but those two together…they kept me hopping." Lars took his seat next to her and put his hands on her arms. "But Strong hasn't been himself. He refused missions, afraid he'd miss some bit of information about you, meaning we didn't go either. He spent the whole time running down every little clue trying to find you before the Mings—especially the son, Wo Ming—found you. When Strong wasn't searching, he was working out in case he had to go hand-to-hand. You must have noticed how buff he is now."

Emma shook her head. "I didn't look at him much. I was afraid I'd give in and…."

"What a mess," Lars said.

Emma dropped her head. "I did that. All this time I thought he…. Oh, God. How could I have been that wrong? Poor Strong— so worried."

"You have no idea. I saw him cry."

Emma couldn't summon words. She looked around the room, searching for the ability to put the pieces together in a reasonable package. Images formed. "Oh! Lars! Now he has gone to her! I've driven him right to her."

"Who?"

"Jo Lynn."

"Of course not. He doesn't love her." He pointed his finger at her. "He loves you."

"He said he's not coming back."

"We can change his mind."

Her eyes welled. "If we find him."

Lars stood up. "I can find him."

"Do you know where he's gone?"

"No. But I can locate him. It may take me a few hours, and I'll have to get Spence's cooperation." He dug into his pants pocket, pulled out the skinny black phone with the red button like Strong carried, and pressed the button. "Spence. We need to talk. Twenty minutes." Lars bent over to speak to her at eye level. "I need to go to…oh hell, I might as well tell you. Remember the clinic you took Strong to? It's our headquarters. Spence is away, but I can go there and get in touch with him. With his permission—"

"Do you guys have a location device embedded somewhere inside your body?"

He pulled his chin. "That I can't disclose. But trust me, I'll find Strong. I'll have to leave you alone for a while. Okay?"

"Fine. Great. Just find Strong. I'm so messed up." The baby cried, and she lifted him to her.

"Okay," Lars said. "Hang tight until I get back."

CHAPTER FIFTY-SEVEN

When Lars left, she put Alan to her breast. Her milk had come in, and she needed to relieve the pressure. She winced when he began to suck, remembering it took a few days to get accustomed to breastfeeding. She also remembered her little breast peccadillo with Lars, making her glad he wasn't there. Then she thought about Strong.

All of the clues had led her to an obvious conclusion. The bullet whizzing past her neck had been the final straw, but now she knew that bullet had saved her life. Yes, there had been convincing clues, but she hadn't listened to her heart. How could she have been so wrong?

Alan's eyes closed, and she laid him on his blanket, marveling at the beauty of a sleeping child. She had refused pain killers after the second day because she wanted to nurse him. Thankfully the stitches didn't hurt like they had the first day, but they still stung. She hadn't experienced a Caesarean before. In her other two deliveries, David Chu had kindly worked a little magic by doing some extra sewing, so she had dealt with stitches, but in a different place and less painful.

Her thoughts stopped when a noise came from outside. Lucky barked at the doorbell. Had Lars forgotten something? Getting up from the couch caused her discomfort, but she needed to move around at least some. She went to the door and looked out the peephole.

She couldn't believe it! She hurriedly unlocked and opened the door. "Susie! How good to see you."

Susie, dressed to the max in a turquoise silk suit and balanced on her usual stiletto heels, held a box wrapped in blue paper, tied with a huge bow. She held it out. "Congratulations."

"Thank you. Come in. I haven't seen you in so long."

Lucky growled and snarled, circling Susie.

"I don't like vicious dogs," Susie said.

"He's not vicious. I don't know why he's acting this way."

Susie leveled her bug-eye at Emma. "Put him up." She stood like a statue, with only her stare darting between Emma and Lucky, who continued his deep, throaty rumble.

"Here, Lucky." Pressing her hand against her stomach, "Stitches," she explained. Emma bent, grabbed Lucky's collar, and pulled the dog out of the living room, into the den. She returned to where Susie stood, wooden, unmoving. "Sorry about that. Please. Make yourself comfortable."

Susie put the gift down and went to the couch where Alan slept. "Aren't babies cute? I never really wanted any myself, but I like to look at them." She shrugged. "I don't particularly like to hold them or anything."

Emma patted the recliner opposite the couch. "Sit down, Susie. Tell me what's happening."

"So, what's up is…I'll be leaving for San Francisco next week with my boyfriend. I've been working for Gianni Latito, and as a final job, he sent me to fetch you."

"Me? How odd. But I can't go anywhere right now, Susie. Plus, I don't want to see Mr. Latito."

Susie left her seat, pulled a gun from her purse, and pointed it at Emma. "But he wants to see you, so no trouble now; I don't want to use this." She shook the gun. "You're my friend, so I'd probably only shoot your knee or something. Gianni wants you alive."

Emma put her hand to her neck and stared at the barrel. "Susie! What does Mr. Latito want with me?"

"I don't ask questions. But to bring you into the office, he's paying me a number with lots of zeros at the end. His friend Mr. Ming is there, and that guy wants to have a chat. That's all I know. So…." She waved the gun toward the door. "Let's get going."

Emma reached for Alan.

"Hold it," Susie said. "No kid."

"I can't leave him here."

"Yeah. You can. And if I have to shoot you, the Samoan man who's waiting in the car will carry you."

Emma put her hand to her head and acted dizzy. "Oh!" She whined and bent over, holding her stomach. As she bent, she slipped her hand into her robe pocket and pulled out the baby's water bottle.

Susie growled her words. "Come on, you wimp. Get up."

Emma straightened up and threw the bottle at Susie's face. When Susie flinched, Emma lunged at her, hoping her perch on the stiletto heels would give. Both of them hit the carpet. The gun went off as it dropped to the floor, hitting the ceiling and showering them with bits of plaster as they rolled. Emma was six inches shorter and fifty pounds lighter than the Mocha Amazon, but she was determined not to leave Alan.

They were still tangling when a huge man rushed in. He bent over and grabbed Emma. Before he could pull her from Susie, the man let go. Emma still fought Susie and didn't have time to think about what was happening, but within a few seconds, she heard a familiar voice.

"Get off her, Susie," Strong said.

Susie, on top of Emma, ceased her actions and turned her head. Emma could see the Samoan man groaning on the floor while Strong pointed his gun at Susie.

Susie rolled to a point where she could stand. She brushed her skirt smooth as if nothing had happened.

Strong, still pointing the gun, squatted and helped Emma up and over to the couch. In emotionless words, he told Susie and the Samoan to lie face down on the carpet with their hands over their heads.

Passing the gun to Emma, he said loudly so everyone could hear, "Keep this trained on them, and if either one moves, shoot them both." He removed the skinny black phone from his jacket and pushed the button. "This is agent seven-three-four-two. Send two unmarked to my location." He sat down next to Emma and took the gun from her. "You okay?"

She touched her lip and saw blood. "I'll live." She ran her hand over Alan's head. "I'm so glad Lars found you," she whispered.

"Lars didn't find me. I camped in that vacant house down the street to watch."

"Watch? What for?"

He took his attention off the captives and gave her a swift glance, his eyes steely, like lightning in a night storm. "Just watch."

"You said you weren't coming back."

"On occasion, I *do* change my mind."

"Really? I didn't think that was your style."

"Not normally, no. But this isn't normal. I saw Lars leave, and then Susie's BMW pulled in. She had no business here. Then I heard the shot and saw that hippo get out of the car." He checked on the two figures still on the floor. "Man," he whispered, "it felt like I tackled a refrigerator. That guy didn't go down easy."

Emma sagged into the soft couch, inches from his back. Strong's shirt sleeves strained at the biceps. Lars said Strong had been working out. She regarded the large man face down on the carpet. Strong's gut instinct had anticipated the need for extra strength. And he *had* needed it.

Still focused on his captives, Strong said, "What are they doing here?"

"Susie wanted to take me to Gianni Latito. She said his friend, Mr. Ming, wanted to chat." She pointed at the large man prostrate on the floor. "She brought *him* to make sure I went."

"That wasn't very nice, Susie," Strong said, throwing the words toward the woman.

Susie's reply, muffled by the carpet, resonated with defiance. "Big deal. I didn't do anything. I was just escorting her to the office."

"Uh, huh. So you know where Ming is?"

"I'm not saying anything."

"Okay," Strong said. "Save it for later, when you deal with

expert interrogators."

Emma wanted to embrace him, to explain, apologize, but this wasn't the time. The huge man, prone and motionless, still looked dangerous, and she couldn't distract Strong even for a second. The mantel clock ticked away, the sound noticeable in the quiet of the room.

In ten minutes, two dark sedans pulled quietly into the drive. Suited men came into the house, pointing their guns as they entered the foyer.

"In here," Strong called. "You might want to put some pressure on this one ASAP." He motioned his foot at Susie. "I'll bet she can tell you where Wo Ming is right now."

The suited men said only a few words. They took the man away and came back for Susie.

Handcuffed and sandwiched between the two agents, Susie looked straight ahead as she neared the front door.

Emma, keeping hold of her stinging abdomen, ran to her. "Wait!"

The agents stopped, and Susie turned her head.

Emma stepped close. "Susie, years ago, you said you researched Strong. You told me he was a government assassin."

"I remember." She shrugged. "He was an arrogant shit, and I liked you. I didn't think you should get stuck with the bastard, so I made it up."

Susie's warning had planted the seed that allowed a thick nasty thorn hedge of lies to grow. Emma pulled her hand back in a long swing, but before it could contact with Susie's cheek, the closest agent stopped the slap with an incredible reflex. He must have practiced the coins and peanuts, too. The man shook his head and gave Emma a look that said Susie faced enough trouble as it was.

Emma backed away, a flush of shame running through her, and let the agents leave with their prisoner. She returned to the couch where Strong sat stroking the baby's dark curls.

"Have we named him yet?"

"Alan for my dad; Benjamin for your grandfather."

Strong's eyes went flinty. "So why is Lars looking for me?"

"To bring you home."

A bit of coldness left his face. "Why am I invited back to my own house?"

She hung her head. "Because I made such a horrible mistake."

"I'm listening."

She gave him the details, stopping every so often to wipe the moisture that she couldn't keep from blurring her eyes.

He only interrupted once to say, "You dated Givens?"

The old Emma would have explained. But the new, formidable woman wiped her tears and blew her nose. "Yes," she said, and continued describing the evidence against him and her conclusion that he was a cold-blooded killer. "I'm sorry. I don't know what to say except that I don't understand how I could think those horrible things about you."

"If I was on a jury and a prosecutor presented the kind of evidence you got, I'd convict, too. No shadow of a doubt."

"Really? You understand?"

"It's my specialty, and why innocent clients who have that kind of circumstantial crap against them hire me. And you know what? If I *had* done those things, I would expect and want you to leave with the kids and not be found."

"Strong, I...I...."

He pulled her close and kissed her head. "Part of this is my own fault. I should have told you more about my work and what I do. It left you vulnerable to misinformation. I'll never keep you in the dark again. Look, we've both been through some bad stuff, but we're together now."

She shut her eyes hard and nodded. She sighed and then looked at him. "I can hardly believe it, but here we are."

"So." Strong tilted his head upward and stared at the bullet hole in the ceiling. "What happens now?" He let out a long sigh. "It's hard to admit, but I don't know what to do."

Emma squeezed his beefy shoulder.

He shook his head. "The Tricky Mice aren't good as a team now."

"Of course you are, but instead of four, there's three." He rubbed his forehead. "Three isn't enough."

Chapter Fifty-Eight

Lars brought Lars Jr. to the daycare quarters. One side of the large room had been sectioned off with padded mats, where several toddlers played, including Katie. The other side of the room had tables where older children quietly worked on their lessons.

Emma held little Lars and kissed his forehead. "What's Lizzie up to today?"

"Inoculations for the recruits."

"And Ditey?"

"Bomb defusing 101 for the agents."

Emma nodded. "Strong and Pete are teaching a small group survival training, and tomorrow those agents will get a week in the wilderness. Knife only."

Grace walked in and gazed at the children in the room. She pointed to a window. "What a beautiful day."

Lars chucked his son under the chin. "They don't call Montana Big Sky Country for nothing. I love it here. I've said it before, and I'll say it again. Emma, you're a genius."

Emma smiled. "You can say it again if you want. I especially like it when Spence tells me how much he appreciates this training facility."

Lars kissed the baby's cheek. "You two ladies have fun teaching the kiddies. I'm off to set up a new obstacle course, harder and longer. We'll whip our replacements into shape."

That night, in their cozy log cabin with the fireplace blazing, Emma and Strong snuggled on the couch.

"Do you miss being in the field?"

Strong shook his head. "Nope. Not getting any younger." He thumped his thigh. "These old injuries are starting to remind me of the good old days."

"But you're still using your skills, your knowledge."

"Yes, I am. And, Princess, you're not only gorgeous, you're brilliant."

"Thanks."

He placed a soft kiss on her cheek. "You've changed a lot since I first met you — back when you were rather...uhm, sedate."

Emma crossed her arms over her chest. "Shy? Meek? Oh, wait a minute, I believe you said trusting, and trusting had the same result as stupid."

"Oh, God. I did say that, didn't I?"

"You did. So, now I'm brilliant?"

"Oh, yes! This idea of using the Newell's property as an agent training school is more than brilliant. Look how it's worked out. Everyone is happy. Dad and Sarah are in constant demand in St. Louis. Lars and Lizzie are here with us. I'm training; you're teaching. And we are all serving our country, doing what we do best. But, Princess, beyond brilliance, you — you are perfect."

"What does perfect mean?"

"Everything. Including the fact that no one pushes you around, especially me. You are just the way I want you, what I would *will* you to be, if I could. I guess you can say you're strong-willed."

Patricia is a former art teacher and high school librarian. She lives in South Florida with her husband and three dogs. She writes short stories, novellas, and novels, mostly fantasy and Sci-Fi. She has also written three Romances, a Sci-Fi, a Victorian, and a Contemporary. Her stories revolve around action and deep relationships, allowing the reader to watch the scene unfold as if present. Patricia is active in three critique groups and often helps new writers learn the ropes. She is an active member of the Florida Writers Association, Mystery Writers of America, and Romance Writers of America.

When not writing, Patricia enjoys painting watercolors and drawing in several media. Currently, she is learning illustration techniques for future books. Her frequent travel provides opportunities to check off bucket list items and sometimes inspires new stories. She is a voracious reader and loves a good book talk.

Check out her Facebook page at Carpewordum@gate.net.

www.ingramcontent.com/pod-product-compliance
Lightning Source LLC
Chambersburg PA
CBHW020346180626
46812CB00001B/356